RISE OF THE RESURRECTED GOD

SAGA OF THE BROKEN GODS
BOOK 3

RYAN KIRK

WATERSTONE
MEDIA

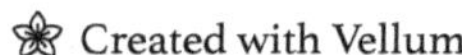 Created with Vellum

*For Sebastian, Joy,
and Fiona*

THE STORY SO FAR

One of the challenges of writing a series is ensuring readers can pick up new entries without having to re-read previous installments whenever a new title is released. Often, authors resort to a standard bag of tricks to help readers. Characters awkwardly reminisce about past events, or we scatter flashbacks throughout the story. Needless to say, such tricks often interrupt the natural flow of a story, so in an attempt to avoid that problem, I've instead tried to summarize the key events of the previous installments. I hope you find it useful.

Band of Broken Gods opens on a father named Hakon searching for his daughter. Once the fearsome leader of a legendary band of warriors, he started a new, more peaceful life with his late wife and now-grown daughter. He is tehoin, a warrior capable of manipulating the mysterious power his people call teho.

His daughter, Cliona, has left home and has been living and studying at an academy in the rapidly growing city of Vispeda. A curious soul, she is one of the foremost interpreters of a long-dead language spoken by the gods of myth and legend, the stamfar. Recently, she disappeared, leaving no clue as to her destination. Hakon braves a vicious wilderness and old foes to seek her out.

As he travels, he hears the first rumors of a possible war, set in motion by a name he hasn't heard in almost a hundred years. Damion is a powerful warrior, an ancient kolma like Hakon, building a force of tehoin far to the west of the Six States in the secluded stone fortress of Aysgarth.

While Hakon searches, Cliona works at an archaeological site led by a cantankerous older scholar from her academy. They seek the home of a famous stamfar, Marjaana, hoping to uncover the mysteries hidden within. She's joined by Zachary, a noble son exiled from his house for murdering his sister's abusive fiancé.

Their dig is a success, and they find the home buried deep underground. Not long after the discovery, Cliona learns the academy didn't fund their dig, as she'd assumed. Their actual benefactor is a mysterious and powerful man named Damion.

Damion convinces Cliona to join him in Aysgarth, where she can study the ancient texts and search for references to an object lost long ago. She agrees, and Zachary accompanies them.

Back in the Six States, Hakon suspects his daughter has gotten entangled in Damion's schemes. He discovers that the academy in Vispeda is run by another familiar face. Solveig, a warrior who was once part of his band, has become an accomplished scholar. She leads him to Ari, a quiet and yet skilled assassin who was also one of the band.

Together, Ari and Hakon find the dig site, as well as the corpses of the academics who worked on it. Damion killed them to prevent word of his efforts from spreading.

There is no love lost between Hakon and Damion. They once fought on opposite sides of a great rebellion, and

Hakon knows that if Damion discovers Cliona is his daughter, her life will be forfeit. Fortunately, Cliona herself doesn't know who her father really is. He's never told her of his long life before he settled down with her mortal mother.

Hakon, driven by necessity, reunites his old band. First, they find the master swordsman Irric, followed by Meshell, the only other kolma who can manipulate teho within her body like Hakon.

Once together, a strange stamfar named Isira visits them. She fought the band in the past and once imprisoned them for the crimes Hakon committed. She is the only foe they fear more than Damion.

The band convinces the stamfar to spare them, though she makes it clear she is watching their every move. Finally, the band travels west to rescue Cliona from Aysgarth.

In Aysgarth, Cliona meets an enormous dragon, a creature that had long vanished from the Six States. Damion controls it, making him an even more fearsome leader. Over time, her trust in Damion erodes. She finally finds the secret Damion has been searching for. Instead of revealing it to him, she escapes Aysgarth with Zachary by her side.

After a dramatic escape, aided by Damion's dragon, Cliona and Zachary meet up with the band on their way to rescue them. Cliona sees her father fight and realizes he is not the man she thought he was.

The reunion between father and daughter is bittersweet. Hakon has his daughter back, but she is wounded by the lifetime of lies he's told her about his past.

Together, the group decides they must travel to Husavik, the place Damion has sought for years. It is an abandoned city deep in the wastes, and Cliona is certain it is the burial place for a stamfar named Ava.

Once they reach Husavik, Zachary betrays them. The young man reveals that Damion has blackmailed him since the beginning. Damion captures Cliona as his troops flood into the old and nearly forgotten city.

Forced to work for Damion, Cliona eventually finds the burial site. As Damion moves to secure it, the band attacks. They intend to both rescue Cliona and prevent Damion from reaching Ava's grave. But they are vastly outnumbered, and Damion has brought his dragon.

It is a fierce battle, and in the fighting, Zachary is gravely wounded. All looks lost, especially when Damion deals a fatal wound to Cliona.

Though her body dies, Hakon is certain some part of her lives on in the dragon, which she freed from Damion's control. Hakon mounts the dragon and in one final blow, ends Damion's life.

After, Isira appears on the scene and agrees with Hakon that there is something strange surrounding the events of Cliona's death. She takes Cliona's body for safekeeping. The band is victorious once again, but at a cost much higher than anyone was prepared to pay.

Fall of Forgotten Gods opens eight months after the conclusion of *Band of Broken Gods*. Hakon and Zachary are both struggling with Cliona's apparent death, each in their own way. Hakon has traveled the width and breadth of the Six States, searching for clues that might explain what happened that fateful day in Husavik. Zachary journeyed west, seeking any sign of the elder dragon. Both are frustrated by their inability to find answers. There's been no sign of the elder dragon nor any evidence supporting their desperate belief that Cliona still lives.

Meanwhile, the situation in the Six States grows direr. The wild is launching coordinated attacks, destroying caravans and young settlements. There are fewer and fewer tehoin to protect the brave settlers. Worse, there is evidence that dragons are returning to the Six States after being driven far away.

In Vispeda, a dragon appears in the sky just as Ava breaks free from her long confinement. Ari and Solveig attempt to fight, but their efforts are futile. Both Ava and the dragon are far too strong.

The Band, plus Zachary, gathers in Vispeda to discuss the challenges facing humanity. Though Solveig continues to ask for help from the more populous cities to the east, her requests are always denied. The cities believe their distance from the frontier will protect them, and they fear suffering the same losses the western militia units have experienced.

At the meeting, Hakon argues that they are stretched too thin. There are only five of them, and they can't possibly protect the entirety of the Six States. Instead, they should strike out west, seeking the home of the dragons. Though he hopes to find Cliona there, he also believes they may find the answers to save the Six States. The others believe he's only holding onto a foolish hope, but Hakon refuses to listen to reason. He storms out of the meeting, set upon his path. Meshell agrees to accompany him and keep him safe.

The meeting represents a turning point for Zachary. His father has been demanding that he return home, but Zachary has little interest in Mioska. In secret, he's been approached by Hel, the head of the new ruling council at Aysgarth, hastily formed after Damion's death at Hakon's hands. They want to recruit Zachary, and their offer is more tempting than his father's. When he tells the band he'll be traveling to Aysgarth, the remaining warriors decide to join him. They hope to recruit more tehoin to the defense of the Six States.

Meshell and Hakon endure a brutal journey into the deep wilds. On their quest, they discover more mysteries, including strange tunnels dug by the stamfar and evidence of a dragon killed by its own kin. Eventually, they stumble upon a massive structure unlike any they have seen in their long lives. Unfortunately, Hakon is seriously wounded on their journey. Just beyond the structure, Hakon senses his daughter within the mountain nest of the dragons. He attempts to assault the mountain, leaving Meshell no choice but to knock him unconscious and return him to Aysgarth.

The arrival of the band in Aysgarth results in mixed reactions. The fortress has been attacked by dragons, and they know they don't have the food to survive the winter. Some are excited that help has arrived, but several of Damion's closest surviving commanders view the band's presence as an affront to their founder's memory. The situation grows more complicated when both Isira and Ava appear, dueling in the skies above. The battle results in an uneasy alliance between Isira, the band, and Aysgarth. Isira sticks stubbornly to her beliefs, refusing all responsibility and telling the Aysgarthians that if they want a leader, they should turn to Solveig.

Isira's proclamation sets off a fierce debate. Zachary risks his life to disagree with the ancient stamfar, an outburst that forces Hakon to explain the events of the band's past. He tells the tale of the band's birth, forged in battle against an elder dragon over a hundred years ago. He talks about the years of dedicated service to the empire, followed by Torsten's and Damion's corruption, which led to them joining the Rebellion. And finally, he talks about his decision to kill Torsten after the war was over. That decision was the one that broke the band apart and led to their long imprisonment. After hearing the story, Zachary is not impressed. He argues they're still so wrapped up in the past that they can't fight for the future.

The events at Aysgarth result in two decisions: the band will once again travel to the nest of the dragons to find Cliona, and Zachary will return home to Mioska in a bid to find food for Aysgarth.

Far to the west, the band explores the enormous structure, finding mystery after mystery within. They watch the dragon nest, only to have Ava appear and go within. Hakon, worried for Cliona, leads the band in an attempt to rescue his daughter. Inside the nest, they find the elder dragon from Husavik, bound by invisible chains of teho. Hakon confirms that some part of Cliona lives within the dragon. While he struggles to free his daughter, the band fights Ava.

In Mioska, Zachary finds that much has changed in his absence. His father is dying and his younger brother, Tollak, is unfit to take charge of the family affairs. Upon Zachary's return, Tollak tries to assassinate his brother, an attempt that fails miserably. Zachary exiles his brother to the western frontier and takes his father's seat on the council, only to find himself stymied by the more established nobles. Before he can even discuss a deal with Aysgarth, two dragons appear in the skies above and attack the city.

Back at the dragon nest, Hakon has freed the elder dragon and rides it into battle. Despite his heroic efforts, Ava deals a fatal blow to the dragon. The band, for all their strength, is helpless before her. As she is about to deliver the final blow, Isira appears and drives Ava away, though at a great cost to her own body.

Zachary loses all hope in his fight against the dragons. He saves whom he can, but Mioska has no defenses. Then Hel arrives with the remaining Aysgarthians, and they fight the dragons off. Zachary and Hel are hailed as heroes, and a deal is struck between Mioska and Aysgarth. The former rebels will provide protection in exchange for food.

The elder dragon and Cliona ask Hakon to kill them, and after fighting against the inevitable, Hakon acquiesces. He drives his sword into the dragon's heart, ending its agony. He believes his daughter is lost for good.

But Isira is not so sure. Secrets lie buried deep within her, and she believes Cliona is walking a path no tehoin has stepped foot on before.

All of which leads us to the present moment...

1

Hakon let go of Isira's small hand the moment the transport completed. Ari, on his other side, did the same. Hakon almost fell forward as vertigo assaulted his senses. Isira hadn't said anything about their destination before leaving, so Hakon was unprepared to find himself standing near the edge of a long drop. A moment before, he'd been on a flat and safe stretch of ground underneath the mysterious structure Isira called a ship.

He caught his balance as a sharp wind rose from the valley below. It cut through his clothing like daggers, and he summoned a small amount of teho to keep his body warm. Ari, who lacked the ability, wrapped his arms around his chest and hugged himself tightly. Seeing the impressive assassin shivering like a child climbing out of a river brought a smile to Hakon's face, though it didn't last long.

"What are you grinning at?" Ari asked. "Do what you need to do but make it fast. Otherwise, I'll leave you behind."

"You'll do no such thing," Isira snapped.

Ari didn't argue. The stamfar had been grumpy since

their battle with Ava, and even the most feared assassin in the world knew when to hold his tongue.

Hakon focused Isira on their reason for coming. "Let's hurry before Ari turns into a decorative icicle."

Isira fixed Ari with a glare. "Don't you even consider making your own transport point here. If I sense the slightest hint of one, I'll kill you and deal with Solveig's wrath later."

Ari waved her away, then turned to enjoy the view.

Part of Hakon wished he could stay and do the same. He was no stranger to mountain peaks, but Isira's shelter had a vista that surpassed any place he'd been before. The mountains here were jagged points of granite, too young to be softened and weathered by the ages. Hakon couldn't guess where they were, but he suspected it was a long way from the Six States.

A really long way.

He heard Isira turn behind him, and he gave the vista one last parting look before he followed after her. A cave, its edges too round to be natural, had been dug into the side of the mountain. It reminded Hakon of the caves he and Meshell had found on their last journey west. Questions danced on the tip of his tongue, but he kept silent. Isira wasn't conversational at the best of times. Now that she was finally allowing Hakon into her home, she was even less so.

About twenty feet into the cave, they came to a wall made of a material Hakon couldn't name. It was something the stamfar had built with. It was lighter than wood but stronger than steel. Hakon ran his fingertips down the smooth surface. One question came to mind that he hoped Isira might answer. "Why build here?"

"It's far away from everyone."

He was sure privacy had something to do with her

choice, but that couldn't be all. He let his gaze rest on her until she relented.

"I've always liked mountains. The high places few people visit. There's something—eternal—about them."

Hakon thought he understood. "Like how I feel when I look up at a starry night sky. They'll last far longer than I will."

"Exactly." She ran her hand over a small panel, and a door appeared in the wall and opened silently. "Welcome."

Hakon followed her in, curious about what her home would be like. Back in the years of the Rebellion, they'd spent months searching for any clue of this place. Now, even though he was here, he wasn't sure he'd ever find it again.

Once he entered, she ran her fingers over another panel, and the light of the stamfar flooded the small space as the door closed. Hakon focused his senses, but there was no teho flowing through the ceiling. All he felt was the faintest of vibrations beneath his feet.

Isira saved him from fighting back his questions. "Electricity. A science that has long been lost to you. I don't know how to recreate it. I'm but a recipient of my ancestor's gifts, the same as anyone else."

"It's true, then? Everything you told me?"

"As far as I know."

Hakon shook his head, unable to work through all the implications. He distracted himself by studying the rooms. Paintings hung on the wall, and two large bookcases filled a whole side of the living room.

Hakon recognized the letters of the stamfar along the spines. "Cliona would love it here." He gestured to the books. "She's obsessed with stamfar tales." Too late, he caught his mistake. "I mean, she was."

It felt as though he'd swallowed a rock that had gotten stuck in his throat.

He closed his eyes and tried to think of anything else.

Instead, he was back on that damned mountain, driving his sword into the dragon's chest. Into his daughter's heart.

He opened his eyes to flee the scene, only to find Isira staring at him.

"Why?" she asked. "Perhaps not like this, but you had to know the gates would steal them from you someday."

It was always the same question. The immortal tehoin had never understood. Instead of embracing joy, no matter how fleeting, they fled from pain. Too many were like Isira, frightened of any relationship. Nothing Hakon could say would ease that fear.

But he always tried anyway. "It's worth it. For all the pain today brings, raising Cliona is the feat I'm most proud of. Our moments together mean more to me than any other accomplishment I could claim." He swallowed hard, trying and failing to budge the rock. "Every moment was worth it."

Emotions threatened to choke him, and he took a deep, shuddering breath.

Isira looked at him like he was a fool. The immortals always did whenever the subject came up.

He'd hoped for more from Isira, but her reaction had at least had the effect of sapping some of the strength of his grief. No matter what he endured, life continued on.

"Can I see her?" he asked.

"Of course." Isira led him deeper into her house, and he let his eyes wander over the different furnishings.

The bedroom held another bookcase and an unmade bed. Paintings hung within, too, giving the windowless space a sense of warmth and openness it would otherwise lack.

It felt unreal to walk through these rooms. Isira had always been a mystery. If anyone knew why she had halted her aging as a child, they were long dead. Until Ava's escape earlier that year from the academy in Vispeda, Isira had unquestionably been the strongest tehoin in the world, yet she made almost no use of her power. Most ahula didn't even know she existed. She had no legend, unlike many of the stamfar she'd outlived.

He'd expected her house to reflect that mystery. But beyond the stamfar construction and the location, it was as mundane as any home he'd ever stepped into.

She led him all the way to the back, into a storage room. For the first time since their arrival, she used teho, filling a door along the back wall with enough to level a small village. Hakon gaped at the strength she so casually wielded. The door slid aside so fast it was as if it was jumping out of her way.

Inside the secret room sat a glowing cylinder, the design all too familiar. Hakon clenched his fists at the sight. Isira had imprisoned him and the band within chambers like the one in front of him for generations. Such had been her judgment for Hakon's murder of Torsten.

His years within that cage had been a living hell. Awake but unable to move. But now, the cursed chamber was the only hope he had left.

Isira's childish hands ran across the controls, their movement too experienced for their size. She watched over the readouts with a close eye, information scrolling rapidly across the transparent material that enclosed his daughter's body.

She finished and looked up at him, still frozen by the door. "Is something wrong?"

"No." Hakon tried to move his feet, but it was as if they'd sank into the stone of the mountain.

The air felt thick and warm. His left hand was shaking, so he balled it up into a fist. He took one step forward, and it was as though he was pulling a cart laden with bricks. Finally, he reached her chamber and looked down at her body.

The tears fell before he could stop them. Though the body before him was that of a young adult, he couldn't help but see her as the little girl she'd once been. The stone in his throat grew bigger. His knees trembled as he placed his hand on the cylinder. It was cold to the touch.

He could leave. Pretend there was still some kind of hope left. He'd already held on beyond reason and been proven right. If he left now, perhaps history would repeat itself. Maybe ignorance was less painful.

He swallowed his fears. His past already consumed too much of him. If he wanted any future at all, he needed to know.

"Open it, please," he said, his voice hoarse.

Isira's hands danced once more, and the transparent lid slid away.

Hakon hesitated one more moment, then put his hand on his daughter's shoulder. He closed his eyes.

Tears dripped from them onto the cold body.

Before, in Husavik, he'd felt the ghostly tendrils of teho whispering their way through her body. Not life, exactly, but not death, either.

Now there was nothing at all.

He pulled his hand away. "Would you?"

Isira reached out and placed her own hand across Cliona's forehead, like a concerned mother taking her child's temperature. After a moment, she pulled her hand away. "I'm sorry, Hakon."

He wiped the tears from his face. "How long do these last?"

"This type has its own power. If nothing happens to it, it should last until these mountains are worn down to hills."

"Can you help me carry it out?"

"Sure."

Isira sealed the cylinder once again, then wrapped thin but powerful strands of teho around it. It rose as though supported by invisible pallbearers. Together, they retreated through Isira's home, back to where Ari waited. The assassin looked halfway frozen, but he uttered no complaints when he saw the procession. Isira used her teho to lay the cylinder down as gently as a leaf falling onto thick grass.

"Thank you," Hakon said.

There was so much history between them, he didn't know what else he could say. She owed him less than nothing yet had helped him in a desperate hour. He bowed deeply, holding the posture long enough that Ari started to shuffle his feet to stay warm. When he rose, he received a brief nod from Isira in return. She went back into her home without another word and shut the door behind her.

Ari didn't need to ask. He could read every expression on his old friend's face. "I'm sorry," he said.

Hakon's tears were already freezing in his beard. "Thank you."

He looked around, taking in the vista one last time.

She would have liked it here.

"It's time to take her home," he said.

2

———

Zachary had attended his fair share of funerals over the years, but Cliona's stood apart not just in manner but in impact. She wasn't the first close acquaintance he'd lost, but her loss cut him deeper than any of the others.

The band was gathered outside Cliona's childhood home, hidden deep in the great woods to the east of Vispeda. Zachary had glimpsed the cabin when Ari had transported him and Hel in. It was a simple design, squat and sturdy, but with room enough for a small family. Perhaps most interesting, though, was that there were no neighbors nearby.

Knowing what he did about Hakon now, the decision made sense, but it forced him to consider Cliona in a new light. Everyone grew up with neighbors. To do otherwise was to invite the wilds to attack. Had anyone but Hakon built and defended this house, the wilds would have devoured the family and structure long ago. But Cliona had grown up out here, alone, with this old forest as her playroom and classroom. It was little wonder, then, as to why she'd been so independent and stubborn. She'd never known any other way.

It seemed a shame that he only understood this about her now that it was too late.

The funeral was small. Far smaller than Cliona deserved. Besides him and Hel, only the five members of the band had gathered. And apparently, Hakon had needed to be convinced about allowing the two of them to join.

There should have been more people here. He'd been to plenty of funerals of people who'd achieved less but had been more honored in death. Cliona hadn't even known most of the people attending her funeral until near the end of her life. Where were her friends? The people she was closest to?

It was only upon reflection that he remembered she hadn't been close to many people, not even at the academy. She'd been missing from the grounds for over a year, and almost no one had noticed. She had traveled lightly through the world, barely leaving a trace on most people's hearts.

He pushed the dark thoughts aside as he returned his attention to the hole he helped to dig. He worked beside Ari and Irric, two tehoin who could have scooped out this hole using teho with little more than a thought. But they hadn't even discussed the possibility. They'd just transported in, collected the spades, and started digging.

The location was a few hundred feet south of the house, in a small sunlit clearing. A stone marker told Zachary that Cliona's body wasn't the first one buried there. He assumed the other was Sera, Cliona's mother. Tears blurred his vision, but he didn't dare wipe them away with his grimy hands. Cliona was gone, and now Hakon had no one left but the band.

They worked in silence, not finishing the hole until just

past midday. Zachary climbed out of the hole, then helped Irric and Ari out. They all turned to Hakon, who kneeled beside the strange cylinder that held Cliona's body. The giant warrior wept, practically draped over the transparent material that formed the top of the cylinder.

Zachary glanced over at Irric and Ari, hoping for some guidance as to what to do next. But their faces were expressionless. Ari went to Solveig, and the two of them wandered off a way.

Irric gestured to where Hel stood, alone near the edge of the clearing. "Be with her. Hakon will let us know when he's ready." With that, the swordsman walked to Meshell, who also stood alone.

Zachary put his spade down and went to Hel. She reached out her hand and he took it. The simple feeling of her hand in his grounded him. Though the band had shown him nothing but kindness, there was no denying the distance between them. They were ancient warriors, already shrouded in legend. He was a middling vilda who had stumbled into their lives. They looked at the world in ways that fundamentally would never be reconciled. His interactions with them felt unreal.

Hel, it seemed, felt much the same. "It's strange, seeing them like this. I can't even tell if any of them besides Hakon care."

Harsh as the words sounded, Zachary agreed. Hakon's grief was real and raw, but the others barely seemed interested. They seemed to be here more as a kindness to an old friend. When he looked at them, he was reminded of a funeral he'd attended with his father many years ago. It was for some council member his father had worked closely with. That whole afternoon, his father had grumbled under his breath about the length of the ceremony.

Zachary reminded himself that only Solveig had known Cliona at all. He knew none were as shallow as his father. "Sometimes, I try to imagine what it's like, being them. What it would be like to be alive so much longer than anyone else. To watch so many people, friend and foe alike, die before them."

He sighed. "I try, but I can't put myself in their position. I can't even begin to guess what they're feeling right now."

She squeezed his hand but had no answer to his observation.

After a considerable time, Hakon rose and nodded. Ari and Irric came forward and wrapped the cylinder in teho. Together, they lifted it, carried it to the hole, then placed it softly within. The others gathered around, and Zachary looked down at Cliona's body. Thanks to the advanced design of the tube, her features were well-lit. In his experience, dead bodies had always seemed dead, as though something vital had leeched off their features. Cliona didn't look that way. To his eyes, she was merely sleeping. He wasn't sure if that reflected his own desires or was simply another effect of the cylinder.

She looked much the same as when he'd first seen her, nose-deep in a book at the academy. She'd wanted little to do with him in Vispeda, and he couldn't say he blamed her. It wasn't until the dig that she paid any attention to him.

He was so focused on her features, he almost missed the movement beside him. Hakon, Irric, and Ari had grabbed their spades and were waiting for him. He picked up his own and nodded.

There were no words shared. Hakon tossed the first spadeful of dirt on the cylinder, and the others followed after, working in silence until the hole was once again filled.

When it was done, Irric collected the spades and returned them to Hakon's house.

They all stood around the grave, and eventually, Hakon spoke. "Thank you all for coming. It means everything to me to have you here today."

He lapsed into silence. Then, after a time, he gestured to Solveig. Zachary frowned when he realized the funeral was already over.

Solveig nodded, then turned to the others. "The question is, what do we do next? Ava seeks to destroy what remains of humanity, and Isira is dying. For the first time in a long time, our fates are truly ours to decide. No path is denied us."

When Ari had arrived in Aysgarth to find Zachary and Hel, he'd caught the two younger tehoin up on the events that had happened far to the west. In return, they shared their tale of the attack on Mioska and the alliance that had resulted. The exchange had been brief, but it was the first Zachary had heard of Cliona's true death. He hadn't yet had time to consider what came after. He still reeled from the news, and the short funeral hadn't brought a hint of closure.

"You have to help!" he blurted. At their answering looks, he retreated a pace. "Don't you?"

Ari glared at him. "We don't *have* to do anything. Not anymore."

Zachary gulped and held up his hands.

After a few moments of tense silence, Hakon cleared his throat. "I'm going to find a way to kill Ava."

Zachary started to object, but the expressions on the faces of the band stilled his tongue. They'd expected this. But would they follow? From Ari's brief description of the events on the mountain, it sounded as though Ava had made short work of the band the last time they'd fought.

Meshell said nothing. She stepped closer and took Hakon's hand.

Irric rolled his shoulders back. "Never is boring, having you around."

The three looked to Ari and Solveig. Of the band, those two had been the most active in shaping the current course of the Six States. They'd also built a relationship with each other that had spanned no small number of years. They had the most to lose.

The two shared a look that tore Zachary's heart in two. He couldn't guess what passed between them, but it encompassed more history than he'd been alive for.

When Ari answered, his voice was barely louder than a whisper. "We'll join you."

Hakon bowed toward them. "Thank you."

Zachary stepped forward. "I'd like to come, too."

He heard Hel shift her weight behind him, ready to object. But Hakon shook his head first. "No. Our paths part here."

"I want revenge, too."

"Sure, and what's a vilda going to do against an ancient stamfar?" Irric asked. "I seem to recall your last plan nearly ended up with you flattened like a pancake outside of Aysgarth."

Shame flushed Zachary's cheeks.

Irric's tone softened. "From what Ari told us, you have a real chance to do some good in the Six States. Why throw that away on this foolishness?" The swordsman glanced meaningfully at Hel. "Stay here and build something better."

Zachary was about to protest, but Ari ended the argument with his customary finality. "I'm not transporting you anywhere, kid, so you might as well drop it."

Zachary growled, but he wasn't going to intimidate any of the band. If anything, they looked amused at his attempt. Hel reached out and grabbed his hand. She pulled him back toward her, breaking the pointless stalemate.

He admitted defeat. "Will I at least have the chance to see any of you again?"

Irric shrugged. "Seems unlikely, but there's never any telling, is there?"

He wanted to plead with them to stay. To insist, despite everything they knew, that there had to be another way. Instead, he bowed. "I hope you're successful and that when you've defeated Ava, you find me wherever I am."

The band gathered closer together and grasped one another's hands, preparing for transport.

Soon, only Hakon stood apart from the others. He looked at Zachary. "Everything with the dragons will only get worse before it gets better. And if we fail, it might never get better. The Six States will need a steady hand. Someone who will make the hard choices."

"And a whole lot of luck," Ari grumbled.

"And that," Hakon said. "I think that person might be you."

"I'll try," Zachary promised.

"It's all any of us can do." Hakon looked back at his house and at the graves that marked the family he had lost. To Zachary, it appeared as though he was saying goodbye. Then Hakon stepped back and clasped Meshell's free hand.

Ari looked around the group, and when he was sure there was nothing left to say, he transported them away.

After a moment, Hel coughed. "Not quite as helpful as I'd hoped."

Zachary understood but wasn't concerned. "They don't

have any better ideas about the Six States than we do. What they do is the most useful thing they can."

Hel nestled into his side. They looked down at Cliona's grave. "How are you?" she asked.

"Sad," he admitted. "I'd always hoped there would be a way to get her back."

"Ready to return yet?"

"Not quite."

He kneeled next to Cliona's grave. He felt a bit self-conscious, but he needed to say the next part out loud. "You were the one that taught me to fight. I promise not to stop fighting until the day I walk through the gate and join you."

He waited as though his patience would result in some response from the dead. But there was nothing except the sounds of the woods beyond the clearing. The sun was falling, and the wilds grew more active.

He stood. "Now I'm ready."

A hint of a smile played across Hel's face. "You sure? Because they went to kill a god, and I still can't help but think they left the hard work to us."

That drew a chuckle out of him. "True. But someone needs to pick up their slack."

He reached out again and took her hand, and she transported them back to Aysgarth.

Back into the heart of the chaos.

3

Ari transported them to the camp they'd built beside the giant ship. It wasn't their first choice of location, but it was where Isira had said that she would meet them once she was sufficiently recovered. This far west, the sun was still high in the sky, so they had plenty of time to fall into their accustomed roles. Solveig started a fire while Irric carved up the meat he planned to cook.

Hakon left them, shaking his head at Meshell's questioning glance. He didn't plan on going far.

His steps carried him underneath the ship. He reached up and brushed his fingertips along the surface, just as he had at Isira's home. The materials weren't the same. Whatever this ship was made of, it was far stronger than Isira's walls. But it was similar.

He swore. If what Isira had hinted at was true, this ship had carried humanity between the stars. It had withstood forces only a stamfar could hope to wield.

The skill to make it had been lost, and instead of seeking it, he'd spent his life fighting and destroying.

When he saw this ship, he was awed. But he was also ashamed.

He'd always wanted to create a better world. And there had been plenty of days when he'd thought he was carving out the shape of that world with his sword. But all that time, this had been out here, pointing in a different direction.

Had he wasted his life?

He didn't know the answer to that. He wanted to believe the answer was no, but the rational part of his mind wouldn't let him off the hook so easily.

On the other side of the ship, the mountain that had once been filled with dragons was silent. They'd all expected the dragons to return after the battle, but none had. Hakon didn't know if that meant all the dragons had died or if they remained away for some other purpose. He leaned toward the latter. Despite Zachary and Hel's impressive victory in Mioska, Hakon couldn't believe that all the dragons had fallen.

He stared up at the mountain until the smell of roasting meat pulled his gaze away. He returned to the fire and sat down beside Meshell. His return silenced the conversation the others had been in the middle of.

"No need to stop on my account," Hakon said.

"Can't blame us for being worried about you," Irric replied.

"It's appreciated but unnecessary. The grief will run its stages in time."

"Are you good to fight, though?" Solveig asked. "Can we depend on you if things get hairy?"

His glare answered that question. The others let the matter drop.

"We were talking about Zachary," Irric said. "Most of us

expected him to fight harder to join us. We were wondering if maybe we were too hard on him."

Hakon shook his head. "He has no place here, and we all know it. Better we make that point clear than delay the inevitable."

"Do you think he has any chance at making a difference in the Six States?" Meshell asked. "My feeling has always been that they're too divided."

"I don't know," Solveig answered, "but if anyone can, it's him. He's grown a lot in the last few years, and his heart is in the right place. And he's the only one that has any say in both Aysgarth and Mioska. He'd do better than any of us."

"Doesn't make me feel all that good about leaving him on his own, though," Ari admitted. "His task will be almost as difficult as ours."

Hakon grabbed one of the roasting pieces of meat. It was barely cooked, just the way he liked it. "Then we might as well finish this so we can help him."

Meshell let out a bitter laugh at that.

They ate well that night, and for a time, Hakon was able to think about more than just Cliona. Her absence created a void in his heart that he knew the rest of the band was trying to fill. But for all their efforts, they couldn't. Sera and Cliona had been the best parts of his life, and his family his greatest accomplishment.

Eventually, the fire burned low, and there was still no sign of Isira. Before retiring, Solveig checked on every member of the band. They'd suffered their fair share of injuries during their last battle, and Solveig refused to let them fight Ava again before they were fully healed. But even she had to admit that they'd all healed faster than she expected. If Isira was to lead them into battle tomorrow, they'd be ready.

Before long, the others were softly snoring beside him, and Hakon lay awake, staring at the stars as they twinkled in the dark sky far above. When his eyes finally closed, his dreams were of his family, back when they'd been whole.

He woke up the next morning later than the others. By the time he'd rubbed the sleep from his eyes, he had a plate of breakfast in front of him. The scents of the food made his mouth water, and he devoured everything on his plate and anything the others had left unfinished.

In the middle of stuffing his face, Isira appeared.

Hakon tensed at the sight of her. The combination of her nearly eternal childhood and unbelievable power made him uneasy in a way that no one else did. Even dragons had a fearsome visage to accompany their strength.

Isira hardly seemed like the stamfar they knew. She shuffled into their camp and flopped onto a stump next to the coals of their fire. She held out her hands to warm them, ignoring the band as though she was the only one in the camp.

Hakon met Solveig's gaze. He sensed it as well. Isira's teho came and went, like waves crashing powerfully against a shore and then pulling away. When it vanished, she felt nearly as weak as an ahula. But when it peaked, it was stronger than Hakon had ever felt it.

After a few tense moments, Isira spoke. "Ava needs to be stopped. She plays with forces better left alone."

"Is she doing *that*?" Solveig asked, gesturing at Isira.

"I don't believe so. This is my body failing. It can't hold teho the way it once did. But this is about as bad as it gets. I wouldn't normally appear before you in such a state, but I fear Ava won't leave us much time."

"We've decided to help," Solveig said. "However we can, we'll help you kill Ava. It's the only way to protect the Six States."

Isira looked up sharply at Solveig. "Ava is only half your problem."

"But she was the one who commanded the dragons to attack the states," Solveig said.

"True, but she isn't responsible for the wilds, though I think she seeks to take advantage of and influence those events as well. Remember, she wasn't free when the wilds began encroaching on the western frontier."

After the numerous battles of the last few years, Hakon was embarrassed to admit the thought had never occurred to him. He'd always assumed that Ava's growing power had been responsible for everything, even though she'd been completely imprisoned until the battle at Husavik.

The others were similarly taken aback, and Hakon took some small solace in knowing he wasn't the only one caught by surprise.

Solveig recovered first. "Perhaps it would be best if you told us everything you know." She pointed up to the ship, towering over their heads. "Everything."

Isira looked up at the ship, her gaze lost in a past Hakon couldn't begin to imagine. Finally, she nodded. "It might feel good to let go of this burden."

She grabbed a stick next to her feet and poked at the fire. "You should know, a lot of what I know is guesswork, nothing more than tales and rumors I've stitched together over the years. I was born near the end of the age of the stamfars, and much had already been lost."

She looked up again at the ship. "As I've told you, we are

all descended from ancestors who came here from the stars. I don't know where they came from or why, exactly, they traveled here, but I believe they were fleeing from something. All across the continent, one can find tunnels buried deep underground. That dragon nest in the nearby peak began as such a tunnel. So did my own home. Perhaps those star farers had another purpose, but I can't imagine another reason one would fly between the stars, only to bury their new cities underground on a beautiful planet."

Hakon thought of the cave entrances he and Meshell had found on their way here and shuddered. He'd found them spooky before, but Isira's tale made them more ominous. What did one flee when one had the power to travel unimaginable distances?

"What happened?" he asked.

"As far as I know, nothing," Isira answered. "Eventually, they left the caves and became the parents of the first generation of stamfar. The children born on this planet had the ability to use what we now call teho. They spread out and founded cities, establishing many of the legends we still tell today. But something happened, and the cities collapsed, and the stamfar turned against one another. There were cycles of war and peace, but with every war, more of the past was lost. Teho replaced the knowledge and skills the star travelers had used, but over the generations, the strength of the tehoin began to fade."

She paused and swept her arm out to encompass the wilds surrounding them. "And through it all, the world never stopped fighting us. As we lost both our ancient knowledge and teho, the world became more dangerous. Torsten understood this. He saw the long arc of history bending toward our inevitable demise. He believed, like the emperors before him, that the only way for humanity to survive was to unite. He hoped to establish an empire that would no longer contract. From there, he hoped to rediscover the knowledge of the travelers and bring about a new age of human flourishing."

Torsten's dream was an uncomfortable echo of Hakon's recent thoughts. "Why didn't he just say so?"

Isira's face twitched. "A dozen reasons and more. For one, he didn't think enough people would believe him. He was young by stamfar reckoning, and many of his beliefs were based on the stories I had told him. There was no proof within the empire that any of what I tell you today is true. Perhaps more importantly, though, he didn't believe the empire he served was strong enough to push the wild back. The emperors were too weak. Thus, he believed the only way forward was to become a benevolent tyrant, one who had the strength and the vision to force humanity into the future."

"There's been more progress in the last forty years in the Six States than there was in the hundred and thirty years of the last empire," Solveig pointed out. "Tyranny rarely breeds innovation."

"I'll not deny it," Isira said. She poked at the fire again. "When I first knew Torsten, he was a singular man. He was well-read, intelligent, and thoroughly grounded in reality. If anyone was capable of achieving the future he envisioned, it was him. But thanks in no small part to the band, the task was beyond even his skill. The more you pulled his vision away from him, the more detached from reality he became. By the end, he became more tyrant than visionary."

"Is that why you left?" Hakon asked.

Isira nodded. "It was one of the hardest decisions of my life. Torsten was one of the few who was ever able to look beyond my appearance, and I do believe that his purpose was noble, even if his means were ruthless."

Ari interjected, brusque as always. "An interesting story, but what does any of it have to do with us killing Ava?"

"You can't kill Ava. Not as you are. The only solution is the same as it has always been. We need to learn the truth about this planet. That's the only place you might find the key to defeating Ava."

"And what will you be doing?" Ari asked.

"Preparing to fight Ava, too. Should you fail, I will do what I can. I still have some allies, and my body hasn't failed me yet. But I do not think I am much longer for this world. Time is one of your many enemies," Isira said.

"What, specifically, do we need to do?" Solveig asked.

"If the stories are to be believed, far to the west, you will find the remains of the traveler's original civilization. There are rumors that they uncovered an incredible power there. Torsten thought the stories referred to teho, but I've never been so certain. I believe it's your best place to find the answers to defeating both the wild and Ava."

Ari laughed out loud. "You want us to wander even farther west? Just getting here almost killed Hakon. Now you want us to find some mythical city? Why not transport us there?"

"I've never been. I don't dare."

"Why not?" Ari's voice was drier than the logs in the fire.

"There's an enormous nest of dragons that way. This is about as far west as I've ever dared transport."

Ari stood and walked away from the fire, shaking his head and muttering.

Hakon agreed with his old friend. "You're asking us to take a lot on trust. This is a gamble, even for us."

"Why would I lie?" Isira asked. "If I wanted you dead, all I'd have to do is snap my fingers."

Hakon couldn't argue that, either.

Solveig, as usual, was the one who kept the coolest head. "Do you think that this is a better plan than joining forces to attack Ava?"

"I've come across her twice, and both times I've only survived because of your heroic antics. I'd rather have something more certain for my third attempt. Remember, if we fail, there's no other plan. The humanity you've fought so long for will be no more."

Solveig looked to Hakon, as though he had any answers.

He rose from his own seat and kneeled before Isira. He took her tiny hand in his and looked into her eyes. "Tell me this is the way."

She didn't flinch. "It's the way. The only one I've thought of."

"You'll protect the Six States or grab us if we're needed?"

"I will."

Hakon looked to Solveig. "I say we do it."

Solveig only debated for a while longer. Then she nodded. "Tell us everything we'll need to know."

4

———

Zachary tensed as soon as they appeared in Aysgarth. It was an old habit he hadn't kicked, back from the days he'd transported in with Cliona. Though his fear was groundless, he kept expecting Damion to be hiding behind the next corner, a predatory smile on his face.

Damion had died over a year ago, but his legacy lived on in Aysgarth, and there were more than enough of his devoted followers remaining to keep his vision alive. That fact was a constant thorn in his and Hel's sides as they searched for a way forward for the Six States.

Zachary forced himself to relax his shoulders. The transport room was empty. Damion was dead. He had Hel by his side and the remnants of an empire to save. It was true he hadn't sorted through all of his feelings around Cliona's death, but she'd been out of his life for far longer than she'd been a part of it. He had no time for the fears of his past. He had to focus his gaze on the future.

"I don't suppose you want to take a quick break before tackling your work for today, do you?" he asked Hel.

"Tempting, but I'd only pay for it later tonight if I did."

He grinned mischievously. "I'm sure I could make it worth it."

Hel shook her head. "Fine. But if it means a late night, you're staying up with me."

"On my honor," Zachary said.

Hel snorted. "You left that behind a long time ago."

Zachary pretended to be wounded, and they left the transport room ready to face the day ahead. Their enthusiasm lasted just as long as it took for them to leave the room. Two of Aysgarth's precious tehoin guarded the door on the other side, and they stopped the pair as soon as they stepped into the cold mountain air. The commander of the two held out a message for Hel.

She took it and opened it. Zachary, raised since birth to closely study people's reactions, saw how she carefully kept her face a mask. But her eyes flared and narrowed. Not good news then, but it seldom was. She thanked the guard and pulled Zachary away.

Aysgarth was quieter today, though that wasn't unusual. They'd already collected their meager harvest for the year, and the cold winter air kept most people inside. Combine that with the absent tehoin stationed in Mioska, and it was no wonder the mountain keep felt abandoned.

Despite this reincarnation of Aysgarth being Damion's creation, the quiet saddened Zachary. One of the defining characteristics of Aysgarth under Damion had been the constant bustle and energy of the fortress. It had reminded Zachary of the streets of Vispeda during the height of summer, except directed toward one end: establishing a new foothold for civilization to flourish, a place where tehoin were welcomed instead of excluded.

He disagreed vehemently with Damion on most other matters, but Aysgarth had been a noble dream. To see it pricked and bleeding out brought him no joy. His own dream would see Aysgarth flourishing as an outpost that eagerly cooperated with the governors of the Six States. In time, he might yet see that dream come to fruition.

Once they were out of the guard's hearing, Hel whispered. "Valdis has been causing trouble on the council again."

Zachary stifled his own curse. The dream he held of Aysgarth threatened to become mist and blow away as he thought of the troublesome nelja. Valdis had been one of Damion's closest and most trusted commanders, and at times it seemed she honored her former master by obstructing anything or anyone that might prove useful.

In his more charitable moods, Zachary reminded himself that Valdis wasn't obstructing them because she could. She had her own beliefs, twisted as he considered them. He wasn't feeling all that charitable now, though. "What's she doing?"

"Demanding that we reconsider our alliance with Mioska."

That stopped Zachary in his tracks. "What?" He shook his head, trying to wrap his head around the idea, but failed. "How?"

Hel crumpled up the note and stuffed it in her pocket. "I'm a little short on details myself, but I plan to find out. You should come with me."

"Of course." He couldn't quite keep the disappointment out of his voice.

"Look at the bright side," she said. "If we can figure this out, maybe we can call it an early night."

Zachary tried to match Hel's optimism but failed. If Valdis was causing trouble, they'd spend the rest of the day solving it, and then they'd still have the mundane problems waiting after. There was nothing for it, though, so he followed Hel.

She led him straight to Valdis' private chambers, a place he'd never been, and for good reason. More than once, the nelja had promised to kill him in a duel if she ever found him alone. He could never tell how serious she was, but he'd decided she was serious enough to avoid whenever possible. The only times he saw her were during council meetings, and even then, he sat as far away from her as possible. It occurred to him, as Hel knocked on Valdis' door, that Hel wouldn't be strong enough to protect him if Valdis made good on her promise.

Valdis opened her door, and Zachary tensed again. He swore Valdis noticed, and he prepared to run if she tried to attack him. She settled for glaring at him, then stepped aside to let them in.

Valdis' room was one of the few in the fortress that possessed a south-facing window, and the late-season light poured into the space. A writing desk had been pushed against the window, and from the position of the chair and the unstopped ink bottle, Zachary assumed they had interrupted the seasoned warrior as she'd been writing. For some reason, he found the sight ridiculous.

He stifled his laughter. His reaction was due more to his own exhaustion than the idea of Valdis spending long hours at a writing desk. If he was going to be any help to Hel, he needed to focus.

"I got your message," Hel said. "Care to explain?"

Valdis gestured at Zachary. "Does he need to be here? I still don't trust him."

"If your proposal involves Mioska, it seems appropriate to have him here."

Valdis grumbled. "Fine. We'll need to break our agreement with the city."

Zachary noted that she wasn't gloating.

"So your note said. Why?" Hel asked.

Damion's nelja jabbed her thumb in the direction of her writing desk. "We don't have enough tehoin to repair Aysgarth and defend Mioska, and if you think I'm going to allow us to abandon this place—"

Hel held out her hands to placate the warrior. "Hold on. I'm not following. No one is suggesting abandoning Aysgarth."

Zachary heard the fear in her voice at the thought. He sometimes forgot, as Hel was most often a voice of reason on the council, that Aysgarth was just as important to her as it was to Damion's most fanatical devotees. He hoped that the day never came when that love became a problem.

Hel asked, "What do you mean, we don't have enough tehoin?"

Valdis said, "When we agreed to the treaty, we didn't think through what it would mean for us long-term. We knew that we needed food and could spare the tehoin. But now that we've been cycling tehoin in and out of the city for a couple of weeks, we're starting to see the cracks in our plan. Most of the problem is that our tehoin here weren't acting solely in their official capacity. They were donating their spare hours to repair walls and prepare the fields for the spring, among a dozen other tasks. But now we've lost all of that. We can still guard our walls, but little else. I've been sitting here searching for a way to make the numbers work, but they don't. Either we pull away from Mioska or quit work on essential projects."

"And you believe our focus should be here," Hel finished the unspoken thought.

"Of course."

Valdis' conclusion didn't surprise Zachary, but her reasoning did. He understood it, even sympathized with it. This wasn't at all like the Valdis he was used to dealing with, who assumed most of her problems should just be killed.

Hel's first objection was the most obvious. "What about food? Mioska hasn't given us enough to last through the winter."

"I'm not so sure," Valdis answered. "It would require going back to our rationing plan from earlier, but with some good hunts, I think we could make it."

Zachary grimaced. He'd been here during their rationing period, and the food had been horrible. If the citizens were forced to endure a whole winter of that, the council would have a mutiny on their hands.

Hel clearly thought the same. "You run a terrible risk."

Valdis didn't deny it.

Hel considered for a moment longer. "I don't intend offense, but may I look over your numbers? There's always a chance a fresh pair of eyes may pick up something you missed."

Zachary prepared for violence, but Valdis looked relieved. "Please. As much as I despise our agreement with Mioska, I recognize how important it is. It's why I voted with you despite my misgivings."

She returned to her writing desk and gathered the relevant papers. Zachary used the time to look around the room, knowing full well he might never have such an insight into Valdis again. Unfortunately, there was little to see. The walls were bare of decoration. Zachary understood that when Damion had been alive, he'd sent Valdis hopping all around the Six States doing his bidding. She'd never used this place as anything more than a place to sleep.

It seemed a shame, given how much she sacrificed for it.

His thoughts tickled an idea in the back of his mind, but it took him a few more moments to draw it out. "There might be another way."

Valdis glared at him for daring to speak in her room, but she didn't lash out like he expected. "What?"

"Bear in mind, I'm not sure this would work, but I might be able to convince the Mioska council we don't need to have your tehoin stationed within the city walls. We might make do with just a handful of transporters. In case of attack, they would summon you to the city, and our agreements would be fulfilled."

Valdis was not impressed. "Such was discussed before the treaty was signed. Your nobles didn't agree then."

"It was right after the dragons attacked," Zachary argued. "They were terrified."

"And you believe they've found some deep well of hidden courage in the last few weeks?" Valdis asked.

Zachary found himself in the uncomfortable position of agreeing with Valdis' point. But he didn't back down. If Aysgarth withdrew, it would doom everything he hoped to accomplish. They had to stand together. "I'm not saying I'll succeed, but I'm willing to try if it would keep our agreement intact."

Valdis stepped close to him. "You would extend such trust?"

Zachary forced himself to meet her gaze. "I would."

For a moment, he wasn't sure if Valdis was going to stab him or embrace him. Fortunately, she did neither. She handed all her papers over to Hel. "Fine, try it. You have my word we would honor such an agreement."

The next thing he knew, he and Hel were standing outside Valdis' door.

"That went better than it usually does," Hel said. "I'm sorry to see you go so soon, though. I was hoping we might spend at least some time together before you had to return."

"You could always come with me," Zachary tried.

Hel turned her gaze down to the pile of papers Hel had dumped in her hands. "I can't."

"I know. I'll try to return as quickly as I can," Zachary said. He bent down and kissed her.

"Come back safe," Hel said.

"I will."

Hel returned to her rooms alone, and Zachary turned around to walk straight back to the transport room, where he would find someone to take him to Mioska.

He glanced back at Hel's departing figure. Sometimes he couldn't believe he had ever wanted a position of authority.

5

Their first few days of travel brought few difficulties. They had all remarked, during their time at the camp underneath the ship, how few visits they received from hungry predators. It was as if the foreign nature of the ship had driven the wild away.

The band had expected to run into trouble soon after their departure. They all knew the difficulties Meshell and Hakon had endured just to reach the ship, and they saw no reason why traveling farther west would be any easier. But for three long days of travel, they didn't come across a single curious predator. They found plenty of smaller creatures, from songbirds to squirrels, but none seemed interested in the band's passage. At night, they would place their defenses, but when they woke in the mornings, the wards hadn't even been tested.

It was so different from Hakon and Meshell's experience that Hakon could tell the other three were starting to entertain doubts about the story they'd been told.

Meshell's unease matched Hakon's. He saw it in the way her eyes never stopped roaming and in the way her gaze darted toward any sound she didn't recognize. He wasn't much better. Though their own journey was now weeks in the past, they still carried the scars from it.

Neither of them spoke much about their concerns. They'd known each other long enough to see the signs of distress in each other, and the reasons were simple enough to discern.

On their fourth day of travel, Meshell broke her silence. "I keep trying to figure out what's different, but nothing I think of makes any sense. Was something trying to keep us away from the ship or the nest? And now it doesn't care?"

Hakon's own thoughts had traveled in much the same direction, but he'd focused on a different aspect of the attacks. "When Isira reminded us Ava wasn't behind the changes we've seen in the wild, it made me think again about how the wild reacted to us on our last trip. I had a thought, back then, that I'm not sure I shared with you."

Meshell's expression told him she was in no mood to guess.

"I had the thought that no human intelligence would attack us the way the wild did."

Her eyes lost their focus as she recalled the attacks. Those days had been difficult for her. With Hakon unable to manipulate teho outside his body, she had borne the brunt of the assaults. She'd been the only one who could ward their camps, and those wards had been under relentless assault. When each new morning came, she'd been more exhausted than the night before. His inability to help had been one of the reasons why that trip had almost been the end of them.

"As trying as those attacks were, they were almost childlike in their simplicity. Whatever was near lashed out at us, big or small. It occurred to me, then, that if our antagonist had been even a little smarter, there would have been little we could do in response. We would have been forced to turn back," he said.

"I could agree with that," Meshell said. "But what does that have to do with us now?"

"It's not as much help as I'd like," he admitted. "But we keep thinking of our antagonist as something human, or at least something with human-like intelligence. If that's not the case, there may not be any reason we can understand for the lack of attacks now."

Meshell considered that for a moment. "That's not helpful."

"Sorry. I'm just not sure there's anything to anticipate or predict. All we can do is be prepared for whatever the world throws at us."

She arched an eyebrow. "That's also not helpful."

Hakon shrugged, and they continued on.

Their journey returned the band to a familiar routine, but one they hadn't employed since before the Rebellion. As servants of the empire, one of their regular duties had been to explore and map uncharted lands, many of which had been on the western fringes of the empire. Their purposes today were different, but the approach was the same.

Ari used his ability to transport to both scout and jump the band ahead. For the first two days, they used Ari's ability frequently, covering enormous swaths of ground, until they spotted the first dragon in the air farther to the west. Transporting the whole band consumed a fair amount of teho, and they didn't want to attract any dragons if they could avoid it. Ari still used his ability when he believed it was safe, but only to scout ahead for dangers. Though that started to happen less.

Once the first dragon appeared, Hakon and Meshell

became the primary scouts of the party. Thanks to their ability to fill their bodies with teho, they could run farther and faster than the others, and their scouting ran little to no risk of attracting a distant dragon's attention.

Irric and Solveig, then, assumed most of the responsibility for warding and shielding the band when it was necessary.

In this way, traveling together was relatively effortless, each of the band able to support the others with their strength. Hakon was grateful that all of them traveled together. They'd always been strongest when all five of them worked as one.

Their journey took them through rugged highlands. The ground here was rocky, the uneven terrain requiring them to watch their footing carefully. More than once, Hakon worried that a mistimed step would twist an ankle and slow their progress.

The weather did them no favors, either. During the day, when the sun shone brightly in the sky above, the temperature was still high enough that they were comfortable in lighter clothing. But when the sunlight faded at night or when thick clouds passed overhead, the air became cold enough that it bit at any exposed skin. Nights were freezing, and sleeping wasn't a simple matter. They built warming fires, but the winter was coming, and they weren't prepared. One evening it grew cold enough that Ari suggested transporting back to Aysgarth for the night. If the constant threat of dragons hadn't worried them, Hakon thought they might have done it.

Winter was coming, and storms grew more frequent. Precipitation fell as either freezing rain or snow. Rain made the exposed stone slick, and the snow made finding secure footing even more difficult. The band bore it all without much complaint, but their moods were already dark, and the stormy weather did nothing to improve their outlook.

Thankfully, there was no serious talk of turning back. They were all of the opinion that the only way was forward, and not even the storms changed that.

There was a day or two, though, when they stood high in the mountains as snow swirled around them and dragons circled overhead, that Hakon worried they might break.

The high elevation left him feeling exposed, as though there were eyes everywhere watching their progress. After more than a week of slow travel, they finally started to descend out of the worst weather. As they lost elevation, Hakon looked back at the endless mountains they had crossed. They'd long ago lost sight of the ship, and the Six States seemed like a distant memory.

Six days later, they came upon the remains of a village.

They were nearly within the remains before they noticed them. The woods were thick here, filled with pine trees that looked like they might rival the band for the title of oldest life in the area. Meshell, wandering ahead of the others, found the homes first. The sight brought her to a standstill.

Hakon stopped beside her. It took him a moment to understand what he saw. The village was no longer recognizable as such. The wild had retaken this land. Trees had grown up in the streets between buildings. Hakon looked down and dug a little with the toe of his boot. He found nothing but soil and pine needles.

The others caught up and came to a stop behind him. It was a while before any of them could speak.

"How old do you think this place is?" Solveig asked.

Hakon walked over to the nearest home and ran his fingers down the wall. "It's the material the stamfars used."

They wandered deeper. Almost all of the homes on the outskirts of the village were intact. Hakon chose one at random and went to the front door. It had panels that reminded him of the ones in the ship. He pushed at the symbol for "open" and the door slid away. Hakon stepped inside.

The interior of the house had been destroyed. The front door opened into what appeared to be a living space. The furniture was all overturned, and there were skeletons on the bloodstained floor. Hakon ran his eyes across the scene, but it didn't take a close look to know what had happened here. He wandered through the rest of the home, finding the same evidence in every room. A family had lived here right until the day they didn't.

He left the house and rejoined the others. Ari, Solveig, and Irric had all explored different houses, and from the downcast looks on their faces, they'd found similar scenes.

"They were attacked by other stamfar," Hakon told Meshell. Then he turned to the others. "I don't suppose any of you found any suggestion as to why?"

No one had. It wasn't surprising, but he hated adding another question to the list that was already growing so long.

Meshell led them deeper into the village, and the strangeness of the place made Hakon want to pull his sword out and keep it ready. There wasn't supposed to be anything this far west. The land of the Six States was the only home humanity had ever had. Every child knew that.

Not only had they been wrong, but this place had a history that stretched back farther than they could imagine. The buildings stood, but the wild had overgrown everything else. He was haunted by the thought that if they failed and humanity fell, they'd leave behind even less than the stamfar. Their buildings couldn't last, not like this.

It wasn't long before they found the center of the village. Meshell stopped once again, and Hakon could well understand why. The foundations of several buildings remained, but the wild had completely taken over here. Meshell kneeled next to one of the buildings and examined the remains more closely.

When she stood, she had the same haunted look the rest of them had worn after exploring the houses. "Looks like it was destroyed by teho."

They found bits of bone around, but without the protection of the houses, the corpses had been eaten and carried away.

They wandered around for a while longer, but there was nothing more a quick examination would reveal. Solveig was the most thorough of them. Hakon imagined the intellectual agony such a find put her in. In a better world, she would have Ari transport her back to Vispeda, where she'd round up an army of scholars and return to examine this place one inch at a time.

She confessed as much a few moments later. "If we survive this, I want to return. There must be answers here, maybe to questions we haven't even thought to ask."

Without being asked, Ari created a transport point.

If they survived, Hakon knew Solveig would return.

But he had the feeling they were going to find far deeper mysteries before they were done.

6

Zachary opened his eyes and looked upon the familiar sights of his hometown. After the dragon attack, the Aysgarthians had chosen a transport location in cooperation with Mioska's council, a move that had raised no small number of objections. Several council members, led by Hallr, claimed that allowing a transport point to be established inside the walls would only tempt the Aysgarthians to invade the city at will.

Anyone who considered the argument dispassionately for even a moment understood it was devoid of substance. The Aysgarthians already had secret transport points within the city, as clearly evidenced by their timely arrival when Mioska most needed their aid. Hel had admitted, privately to Zachary, that they maintained similar points in all major cities in the Six States. Even had such points not been in place, it was a trivial matter to create more.

But Hallr didn't appeal to reason. His strategies played upon people's fears. And despite the fact that the Aysgarthian tehoin had saved the city, plenty of citizens struggled to let go of their long-held bias. When he'd last left Mioska, an angry group of watchers had lurked beyond the militia's walls.

Some part of Zachary understood. Beliefs never changed overnight, and the distrust of tehoin had built up over generations. But those fears didn't help. They threatened the shaky foundations of the alliance he hoped to build. The alliance they needed to survive.

Their compromise led to the transport point being established in the middle of the local militia's training ground. It was a wide-open space, which made transport convenient. And it quelled some fears that Aysgarth was going to invade.

Which was also foolish. If Aysgarth wanted to use this transport point to stage their invasion, they would wipe out the local militia within the first few moments. But Zachary kept those thoughts to himself.

Once he was sure of his balance, Zachary stepped out of the arrival circle, only to stop when he saw a familiar face. "Edda?"

Her surprise was almost as great as his. She was part of a group heading to the departure circle, mostly tehoin from Aysgarth returning from their duty in Mioska. She hadn't been paying any attention to the new arrivals, and she jumped at his voice. "Zachary? What are you doing here?"

"I could ask you the same. I've just returned to pick another fight with the council."

Her look fell. "I was coming to find you in Aysgarth. There's been trouble."

Zachary pulled her aside and assured the tehoin it was safe to depart without her. They were drawing a fair amount of attention, so Zachary led them out of the training area. The guards had set up a checkpoint before they could leave the militia grounds, but Zachary and Edda passed through it with only a slight delay. The watchers were still in the streets beyond, and several took notes on Zachary's arrival. They caused no problems, though, so Zachary ignored them.

Once they were clear, Edda explained, "There was another fight last night between one of the off-duty Aysgarthians and a group of troublemakers at a local tavern."

Zachary swore. It wasn't the first time. "How bad?"

"The Aysgarthian injured five citizens and two members of the militia before his friends stopped him."

Zachary cursed again. Edda had been right to brave a transport. "I don't suppose you've established any connection to Hallr or any of his allies?"

"Not yet, but I've been searching. I heard they plan to rush the case to a tribunal, probably hoping to take advantage of your absence."

Zachary took a moment to appreciate his sister. As one of the few people he trusted completely in Mioska, she'd helped him take up his father's mantle. He'd suspected she would be useful but had been surprised by how naturally she'd taken to the role. She had a quick mind that cut through the layers of deception that surrounded anything the council did, and she was decisive. Zachary trusted her judgment, sometimes more than his own. More than once in the past few weeks, he'd wondered if she wasn't the best choice to take father's place. She'd never expressed interest, but that didn't mean it wasn't there.

He relied on that judgment now. "What's our best course of action?"

"Try to free the Aysgarthian from the prison."

Zachary grimaced, and Edda noticed.

"Yes, Hallr will jump on you, but even if the attack was

provoked, there's no doubt of what the tehoin did," she explained. "If it comes to a tribunal, he'll be found guilty. Given that he isn't a citizen and attacked a militia member, they might try to hang him. That seems to me to be the worst outcome."

Zachary weighed his sister's words and agreed. Freeing a guilty tehoin didn't sit well with him, and the cost to his cause would be considerable. But if Mioska sentenced one of the Aysgarthian tehoin to death, the consequences would be both unpredictable and dangerous.

He turned from his path onto one that led him to the prison. Edda followed.

"How's Father?" he asked.

"Sleeps most of the time," Edda said. "The healers still say he should die any day, but he seems to be holding on just to spite them."

"Sounds about right," Zachary said.

Despite his own mixed feelings toward his father, the corner of his lips turned up in a smile. He could well imagine his father clinging to life, not because he had anything to live for, but because he wanted to prove someone else wrong.

Belatedly, he realized there wasn't any need for Edda to join him. Particularly if he ran into trouble. "It might be best if you don't join me for this. Could you dig deeper and see if any of last night's instigators had ties to Hallr or his friends?"

"Of course. Good luck."

She hugged him quickly, then left. He glanced at her as she walked away, impressed by the woman she'd grown up to become in his absence. Then he turned his attention to the task before him.

The prison looked like the sort of place one wouldn't

want to spend any time in. It was a squat, almost windowless building. Two militia guards stood at the entrance, and Zachary announced himself.

They let him into a small office with a thick door on the other side. A militia commander sat at a desk, enjoying one of the few windows that let in light.

The officer recognized Zachary. "Councilman. I wondered if we might be seeing you soon."

Zachary searched his memories for the commander's name but came up short. He'd fallen out of touch in the years he'd been gone, and after the dragon attack, there were far more people who knew him than he knew in return.

He bowed as though showing respect to a commanding officer. "I'm afraid you have me at a loss, sir."

The commander waved away his formality. "No reason why you should know me. I was just one of the soldiers serving the day the dragons attacked. I watched you fighting with the other tehoin. Name's Madoc."

"One of these days, I hope we can meet under better circumstances," Zachary said. Madoc's introduction made him hopeful that the soldier would work with him. "I just arrived and heard about last night. How's the prisoner?"

"Under the influence of a sleeping drought, as per regulation," Madoc reported. "His next dose is in less than a half-hour, though."

"Would you permit him full awareness so that I may speak with him?"

Zachary's optimism increased when Madoc didn't hesitate. "Of course."

"Thank you. Perhaps you could fill me in on what you know of the incident. How are the soldiers who were injured?"

From Madoc's approving expression, it had been the right question. Fortunately, it was also one Zachary genuinely cared about. The militia based in Mioska might not have the same abilities as the tehoin, but they would be no less vital to the protection of the city. And as their councilman, they were his soldiers, no matter what Hallr proclaimed about his true loyalties.

"They are recovering well. Their injuries were minor, and I'd expect to see them back on duty within a few days," Madoc said.

Zachary breathed a sigh of relief. That was something, at least. "And the others?"

"One of them was roughed up pretty bad, but no one is in danger of dying."

Zachary leaned against the wall. Asking the questions he really cared about carried a risk, but he felt confident in Madoc's trust. "May I ask you a frank question?"

"Of course, sir."

"I need to know what the feeling is among the militia regarding the Aysgarthian tehoin. Not the official reports I get as a councilman, but the real version." He nodded toward the thick door. "I don't doubt the Aysgarthian is guilty, and under normal circumstances, I'd let him suffer the consequences. But I fear we'll lose the treaty if he's hung."

Madoc was no fool. Zachary saw that he followed the argument without a problem.

"There's no easy answer, sir. There are probably as many opinions about the Aysgarthians as there are soldiers in the militia. Many of us who fought against the dragons and lost friends are grateful for the tehoin, but they're a pain to have around."

"How so?"

"They think they're better than us, sir. You'll see it when this one wakes, and I could tell you a dozen stories I've heard just in the last week. To them, ahula are little more than the cattle they have to protect. Makes it hard for us lowly soldiers to stay grateful for long."

Zachary rubbed his eyes. Madoc spoke as if he'd forgotten Zachary was tehoin, too. But his opinion mattered dearly to Zachary. The veteran had seen firsthand how the tehoin had saved the city and claimed to be grateful. Even so, he spoke with barely disguised contempt. He had reason, too. Of course the tehoin trained by Damion would think themselves superior. "How would your comrades react if I exiled this one from Mioska forever?"

Madoc didn't answer at first. Then he nodded. "There will be many who want a stricter punishment, but I think most would find it acceptable."

"Thanks for your honesty. Mind if I go back there?"

Madoc tossed him a large iron key. "Turn left, third door down. Call if you need help, though I don't have any tehoin on duty."

"I can handle myself," Zachary said, wishing he felt nearly as confident as he sounded. It looked like it impressed Madoc, though, so he unlocked the thick door with the key and stepped through. He locked himself in.

The hallway on the other side was dark, lit only by a pair of lanterns on a table. Two guards were playing cards. Both recognized him and rushed to stand, but Zachary waved for them to return to ease. "Not here to bother you. I just need to talk to the Aysgarthian."

He borrowed their lantern, then found the door Madoc had indicated. He held the lantern up so he could see inside. A man was manacled within, sound asleep.

Zachary unlocked the door and left it open. If he needed

help, he wanted the other two to be able to reach him as quickly as possible. He took the chair opposite the cot and waited.

It didn't take long. He heard the change in the man's breath. Before there could be any trouble, he spoke. "My name's Zachary. I'm here to speak with you about last night."

The man rolled over and sat up. His eyes were sharp and focused, and Zachary sensed the other man's readiness to use teho. The tehoin studied him for a moment, then recognized him. He spat on the floor. "You're the one who came with the band."

"I was." Apparently, Zachary wasn't a friend, but at least he had the tehoin's attention.

The Aysgarthian relaxed and leaned back. "What do you want?"

"What happened last night?"

"I was out drinking when a group of fools started a fight."

"How did they start the fight?"

"They compared tehoin to their shit."

Zachary sighed. "Why were you even in a tavern? Everyone's orders are to avoid them for exactly this reason."

The tehoin glared. "I was off-duty, and I was thirsty. Besides, if we all stopped going to taverns, they would just bother us somewhere else."

Zachary conceded the point.

The tehoin watched him, then casually formed a long teho blade and cut open his manacles. "So, what are you here to do?"

He didn't disguise the challenge in his voice.

Zachary wanted to knock him unconscious and send him to the tribunal. There wasn't a sliver of repentance in him. It didn't matter if Hallr and the others had set this up. Zachary had the feeling this tehoin would have attacked anyone who looked at him the wrong way.

The Aysgarthian's hostility limited Zachary's already terrible options. "I guess I'm getting you out of here and letting you return to Aysgarth."

The tehoin's smile was wicked. "I was hoping you might say that."

The next day, Zachary came to the council meeting prepared for a battle. When he entered the council chambers, he let his eyes drift from councilor to councilor and decided it was worse than he expected. Hallr looked as though he was ready to jump in glee.

Zachary ignored them all and bowed to Agnar, the wizened governor of Mioska. The bow was returned with a slight nod of the head.

Agnar's moods were difficult to decipher, but Zachary thought he looked tense. That also didn't bode well. Though Agnar remained aloof both in council and in public, Zachary believed him to be an ally. Though that belief was never as certain as he wished it was.

Zachary strode in. When he took his seat, Hallr looked like a trapper who'd just caught the biggest prey of his life.

Agnar called the meeting to order, and Hallr stood immediately. He was so eager that it was pathetic. "Sir, we need to discuss the Aysgarthians and councilman Zachary's criminal behavior."

Zachary didn't have to pretend to act surprised. He'd expected an attack, but not one quite so vicious.

Agnar didn't seem pleased, either. He recognized that

infighting was almost impossible to stop among his councilors, but he tolerated little of it in the open. "Explain yourself."

Hallr was delighted to. "Two nights ago, there was an altercation between an Aysgarthian tehoin and a group of citizens. In that altercation, several citizens were injured, as well as two of the militia who responded to the fight."

Zachary doubted any of this was news to Agnar, who was as well-informed as anyone. But he feigned surprise. "I see. We've had several of these incidents in the past few weeks."

Hallr took the statement and ran with it. "Indeed we have, sir, and this one was by far the worst of them. The incident was terrible enough, but it was councilman Zachary's behavior afterward that surprised me. I'd go so far as to suspect him of treason, as much as the accusation pains me."

It took most of Zachary's self-control not to laugh. The council had a fair number of fools, but no one here believed for a moment Hallr would be anything but pleased at Zachary's misfortune.

Agnar remained aloof. "A serious accusation, councilman. One that requires considerable evidence of wrongdoing."

Hallr was unfazed. "I agree, governor, and I hope we can resolve the matter quickly. There are plenty of witnesses willing to testify under oath, but I hope that won't be needed. It has come to my attention that yesterday, councilman Zachary freed the accused prisoner and sent him back to Aysgarth. It's the equivalent of a pardon, after one of these tehoin hurt our citizens!" Hallr almost spit the word tehoin.

Agnar turned his gaze to Zachary. "And what do you say

to these accusations?"

"The substance is true, though much is left out," Zachary replied.

"Perhaps you can be troubled to explain?" Agnar sounded frustrated, and Hallr could barely contain his glee.

"What Hallr says is largely true. I returned yesterday to news of the attack and resolved to explore the matter. When I spoke with the accused, I determined the best course of action for Mioska's immediate and continued safety was to exile the warrior back to Aysgarth."

"Why?" the governor asked.

"Two reasons. The first is that I feared he would have tried to escape had he not been let free, and we do not have enough tehoin to stop him if he tried."

"That hardly gives you the excuse to release him!" Hallr cried. "Your actions brand you as a coward!"

Zachary fixed him with a hard stare, and Hallr flinched.

He turned back to the governor and continued as though he hadn't been interrupted. "Second, I feared what the consequences of a tribunal would be upon our fragile treaty. It was, perhaps, inappropriate of me to act without consulting the rest of the council, but I believed haste was necessary."

Hallr had regained his courage, and he addressed the governor again. "Sir, if we must bend our own laws for the sake of this treaty, perhaps the treaty itself needs to be questioned."

Zachary had to fight not to smile. "I agree, sir."

"You—what?" Hallr stared at Zachary as though a stranger stood in Zachary's place.

Even Agnar seemed surprised.

"I agree," Zachary said. "I also believe the treaty was poorly written, and I accept my own share of the blame.

Especially given this recent event, I believe that we should no longer allow the Aysgarthians to maintain such a large presence within our city walls. Don't you agree, councilor Hallr?"

Hallr couldn't think through Zachary's attack fast enough. He looked like a fish, knowing the worm before him contained a hook, but he had no choice but to bite. He'd spoken too often about his misgivings about the treaty. "I do."

All eyes were on him now, Hallr's accusations forgotten in this new development. Zachary addressed the governor. "I just returned from Aysgarth, and there is concern there that they do not have enough tehoin to make their own repairs and maintain their forces here. In cooperation with Hel and their council, we believe we've found a solution."

He went on to explain their reasoning, adding to it the fact that it would remove the troublesome tehoin from their streets.

Hallr, after long voicing his objections to the Aysgarthian presence, couldn't protest. Agnar, though, asked the obvious question. "What's to say they'll come if we call?"

"For that, we have little choice but to trust," Zachary said, knowing how weak the argument was. "I do." He paused. "But even if they don't come, I believe it's right to uphold our half of the treaty. Their people are on the brink of starving, and we have food to spare. It's the right choice, whether they honor their payment or not."

Hallr scoffed. "Such nobility is wasted on them, councilor Zachary."

Zachary bit back his first response. "You and I don't agree on much, councilor. But saving others is never a wasted choice."

7

More than a week of journeying carried them through the rest of the forest and below the foothills of the impressive range of mountains. The air grew warmer, and their travel more pleasant. Though they encountered their fair share of wild creatures, none were as antagonistic as those near the frontier of the Six States.

They debated at length the possible reasons for the difference. Solveig wondered if there was something about the Six States attracting the wild's attention. Ari, always willing to see the dark side of any hope, suspected the wilds here were simply massing their forces for a more dangerous attack later. Hakon told the others of his own theory, that the intelligence directing the wild wasn't one they could ascribe human motivations to.

The arguments filled their time but brought them no closer to an answer. They walked deeper into unknown lands, treading ground no human had walked for hundreds of years.

They followed a stream for the last of their days in the forest, which brought them across another destroyed and overgrown stamfar village. Inside the homes, evidence of violence was easy to find. Whatever force had committed the atrocity had been thorough, searching every house from top to bottom. The band explored for a bit but didn't stay long. Ari obediently placed another transport point for Solveig, and they continued on.

As the trees thinned near the edge of the woods, the band looked upon an endless vista of rolling hills. They followed the stream, which meandered west at a leisurely pace.

The wild launched its first attack two days after they were out of the woods.

Meshell had spotted the creatures well before, a pack of perhaps a dozen animals they didn't recognize. They were larger than shadow wolves, but leaner. When they caught the scent of the band, Hakon understood their strengths well enough. The pack charged toward the band, running faster than any creature Hakon had ever seen. He could think of a few birds that moved slower. They made a loud hissing sound as they neared and revealed fierce fangs.

Imposing as the creatures were, they posed little threat to the band. Hakon and Meshell filled their bodies with teho and met the pack head-on, cutting down a third of the creatures on the first pass. The creatures that survived were stuck between Hakon and Meshell and the rest of the band. The others checked the sky, then risked using teho to end the battle quickly.

"Remarkable creatures," said Ari as he kneeled beside one. He ran his hand along its body, checking its paws and jaw with particular interest. "I didn't know anything alive could run that fast." He looked up at Solveig. "Have you ever heard of these?"

"Never. I'm not the most informed scholar when it

comes to stamfar myths, though." She risked a glance at Hakon but didn't say what she was thinking.

Hakon knew well enough. "Cliona might have known."

He searched his memories, wishing he'd held on tighter to her as she made her new life in Vispeda. She'd wanted space, and he'd only wanted to honor her wishes. At the very least, though, he could have written more often.

"She never told me about anything like this, though."

"Interesting, isn't it?" Ari said, half to himself and half to the others. "All our myths about the stamfar, and there's no mention of any creature like this. No mention of towns wiped out by a mysterious faction. There are stories of dragons and shadow wolves, but nothing of what we've seen."

"What are you getting at?" Irric asked.

Ari stood. "We have no legends of this place. I don't know why, but I would bet we know nothing of what happened here. Not even a myth."

Solveig didn't contradict him, which meant Ari might be right.

"We have an even more pressing problem," said Meshell.

All eyes turned to her, and she swept out her hand. "Where exactly are we supposed to go? In the mountains, our only goal was to travel west, and there weren't many options. Now we can go anywhere."

"Isira seemed to believe that if we just headed west, we would find the ruins we were seeking," Hakon said. "I say we keep following the stream. We already know the stamfar who lived here built near the water."

He understood the weakness of the argument as well as anyone, but they needed to keep moving. If they stopped or debated too long, he feared they would give up and look to return to the Six States. He certainly fought the temptation.

All they had was Isira's vague guess, and when he stared out across the expanse, some part of him cried out, shouting that they had been sent on a hopeless task.

No one argued against him, which was another ominous sign. They would have debated the best course of action if they'd believed in this journey. Even Meshell, who had raised the question, nodded and accepted Hakon's suggestion.

They cut meat from the animals while Irric prepared a fire. The meat was too lean to be tasty, but they wouldn't waste the bounty the wilds granted them. They ate their fill and resumed their journey. The miles passed underfoot, quicker now that they weren't fighting inclement weather and rugged terrain. Hakon kept a sharp eye on his surroundings, seeking any sign that would point them in a specific direction.

At a glance, the prairie appeared almost devoid of life. There were wild grasses and small trees, but there were times when it seemed the band was the only source of movement for miles.

Hakon was no stranger to prairies, though, and understood that they only whispered their secrets to travelers with the patience and attention to appreciate them. The band spooked a pair of large birds that had buried themselves deep in the grass, sheltering for the evening. By one bend in the river, they found a new species of turtle sunning itself on a stone. Once, he spotted a deer bounding far off in the distance. There was as much life here as in most other places. It just tended to keep out of sight.

For all that he saw, Hakon still had no better answer to the question of where they should go. Though it was doubtless on everyone's minds, the discussion didn't come up again as they set up camp and prepared for an evening of rest. They spoke little, and most were quickly asleep. He and Meshell were the only two who remained awake, and at her look, he stood up and followed her away from the others.

"You've been more pensive than usual today," she said.

"Can you blame me?"

They were far enough away that they wouldn't bother the others. He took her hand and pulled her toward him. Their lips met, and for a precious few moments, it felt as though the years and worries had fallen from his shoulders. She'd always had that effect on him, and he'd never understood it. They'd been together for more years than many people had lived, but it often felt as though they'd just met.

She buried her head in his chest, and he wrapped his arms around her. She felt small next to him, but he was the one drawing strength from her.

"Tell me," he asked, reaching up with one hand to run his fingers through her dark hair, "what do you really think of all of this?"

"It's a fool's errand," she said. "Although that's probably putting it kindly."

He'd expected no different, but the words stung like an accusation. "Why not object?"

"I have no better ideas. We've long argued that humanity doesn't have the strength to fight the wilds, much less war against Ava and dragons. If there was a way, I think you or Solveig would have found it. So this is as good as anything. I'm enjoying the opportunity to explore a new land again, and thanks to Ari, we can always return to the Six States if we're needed."

Hakon shook his head. "Transport is a double-edged sword. Without it, we'd have no choice but to continue on.

The route we took over the mountains will be closed soon, if it isn't already."

"But we might not have made the attempt if we knew it meant abandoning the Six States." Meshell pulled his face down so they were eye to eye. "You don't need to worry about us. We won't turn back until there's no other choice."

She kissed him again and pulled him down into the grass, silencing any objections he still had. He fell asleep with her head resting against his shoulder.

Hakon wasn't sure what woke him. When he opened his eyes, he saw from the position of the stars that he'd been asleep for several hours. But there was nothing dangerous he could sense. Still, something was wrong. He felt the unease in his stomach.

Movement in the corner of his vision caught his attention.

Cliona was there, looking at her hands as though she'd never seen them before.

Hakon blinked, his eyes filling with water. A choked cry caught in the back of his throat, and he started to reach out for her. Before he could fully extend his hand, he pulled it back and cradled it close.

"Cliona?" His voice came out softer than a whisper.

She didn't hear him. Instead, she continued her examination of her hand. When she moved, her image blurred, the edges of her body indistinct. His daughter stood, bending the grass as she stepped forward. She either ignored or didn't see Hakon.

Hakon reached down and shook Meshell. She came awake instantly and sat up. Hakon pointed. "Do you see that?"

Meshell's wide eyes were answer enough.

Hakon cleared his throat and dared to speak louder. "Cliona?"

His call received no response. Cliona walked another ten paces away from them, heading north. A sudden fear gripped Hakon's heart. She was walking away from him, just as she had when she was younger. She was leaving for Vispeda all over again.

This time, he wouldn't let her go so easily. He pushed himself to his feet. Meshell stood beside him. "Cliona. It's me."

Cliona stopped, and he believed she'd heard him.

She turned toward him and Meshell, and Hakon's heart broke again. Where her eyes should have been, there was a pair of dark voids. She smiled, and to Hakon, it reminded him of her smile in the days after Sera had died. The one that told him she fought an unbearable sadness but that she hadn't surrendered yet. Cliona raised her right arm and pointed northwest.

Hakon couldn't restrain himself any longer. He ran for her, arms open wide.

He'd not even crossed a quarter of the distance when she vanished again.

8

———

Zachary gritted his teeth and forced a smile as he reached out for Hallr's hand. He took some small comfort in the noble's reaction. Hallr looked down at Zachary's hand as though it held wet dung. Unfortunately for the noble, switching positions would have been an obvious display of weakness, so he had little choice but to grasp Zachary's outstretched hand. Zachary resisted the urge to crush Hallr's soft hand in a tight grip. He didn't care to admit it, but Hallr as an ally carried far greater value than Hallr as an enemy. This was the only way he could think of to win that ally.

The nelja from Aysgarth gave Zachary a questioning look. The tehoin had spent the last twenty minutes glaring and stomping around the militia training ground, making his displeasure known with every opportunity. Zachary could hardly blame him. Gathering for a transport shouldn't have taken more than a few minutes, but everything related to the council took far longer than necessary. At one point, Zachary had feared Hallr was about to launch into a speech for the soldiers milling about.

Not only had Hallr shown up far after their prearranged time, but he'd also shown up with more people than he'd promised. He treated the transport as a negotiation to be won. Zachary tried to explain that a nelja could only transport so many people, but it wasn't until the nelja had launched a tirade against the councilman that Hallr backed down. As it was, Hallr still traveled with three guards that looked around the training ground as though an assassin was going to leap from behind one of the nearby buildings.

Eventually, Zachary silenced all of Hallr's objections, and the nelja was able to lead them to the transport circle.

Zachary met the nelja's questioning gaze and nodded. Best they transport before Hallr created yet another foolish objection. Zachary closed his eyes. Though he'd gained experience transporting over the last year, his stomach still rebelled every time. Closing his eyes eased the disorientation a little. The air grew colder against his skin, and he knew it was done.

And if there'd been any doubt they'd transported, Hallr vomiting out his breakfast served as the conclusive piece of evidence. Zachary fought the smile that threatened to spread from ear to ear. He was only partially successful. He let go of Hallr's hand and stepped back.

Zachary turned to the nelja. "Thank you."

The tehoin grunted as he turned away. "I'll be here when you want to leave."

Zachary had hoped the nelja would join them as they went into town, but he didn't want to press the matter. He considered it fortunate that the tehoin had agreed to his request and that someone in Aysgarth had a transport point at their destination. Hallr wouldn't have agreed to come if they'd had to leave Mioska for the weeks it would take to travel using more mundane means.

They shouldn't need another tehoin, but even Zachary had to admit that leaving Mioska carried a fair amount of risk. Especially if the stories they'd heard were true.

He waited for Hallr to finish vomiting. It was, undoubtedly, Hallr's first transport. Zachary would have jumped to exploit Hallr's weakness, but he couldn't fault the noble this time. He wandered away while Hallr cleaned himself.

Midvale was less than a mile away, but the nelja's transport point was out of sight of the town, so Zachary couldn't tell if the stories contained any truth. He waited patiently for Hallr, and when he felt enough time had elapsed, he returned to the noble and his guards. Hallr's face was a little more pale than usual, but he looked otherwise prepared.

Zachary pointed north. "Midvale should be about a mile that way."

"Then let's get this over with," Hallr said.

Zachary considered addressing Hallr's dismissiveness, then thought better of it. He'd burned whatever last slivers of goodwill he had on the council to pull Hallr out here. He had to make the sacrifice worth it. With a nod, he led the way. Hallr and his three guards followed, perhaps a dozen paces behind. The nelja who'd transported them was already asleep in the grass.

The only conversation on the walk was between Hallr and his guards. They spoke in low tones so that Zachary could only catch one out of every half-dozen words. Zachary tried at first to listen in but grew frustrated with the attempt after a few minutes. He chose to ignore them and seek what pleasure he could on this beautiful day.

Midvale was colder than Mioska, though that was little surprise. It was farther north enough to make a difference, and it didn't have the moderating influence of the sea. Zachary welcomed the nip in the air. It made the walk pleasant, and the scenery reminded him he hadn't been outside the walls of Mioska in too long. Cities had never bothered him growing up, but he found that after his time on the western frontier, he'd grown attached to wide open spaces. If everything else failed today, at least he'd get a nice walk in exchange.

Despite Hallr's reluctance to be here, he kept Zachary's pace without problem. Perhaps he was only eager to see Zachary's scheme fail, but they made quick work of the remaining distance to Midvale. They crested a small rise, and the walls of the town came into view.

That first sight brought Zachary to a standstill. Hallr and his guards caught up, their laughter at some jest dying as they, too, cleared the rise.

Zachary had never been to Midvale. He knew it from the detailed maps his father had kept in his study, but that had been the extent of his knowledge until yesterday. When the first reports had arrived on his desk, he'd sought to learn more about the town. According to Agnar's records, less than a thousand people lived within its walls, and the town served as a hub for the local farming community. It was one of the dozens of towns that funneled its excess produce toward Mioska.

He could see evidence of what it had once been. Two taller buildings served as enormous storehouses. A third of one had been destroyed, but the other stood unharmed. Farms surrounded the walls, the harvested fields in pristine condition compared to the town that sat in the center of them. What he'd once thought were clouds was actually dusty smoke from half a dozen ruins. Entire homes were gone.

Zachary remained silent, letting the sight make his case for him. He continued on, and after a moment, the others followed behind. The wall on the southern side of the town, where they approached, was still intact, a lone soldier standing watch. Zachary announced them, but the guard barely seemed to hear. His eyes were locked on a sight invisible to the others, and he waved them through with little more than a grunt.

Once inside the walls the full extent of the damage revealed itself. Zachary estimated that almost half of the homes were either destroyed or too damaged to be livable. Several streets were filled with people seeking warmth and food. When they saw Zachary and Hallr, dressed in their fine clothes and warm cloaks, they shuffled toward the pair. Hallr's guards formed a small triangle around him, preventing any supplicant from getting too close.

Zachary spoke with a few of the survivors. He offered his cloak to a young woman with two infants. The few coins he carried in his pocket he gave to the first who asked, though he feared money would do little good. Midvale's survival rested solely on the generosity of strangers and the will of the council in Mioska.

He noted the immediate needs. As an agricultural center, there was probably enough food still in the town to feed the survivors. Unfortunately, most of it was under the ownership of merchants, who had purchased it with the intent to sell to their counterparts in Mioska. The council would have to put itself in the middle of the merchants to ensure the necessary food remained in Midvale.

Shelter would be the other problem. Zachary wondered if a military unit could set up a temporary camp somewhere within the walls. With winter coming, it wasn't a permanent solution, but it would give them time.

Hallr followed behind Zachary, never leaving the protection of his guards. Zachary caught him listening to every conversation, but he kept himself otherwise aloof. After an hour, Zachary felt like he had a clear story of what had happened. They parted from the crowd gathered around them and made their way closer to the center of the town, where they hoped to meet with the town's magistrate.

The farther north in the town they traveled, the worse the damage became. Homes had collapsed on their occupants. Some of the survivors here were covered in mud, dust, and blood. Twice they passed piles of rubble where parts of bodies lay exposed, trapped underneath the wood and stone of their homes. At each, Zachary stopped to express his respects for the deceased. It was a bit of a performance, as there were no doubt countless more bodies hidden from view.

But the great danger here was that Hallr would close his heart to the destruction. In Zachary's experience, most people had a limit to the amount of suffering they could endure. When that limit was reached, when the hurt was more than one could bear, they built walls around their thoughts. If Hallr built such a wall, it would be too easy for him to return to Mioska and turn his back. Zachary couldn't allow that. He needed Hallr to feel the urgency of the threat deep in his bones.

Zachary was hopeful. Hallr was a noble accustomed to comfort and leisure. Everything that had happened since the transport was beyond his previous experience. When Zachary glanced back, he saw Hallr huddled deep within his cloak, eyes peeking out as though the thick fabrics would protect him from the sights that assailed him.

The evidence of dragons was unmistakable. Large claws

had torn through walls and streets with equal ease. The destruction of the buildings had no other explanation.

They reached the center of the town, where a collection of tents already overflowed with the injured. Zachary swallowed hard as he passed by. He was no stranger to violence, but this was beyond his experience. The wounded weren't soldiers, but farmers and merchants, mothers and children. They hadn't volunteered or marched to battle. They'd been at home, tending to their own affairs.

He thought of Edda, safely back within their estate in Mioska. Despite their agreement with Aysgarth, there was no reason that what had happened here couldn't happen there. His knees began to feel unsteady, and he stopped to take a deep breath. He couldn't give in to his fears. Once he did, he was useless, just as he so often had been.

He found the commander, a burly woman named Anwen. She was covered in blood and dust, and it looked like the only reason she still stood was her sheer willpower.

When she saw Zachary and Hallr, her eyes flared. "I don't have time for you, councilors."

"Only a moment, please," Zachary pleaded. "I've come to see what happened so that I may return to Mioska and direct the appropriate aid your way."

Her look held little but contempt, but she relented. "Five minutes."

"What do you need?" Zachary asked.

"For the damned merchants to give us the food we grew. Tents and building supplies to build shelter. Soldiers to help maintain order."

"I'll do what I can," Zachary pledged. "We've heard of the attack from the survivors, but is there anything more you can add? Where did the attack originate, and was there anyone in command of the dragon?"

He knew the last part of the question was unlikely to be taken seriously, but he wanted to know if Ava had been here.

Fortunately, Anwen was too exhausted to argue. "The attack came from the northeast, in the direction of the wastes. And no. There was no woman commanding the dragon that I could see. Though I wouldn't be too surprised if there had been. Nothing about the attack makes any sense."

That was a theme oft repeated by the survivors. It was the same pattern Zachary had seen out west. The wild, attacking as though it was being coordinated. Only this strike had been accompanied by a dragon. One last question occurred to him. "Did you have any tehoin here?"

Anwen shook her head. "No. Not that I knew of."

Zachary hadn't expected any different, but it confirmed the influence of a foreign force. Dragons rarely attacked unless a tehoin was present.

He once again offered as many promises to Anwen as he could, but the greatest gift he could offer her was to leave her alone. He did so, moving to the side of the camp to a place where he'd be out of the way.

He turned to Hallr. "Do you understand? This is all that I care about. This is what we need to fight against. Not one another"

Hallr barely nodded his head, but Zachary waited for him to speak. It took almost a minute. When Hallr answered, his voice sounded like it came from far away. "Please, take me home. I have seen enough."

9

The downside to knowing a group of people as well as Hakon knew the band was that each member's private thoughts were as clear as day. He imagined it was much the same as a marriage that had weathered dozens of years, facing good times and ill alike. Small tics revealed volumes, and whole arguments were had without a word exchanged.

Back before the Rebellion, Torsten had once sent an observer to accompany them on a set of sensitive missions. His name now slipped Hakon's memory, but he'd been a talkative young fellow, eager to follow the famous warriors on behalf of the empire. His excitement didn't last long. Torsten, more amused by the resulting report than informed, had later shared it with Hakon. In it, the observer had said, "They are by far the most taciturn group of warriors history has ever known."

Dramatic claims aside, Hakon understood how their relationship might appear to outsiders. But few understood how time changed people. The band said little because little needed to be said. Ari had once told him "Words are a weapon like any other. I use them only when I must."

They had argued plenty when Hakon and Meshell had reported their sighting the next morning, and the words they'd spoken then still left a bitter taste in Hakon's mouth. He didn't need to be told anything involving Cliona ruined his reason. Every time he closed his eyes he saw her again in that field, and whenever someone tore him away from the vision, he fought the urge to snap at them. The others weren't inclined to believe his story, and if not for Meshell's aid, they'd probably still be following the stream west. He was grateful Meshell had stood with him, but the lack of trust the others expressed was an open wound that refused to close.

Making matters worse, following Cliona's vague directions had done little to help them. For four days they'd traveled northwest for no apparent reason. The prairie remained as featureless as ever, and they'd spotted no more signs of the lost civilization they were supposed to find. No one said anything, but the curse of their years together was that they didn't need to.

Ari kept glancing east, and Hakon knew the assassin was thinking of events in the Six States. He and Solveig had been the two most involved in the creation of the new order, and their absence no doubt pained them both. The temptation for Ari was even greater, as it would take little more than a thought for him to return and soak up the latest happenings. He didn't only because he knew he couldn't afford to split his attention. He also ran the risk, if he returned alone, of abandoning them to any sudden threats that might appear.

It wasn't an idle worry. They'd been attacked twice more, and dragons were a common enough sight in the sky. So far, the dragons hadn't found them interesting enough to attack. Hakon suspected that if Ari transported, though, that would change quickly.

Solveig didn't glance east, but more than once others had to call her name twice or more before she responded. She was lost in her thoughts, though she shared few of them. Meshell was mostly concerned for him, though she never dared say so out loud. Hakon only knew because she almost never left his side.

Irric was the only one who didn't seem too bothered by their change of direction. Hakon saw no sign Irric was bored or frustrated. It seemed as though he was as happy walking in one direction as another. The only time he'd shown any concern was when Solveig had come close to shouting at Hakon during their last argument.

Meshell continued to reassure him, telling him that they would follow this path as long as was required. Hakon wasn't so sure. He trusted that they would accompany him, but only as long as they were convinced it was their best choice. The longer they went without any clues, the weaker Hakon's arguments became. Cliona didn't reappear either, which only fed more fuel to the fire of the band's doubts. Even Meshell didn't seem sure of what she'd seen.

On the third day, Hakon grew more certain that something in the band was about to snap. Ari was almost walking backwards, his glances to the east had become so frequent. Hakon was tempted to take Solveig by the hand and pull her along as her thoughts carried her in other directions. Even Irric looked worried.

Then their first clue found them.

Hakon and Meshell roamed a few hundred paces ahead of the others, though there had been little need of their scouting for days. He spotted the mystery first, and he stopped so he could focus on it.

Meshell noticed his pause. "What is it?"

Hakon pointed to the sky, and Meshell followed the gesture. She stared for several moments, struggling to identify the creature. "It has to be a dragon, right?"

Hakon squinted. The flying beast had to be miles away yet, but the wings were already visible. It looked like a flying rock, but even he wasn't ready to believe something that outlandish.

The other three caught up to their scouts. There was no need to point out their discovery. The sky was clear as crystal, and the odd shape was the only movement either in the plains or above.

"Dragon?" Irric asked.

"Never seen one shaped like that," Ari remarked. He glanced at Solveig. "You ever read about a creature that matches that?"

"No." Solveig had her gaze fixed on the creature. "It's high, though. Very high."

She was right. Had there been any clouds in the sky, the creature would have been well above them. Its altitude didn't reassure Hakon. "It's coming straight for us."

"Anyone used teho lately?" Solveig asked.

The fact she had to ask told Hakon just how distracted she'd been. But no one had.

"It's still coming toward us," Irric observed. "What are we doing?"

The swordsman had aimed the question at Solveig, so Hakon bit back his own answer. Solveig thought for a moment, then issued her orders. "Ari, make us a transport point here. If we have to retreat, I'd rather not have to lose all the progress from the last few days. The rest of you, spread out in the grass and take cover. If it is a dragon that's interested in us, let's not all be in one place for it to attack. Meshell, you stay near Hakon."

Hakon didn't argue. Solveig wasn't making them retreat, and he was encouraged by Ari's creation of a transport point. He ran away from the others, Meshell following him. She would protect him if he needed a teho shield. Thirty paces away from the others, he took a knee in the grass. Meshell kneeled next to him. The others did the same, spreading away in other directions. The only flaw in Solveig's plan was one Hakon approved of. Ari couldn't transport them all immediately. By spreading out, she was committing them to fight, if it came to that.

Hakon pulled his sword from its sheath. Meshell raised a questioning eyebrow.

"Just in case," Hakon said.

"It's at least a mile above us."

"Still."

They didn't have to wait long. The creature never deviated from its path, flying toward them as straight as an arrow. It maintained its altitude, which was even higher than Hakon had first thought. Meshell's estimate, if anything, was low. He crouched deeper into the grass as though it would somehow protect him.

He kept watching, trying to make sense of what he saw. The wings of the creature looked draconic, although they were wider across than any he had seen before. The shape of the body remained all wrong, though. It was too round, and he didn't recognize the profile. All he knew was that it was enormous. It was larger than an elder dragon.

Beside him, Meshell swore softly. "What *is* that?"

Hakon wished he had an answer for her.

As it came closer, he sensed its teho, and it almost

made him drop his sword. He'd fought his fair share of dragons over the years, and they always terrified him. The strength of a youngling was almost unmatched in the Six States. What victories he'd amassed against elders could be chalked up to a combination of luck and heroic sacrifices.

The teho within this beast reminded Hakon of the vast valley between a kolma like him and a stamfar like Isira. He couldn't hope to fight most stamfars, and an elder dragon would fall before this creature with equal ease.

He knew Meshell felt it, too, because she didn't even curse.

His heart pounded in his chest, harder than it had during his first battles as a young recruit in the army. His mouth went dry, and he found it difficult to grip his sword. He looked at the enormous weapon, and it suddenly felt small and inconsequential. If that creature came down, there was nothing Hakon could do. He was as useless as an ahula in a battle between stamfars.

Fortunately, the creature didn't seem interested in descending. If it had, Hakon might have ordered the retreat himself. As it was, he was frozen between wanting to hide and wanting to run. Could the creature see them? If it was a dragon, the answer was almost certainly yes.

Hakon couldn't tear his eyes away from the creature. It still looked like a flying rock, which made no sense.

The creature was a way out when its profile changed. Its belly distended and then split apart from the rest of the beast. Hakon needed several moments to understand what he'd just seen. He hadn't been that far off when he thought he was looking at a flying rock.

The dragon was the largest he'd ever seen, twice as big as an elder. And it had been carrying a boulder at least the size of a house. By the time he understood, the boulder had already fallen halfway toward them.

Solveig was a moment faster. "Run!" she shouted.

Hakon was already in motion. He grabbed Meshell's hand and pulled her to her feet as he filled his legs with teho and sprinted away. The force of his pull dislocated her shoulder. He felt her arm pop out under his grip, but he didn't stop. She grunted against the pain and flailed with her legs, searching for her balance and rhythm. As Hakon ran, he watched the sky, and his stomach sank as fast as the boulder fell toward them. They weren't going to make it in time. He stopped and wrapped Meshell in his arms, twisting so that his back was to the impact site.

"Shield!"

The boulder hit the exact place Ari had located his transport point. Hakon had just enough time to be impressed before the force of the impact struck them. Meshell cried out as the pressure pounded her shield. The ground threw them in the air as though they were a child's ball, then blasted them away. Meshell held her shield for a few moments as dirt and stone pummeled them, and then she went limp in his arms. Hakon squeezed as much teho into his body as he could as they plummeted to the ground.

Even with his teho, they hit hard. He cratered into the ground and rolled, protecting Meshell as well as he was able. Stone shards cut into his hardened skin, and when he tried to breathe, he choked on dust. But when he came to a stop, he was alive. He positioned himself on top of Meshell, sheltering her from any large debris that may fall. With one hand, he pulled his tunic over his mouth and nose, then did the same for her.

He stayed like that for a while, thinking of nothing but protecting Meshell. The dust remained thick in the air, but the other dangers soon passed. He considered calling for the others, but he couldn't hear anything. He felt for teho and sensed at least one person nearby. It felt like Irric, but he couldn't be sure. Regardless, at least three of them had survived. Ari and Solveig had been closest to the impact, though.

More concerning was the great concentration of teho above them. It was falling fast, the dragon swooping down to finish what it had started. Hakon pushed himself to his feet, stumbling as he fought for balance. In the blast he'd lost his sword, and there was no chance he would find it in the choking dust. Without it, he was next to useless. Still, he had to do something. He walked toward the falling teho, hands balled into fists.

The dragon landed with surprising grace, settling its massive bulk with the ease one would expect from a creature a fraction of its size. A blast of teho cleared the air and sent Hakon falling back onto his rear. He returned to his feet, but when he got his first good look at the dragon, he wasn't sure why he had bothered.

The size of the dragon defied easy comparisons. Elders were as big as the tallest buildings Hakon had ever seen, and this dragon made elders look small. Its bulk defied Hakon's attempts to understand it. The amount of muscle required to move such a creature was impossible to comprehend. But when he felt the teho that radiated from the dragon, he understood. It wasn't physical strength that kept this dragon upright.

The power was so intense that Hakon felt as though he stood before a raging inferno. He wasn't sure he could get closer, even if he wanted. Hakon couldn't remember a time in his long life when he'd ever felt so insignificant. He had always mattered. Always been able to change something about the course of events.

Not here. He opened his hands and shook them out. He might not be able to fight, but at the very least he would die standing between the dragon and Meshell. The dragon leaned forward and bared its teeth. He looked up and met its gaze.

Ancient eyes met his, and the dragon stopped.

Hakon waited. There was nothing left for him to do. He stared into the eyes, trying to imagine all the history the creature had seen. All the wisdom it had gathered.

The reptilian eyes seemed to look past Hakon. Or through him. They were so large, it was hard to tell exactly what they focused on. Hakon stood, more relaxed than he thought he would be. Surrender was always easy. It was fighting that was hard.

Then the dragon brought its head back and swept its wings out. It launched into the sky, once again exhibiting that effortless grace that seemed physically impossible. A wave of teho swept over Hakon, but he kept his feet. He watched as the dragon sped high into the sky and northwest.

He grunted softly to himself, then looked behind him to see if Meshell had woken up and somehow threatened the dragon. But she still lay, unconscious, right where he had left her. Something caught his eye, though. Dust was everywhere, and most of the grass where Hakon stood had either been flattened or ripped away by the impact of the boulder. But right behind him and a little to his side was another pair of footprints. They'd stood in one place, never moving.

Before he could think too deeply about it, he saw movement out of the corner of his vision. Irric and Ari carried Solveig between them. She, like Meshell, was unconscious, and looked as though she'd been buried in debris. But she was breathing, which was all that Hakon cared about. Time would let them heal most injuries.

"Meshell?" Irric asked.

"She's out, but she'll be fine. She absorbed the brunt of the impact."

"I've never seen anything like that," Ari said.

"None of us have," Irric pointed out. "Why did the dragon leave?"

Hakon kept his suspicions to himself. "I don't know, but at least we learned something today."

"I feel like we learned a lot today," Irric said. "And I'm not particularly pleased by that fact."

"We learned the one fact that matters, though."

"Oh?" Irric arched an eyebrow. "And what's that?"

Hakon pointed northwest. "We learned that we're going the right way."

10

———

Zachary found Edda in one of her favorite hiding places, a balcony on the third floor of their estate that overlooked most of Mioska. She sat on one of two chairs, twirling an empty wine glass idly in her right hand as she flipped through the day's correspondence with her left. Her focus on the papers was complete, and she didn't notice Zachary enter the adjoining room. He took a moment to watch her.

As often happened, the sight of her today clashed with his memories of her. Since his exile to Vispeda, she'd become fixed in his memory as a young woman, barely of age to marry. But as he'd grown and matured in Vispeda, she'd done the same here at home. Only he'd never had the opportunity to see her become the woman she was today. He still thought of her as his little sister, someone he needed to protect from the world.

Then she let out a vulgar curse, and the spell was broken. Zachary grinned and stepped onto the balcony.

He picked up the bottle of wine. "You need another glass?"

In answer, she lifted her glass and held it out toward him. He filled it with a hearty portion, judging it appropriate for her mood. A second glass had been left on the table for him, and he allowed himself a little. He took the other chair, sipped at the excellent wine, and looked out over Mioska.

"Does Father know you're pillaging his most precious reserves?" he asked.

"I'm not sure Father even knows his own name these days."

"Not saving it for a special occasion?"

"Not sure there's going to be any to save it for."

Zachary glanced over at her pile of papers. As he suspected, some of the pamphlets that had been flooding Mioska the last few weeks were in the pile. "You shouldn't be reading those."

It was the wrong thing to say, and she let him know it. "Why? Because you think it'll worry me?"

He held up his hands in a placating gesture. "Not what I meant. They're trash, is all."

Her frustration died as fast as it had flared up. She rubbed at her eyes, and Zachary saw how tired she looked. He almost asked about her sleep, but she hadn't asked him here as an older brother. He sealed his lips.

"I know what they are," she said.

Her fingers ran deftly over the pile, removing the most recent arrivals. She handed them to Zachary, who skimmed them quickly. Most were the same drivel he'd been reading for the last week, but one new one showed a dramatic sketch of the ruins of Midvale.

She continued as he looked through them, "But I think it's important to know what's being said. If we don't know what we're up against, we can't fight effectively."

"I agree, but if we study them too carefully, we run the risk of taking them seriously."

Edda took a long sip of her wine, and Zachary noticed a fair amount of the bottle was already gone. "I think we should."

"How so?"

"I think we need to ask ourselves if whoever authored these is right."

Zachary set his glass down on the table harder than he'd intended. Edda flinched, and she wouldn't meet his gaze. The pamphlets were everything Zachary stood against, and his first instinct was to forbid their discussion in this house. That was what his father would have done. What his sister was expecting him to do. He would make his proclamation, and she'd ignore it, just as Zachary had ignored Father before his exile. Maybe the disagreement wouldn't spread, but anything that turned him in any way against his sister was unacceptable. Not after he'd lost her for so long. He took a deep breath and sought a different way forward.

When he spoke, he knew his voice sounded strained, but it was as calm as he could be. "Maybe it would be best if you let me know what you're thinking about."

She met his gaze then, and he watched as her body relaxed. That was good. He didn't want her fearing him like she had Father. She pointed to the papers. "To be clear, I don't believe anything about the dragons opening up a new passage through the gate for us. Nor do I believe any chosen few will be selected for some mysterious ascension by the dragons."

Zachary didn't try to hide his relief. Those were among the wildest beliefs being proclaimed by the sect that had risen like weeds in an untended garden.

Edda continued, "But I do think they're asking the question we've been too afraid to confront directly."

Zachary thought he now understood the direction of Edda's concerns. "What if they're right? What if there's nothing we can do to stop the advance of the dragons and the wild?"

Edda nodded. "I know you're working night and day to prevent it," she pointed to the remaining stack of her papers, "but the facts are clear. We're losing land and lives at an alarming rate. The only reason we've avoided panic so far is because no major cities have fallen yet."

"We can't give up hope. As soon as we do, we lose any chance of victory."

Edda didn't capitulate that easily. "A noble sentiment, but hope doesn't bloom without some sort of seed."

"We fought off the dragons here." Zachary knew he was becoming defensive but couldn't stop himself.

"And now the tehoin are gone, and for weeks the only news has been of towns falling, not just across the frontier, but within our own state. We need more." She shot him a warning glare. "And it can't be about the band. I believe you well enough, but you'll sound like little more than a madman to most."

Her words cracked the brittle defense he'd maintained since visiting Midvale. Suddenly, he felt like crying. He sniffled and wiped his nose with the sleeve of his tunic. "I don't know what more I can do."

Edda reached out and took his hand. "I'm not criticizing you. You've done more to keep this state safe than any council member I can think of in the past decade. All I'm saying is that you're so focused on winning that you haven't considered what losing might look like. And I think a good leader prepares for both possibilities."

Zachary knew well enough when he was being led someplace. "And you have an idea?"

"One. I've been asking myself the same question I just put to you. What is the best loss we could hope for?"

"And?"

"If we can't save everybody, are there ways we could save a few? Perhaps we could design a safe and self-sustaining settlement that would allow humanity to continue."

He heard the last threads of hope in her voice, and he hated to be the one who snipped them. "But we can't build a place like that. We have no construction that can withstand the dragons, and no tehoin besides the band that can fight meaningfully against an elder. I know you haven't seen Aysgarth personally, but it's the most defensible position in the Six States, with the strongest tehoin, and it was still destroyed in a single attack. There's no hiding from this. We have to win, or there is no future for us."

She turned away from him, hoping to hide the hurt his words had caused. When she'd recovered, she gestured again to the pamphlets on the table next to Zachary's untouched wine glass. But she couldn't speak.

This time, it was Zachary's turn to comfort his sister. "I know it can feel hopeless. I feel it, too. But we never stop fighting."

She nodded, but words weren't enough to fight the darkness gradually spreading across her thoughts. Zachary knew he needed to do more. She'd spoken true when she spoke about hope. Words alone wouldn't suffice. He glanced down at the papers on the table.

He knew one place where he could start.

∽

When he opened the door to Ingolf's, he was surprised to find the common room full. The mood wasn't exactly boisterous, but it was a far sight better than Zachary had observed on his walk here. Acolytes of the apocalyptic cult had spread throughout the city like wildfire. They came out of their hiding places at night like termites out of rotten woodwork. Zachary had heard the reports, but it wasn't until he walked the streets at night that he understood the power the speakers held over the city.

Agnar had yet to issue any rulings against the acolytes. He believed in allowing his people to speak freely, a tradition held close to his heart since the Rebellion had established the Six States. And the acolytes were careful not to break any laws. If roaming patrols believed the acolytes were too disruptive, the patrols shooed them along. The acolytes always left without complaint, only to appear later in the evening somewhere else.

Zachary didn't like the acolytes, but during the day they had few listeners. He'd dismissed them as little more than an annoyance. Now that he saw them at night, his attitude became harder. Crowds gathered wherever an acolyte spoke, and more than a few guard patrols were among the rapt listeners.

They were a danger, and the council would have to take up the matter of their proselytizing soon. Tonight, Zachary had a more specific task, which had brought him to this inn. Here, at least, there were no acolytes to drag the mood of the room down.

He stood on his toes and looked around the crowded room, finding the subject of his visit easily enough. Ingolf stood behind the bar, pouring drinks, and talking happily with several patrons at once. Though Zachary had the hood of his cloak pulled low over his eyes, Ingolf recognized him. The innkeeper inclined his head, and Zachary tilted his toward the private room in the back. Ingolf shook his head, and they reached the limit of their unspoken conversation. Zachary weaved through the tables and found a corner of the bar he could stand by.

Ingolf finished his conversation, then shuffled over to Zachary. "How can I help you?"

"Busy place tonight. I was hoping to find someplace quiet to share a drink."

"Of course, sir. It'll cost you something fierce tonight, though."

"Money's no object."

That caught the attention of a few of the bar's patrons, but when they couldn't penetrate his identity, they lost interest. Ingolf ordered another bartender to keep an eye on everything, then led Zachary through the kitchen and into a small office. He didn't sit. "Can't say I was expecting you to walk through my door. What do you want?"

"Nice to see you, too."

"Not sure if you noticed, but I've been busy. There's gold to be made and secrets to be learned." Ingolf seemed tense, but Zachary didn't ask about that. Ingolf was always willing to part with a secret, unless it was one of his own.

"Why so busy?"

"The dragons were kind enough to eliminate a significant fraction of my competition. Then they drove people from all over the state toward Mioska because we're the only city that fought off a dragon attack. Now, why are you here?"

Zachary had looked forward to catching up with Ingolf, but he didn't want to be a nuisance. He didn't feel very welcome. "Who's printing the pamphlets that have been flooding the city?"

"What are you paying me?"

"What do you want to know?" Zachary didn't even bother to offer money.

Ingolf thought for a moment. "Will Aysgarth honor their word to return if the dragons attack?"

"I'm not certain. Hel, who you met, is the head of their council. Were it up to her alone, they would come. But she is fighting against several factions within her own people."

"Of course she is. The tehoin hate us. What odds would you put on Aysgarth responding?"

"Seventy-thirty for."

Ingolf scratched his chin, and Zachary wondered what calculations were running through the innkeeper's head. Eventually, Ingolf reached his decision. "Hallr is behind the rapid printing of the brochures."

Zachary wouldn't have been more surprised if Ingolf had told him that Edda was an assassin. Ever since Midvale, Hallr had been a mostly cooperative voice on the council, giving support to almost every idea Zachary suggested. The last couple of weeks had been the most pleasant and productive council meetings of Zachary's short experience. He'd been patting himself on the back for showing Hallr the destructive forces they were up against. But he'd never known Ingolf to lie. It was bad for business. "Why?"

"You, mostly. I heard about your trip to Midvale, and had it been a council member with a functioning spine, it might have worked. But Hallr saw the destruction and concluded there was nothing he could do. That there was nothing anyone could do. When he returned, he sought out one of the acolytes and bought into the cult something fierce. He's been pouring money into their coffers, thinking that he'll be among those who ascend when the dragons return for his soul."

Zachary cursed his own foolishness. If nothing else, he should have realized Hallr's change of heart had been too complete to be true. He'd been blinded by his own pride. Ingolf was casting glances toward the door, so Zachary finished with one last question. "Tell me true. How bad is it out there? How close are we to losing order?"

Ingolf considered for a moment. "It's bad, but I would guess there's a way to go before it breaks. The more esoteric beliefs of the cult don't attract many followers, but they're the only ones offering hope right now, even if it is the hope of the mad and deluded."

"Don't suppose you have any brilliant suggestions?"

"No, and that's why I never wanted to be anything besides an innkeeper. You're the fool who sought out a council seat."

"Thanks."

"You're welcome. Now get out of my inn. I've got paying customers to serve."

Zachary obeyed and found himself once again on the streets of Mioska. He wandered home, choosing streets at random that took him in the right direction. He came across one of the acolytes speaking at a street corner and stopped to listen. As he did, he understood what the acolytes offered. They preached about something better on the other side of the gates, and for those that were worthy, something else entirely.

It was foolish and without reason or evidence. But he sensed the power in their proclamations. The acolytes offered what the council hadn't been able to. At least, not yet.

Zachary couldn't listen for long. As he left, he

understood better what he needed to do. What he needed to offer to the people. He disappeared into the night, his thoughts churning with plans for the future.

11

———————

Hakon sat away from the others, a weathered water skin in his hand. He took another swig, but no matter how much he drank, nothing quenched his thirst. He stared toward the northwest, halfway expecting the silhouette of the monstrous dragon to blot out the stars as the others rested. But the only movement came from behind him as Irric stood up from the fire and walked toward him.

"Mind if I join you?" the swordsman asked.

Hakon shrugged and gestured to the grass next to him.

Irric sat, and the motion reminded Hakon of an old cat coming to rest in a sunny alley. Graceful, but with a weariness that no amount of strength could banish.

"You expecting company?" Irric nodded in the direction Hakon was watching.

"Not really." He declined to elaborate, and Irric didn't press. He changed the subject before Irric changed his mind. "How are the others?"

"Meshell and Solveig will both be fine after a full night's rest. Ari's furious, though."

"Noticed that." It had been one of the reasons he'd left the fire. He'd endured no small number of angry glares from Ari over the years, but tonight he preferred to have the glares aimed at his back. "You think he's going to press the matter?"

Irric leaned back on his arms and stared up at the stars. "He wants to, but he won't."

"What about you?"

Irric didn't answer for a long time, but Hakon was in no hurry.

"You ever get tired? Exhausted in a way you can't quite explain?"

"I do."

"It's all the time for me, these days. No immediate reason. I could sit and read a book all day, then get a full night of sleep, and I'd still wake feeling as though I'd fought a war singlehandedly the day before. Asked Solveig about it once, a couple of years ago. She didn't even look me over. Just told me she'd been feeling the same. Don't think it's as bad for her, though."

Irric drifted off into silence. Hakon knew he was coming to a point, so he waited. It reminded him of old times, the two of them talking late into the night.

"You know, I can't say I believe in fate or destiny or any of that, but I can't tell you the number of times I thought that I was supposed to die with Brynja."

Hakon hadn't thought of his first commander since the day in Aysgarth when Zachary had pushed him into telling the others about the origin of the band. It was no secret that Brynja's death had haunted Irric for years. The swordsman had always felt responsible, and any ambition he'd possessed died that day. But Hakon had always thought the pain of that day had faded with the countless years between then and now.

He'd mistaken Irric's silence on the matter for healing. "Still?"

"Still. There are days where I feel like I'm a ghost moving through the world, leaving no trace."

"Really? Because when I sought you out, you were standing before a roaring crowd of admirers."

"Heroes in the arena rise and fall faster than you can swing the giant sword of yours. I'm certain that if you were to go back today and ask about me, only a handful would even remember I existed. If you hadn't come for me, I would have blown around forever, like a leaf in the wind. Sometimes I think that's how it's always been. You keep pulling me forward, even though I have nowhere to go."

Hakon couldn't tell if Irric was grateful or upset. "What would you have of me?"

"Nothing at all."

Hakon couldn't keep the confusion off his face.

Irric's grin did little to hide the ache in his voice. "Ever since Brynja died, there's been nothing I truly want. I like the band and the bond we formed. Our adventures keep me distracted. Even when you betrayed and abandoned us, I think there was a part of me that always knew I'd follow you again. It wasn't that you gave life meaning, but that you gave it the illusion of meaning, and that was enough. But now, I do want something."

Hakon was able to finish Irric's thought. "You want to die."

Irric made a noise in the back of his throat that Hakon took as an agreement. After a moment, he asked, "You don't think less of me for it, do you?"

"After Husavik, my own thoughts turned that way often.

Meshell grounded me here, and I needed to be sure of what happened to Cliona. Now I know, but I suppose we've been so busy I haven't considered it again. But no. I think I understand."

Irric's gaze was focused on something in the past. "Remember how we were always so confused when the stamfars committed suicide?"

"We couldn't imagine why someone would part with such power."

"I understand now. Our strength is as meaningless as anything else."

Hakon reached out to his friend and rested his massive hand on Irric's shoulder. "You're wrong, there. Sure, strength alone is meaningless. But it still allows us to make a difference."

"Seems like it's rarely the difference we hope to make."

Hakon had no answer to that. "We seem to have gone a long way from where we started this discussion."

"Not really. It's all been me trying to let you know. I'll follow you as far as you lead. You'll never have to fear me changing my mind. But I think that if we figure this mess out and survive it, I might have one final favor to ask of you. Would you be willing?"

Hakon swallowed hard. "Yes."

"Thanks."

Irric lay all the way back, laced his fingers behind his head, and stared contentedly up at the stars. After a moment, Hakon joined him, and they watched the constellations drift on their endless cycle together.

～

The next morning, they rose with the sun. Irric fixed them breakfast, and they ate quickly. They spoke little, but Hakon sensed no hostility or frustration. Ari was the one he worried about most, and the assassin seemed more resigned than upset. When the last bite was finished, they packed up and followed Hakon northwest without question or argument.

Hakon divided his attention between the sky and the land, but neither proved terribly interesting. Patchy clouds dotted the horizon, and it felt like a storm was gathering to the east. The breeze picked up until it was a constant wind. The wind picked up dust and abraded their exposed skin. Hakon decided he much preferred the ceaseless wind over another encounter with the dragon from the day before. Even as the skies darkened to the east, they remained clear of predators.

The storm caught up with them by late afternoon. It started as cold rain that pelted them like small arrows, but before long, it transitioned to snow. Hakon pulled his cloak tighter and used teho to keep himself warm. He frequently checked on the others. They remained warm enough, but they would need to find shelter before long.

The wind whipped the snow in circles around him, cutting off any sight of danger. The first sign he had that something was different was the sudden change underneath his feet. He'd gotten used to pressing grass down as he walked, his feet crunching and shifting with every step. Then the grass suddenly ended, and he stood on a hard and even surface.

He looked down. It was as though he stood on a road, but one far better constructed than anything in the six states. This was perfectly flat, and no grass poked through. A few moments later, the rest of the band discovered it as well.

"A road?" Solveig asked.

"That had been my thought, too," Hakon answered. He pointed north, his finger following the direction of the road. "I say we follow it. There's bound to be shelter eventually."

There was little reason not to, and the road seemed to travel in the rough direction they were going.

Ari crouched and put his hand against the surface. "It's warm."

"What?" Hakon took a knee and did the same.

Ari was right. Now that Hakon looked for it, another detail stood out. The blowing snow tended to collect in drifts, but there were none on the road. The snow that landed on the road melted and trickled off the edge. Hakon had never seen anything like it.

Ari's observation made the choice even easier. They followed the road north as the storm raged. In time, the heat of the road worked its way through Hakon's boots, and his feet were warm even as the wind tried to freeze his face and arms.

Thanks to the road, they made faster time than they had in the grass. Their direction was set, and every step was the same as the last. The demanding pace kept them warm, and before it turned dark, the wind from the storm died down. The blowing snow started to fall gently, and then it was over. The clouds moved west, and the gray skies with them.

As the storm cleared, their horizons expanded. Off in the distance, Hakon could see buildings taller than any found in the Six States. But that wasn't what caught his attention and stopped his advance.

That honor went to the skies above the city. From this distance, they didn't appear to be much. More like a group of bees buzzing around one of their hives. But the buildings gave Hakon and the others some sense of perspective. Small as they seemed from here, the creatures were large.

Very large.

Meshell stopped next to him and swore. "That's an awful lot of dragons."

12

Agnar's servant found Zachary in the gallery. It was a square room with polished wooden floors. The walls were filled with commissioned paintings of the governors of Mioska, from Lieve, the first governor after the Rebellion, all the way to Agnar. They were an eclectic group, with little to link them except the position of authority they'd all shared. Lieve had been a Rebellion commander, rewarded with the governorship after a brilliant campaign in the south. Zachary's childhood lessons had taught him that she'd been a more than competent governor. She'd focused on repairing and rebuilding Mioska, and much of the state's current wealth could be traced back to decisions she'd made in those early years. Zachary idly wondered if any of the band had known her. He suspected the answer was yes, which made his head spin.

Not all governors were as well regarded. Two paintings down from Lieve was Jabez, a beady-eyed governor whose painting looked like it had been created out of spite. He'd brought Holar to the brink of ruin during a drought, and it was only thanks to his timely death that the state hadn't suffered worse.

When Agnar's servant entered, Zachary was staring at Agnar's portrait. He imagined the servant saw it as some sort of fawning, but Zachary was genuinely curious. In his own time, Agnar was liked well enough, and he'd made no great mistakes as governor. Zachary couldn't guess how history would remember Holar's current governor. He wondered, too, how Agnar considered his own reign. Unfortunately, his portrait couldn't answer any of Zachary's questions.

"He's ready to see you, councilman," the servant announced.

Zachary gestured for the servant to lead the way, and before long, he found himself in Agnar's receiving room. Today it was just the two of them, but the space was large enough to allow many of Agnar's advisors to observe if needed. It was an opulent room designed to instill in visitors a sense of Mioska's wealth and strength. Bands of gold wrapped around the columns, and expensive silks were draped around the walls. Zachary bowed toward Agnar, wondering if there was any significance to the decision to meet here. He looked around again, ensuring the two of them were alone.

The governor waved for him to approach. "Sorry for meeting here, but the only time today was between more official receptions. I've ensured our privacy, so we may speak freely."

"The apocalyptic cult is becoming a problem we need to address. Hallr has been cooperating with them."

Agnar didn't appear surprised, which Zachary took as confirmation that he'd already known. Agnar leaned back in his ornate chair. "And what would you do?"

Zachary told him, and Agnar's eyes went wide. From the

veteran governor, such a reaction meant Zachary had truly caught him by surprise. "A bold plan. I thought you were going to demand I take some action against the cult."

It wasn't the enthusiastic support Zachary had hoped for, but Agnar was nothing if not cautious and measured in his decisions. That was why he'd survived on the throne through as many tumultuous years as he had.

"Attacking them only increases their legitimacy," Zachary said. "So long as their assemblies are peaceful, they are best left alone. Force won't win this argument."

"I agree. But why come to me? Your plan doesn't require my support." Agnar's sharp eyes shone, and Zachary guessed the governor already had some idea what Zachary had come to ask.

"I disagree. I want you to support us, publicly."

He met the governor's gaze. Agnar had little to gain and much to lose by acceding to Zachary's request, and the request made Zachary's own ambitions clear. Agnar was right. Zachary could follow through on his plan without Agnar's help, and it might do some good. But the plan only worked if Agnar threw his support behind Zachary. It was the sort of decision Agnar never agreed to. It would put him in a corner. But that was exactly why his support was so valuable. Why it was necessary.

Agnar tore his gaze away and looked out the window to his left, the one that looked over Mioska. "It's never been written into law, but you know as well as I there will be questions about you being tehoin. It is not our way."

"Would you support this if I wasn't?"

Agnar thought for a moment more. "I think I would, yes."

"Which is why I need you now. This is how we fight back

against the cult. We bring hope instead of despair. Together is the only way we sway the council."

"Hallr will object," Agnar pointed out.

"I'm not so sure he will. If his new beliefs are genuine, he might not see any point."

Agnar's features hardened, and Zachary felt like a student who had given the wrong answer to his tutor. But the governor's next question didn't reflect that disappointment. "If I do this, I'm not going to find any poison in my meals, am I?"

The thought hadn't even occurred to Zachary.

Agnar shook his head. "You're going to need to think of such things if you want to sit here."

He went silent as he looked out the window again. At this angle, Zachary thought he looked almost exactly like his portrait back in the galley. Strong and thoughtful. Just not quite bold enough. Finally, he nodded. "I'll consider it. I'll need to speak to her, too, before I commit. Have you asked her yet?"

"No, sir. I figured this would be the more difficult ask."

"Then, assuming you succeed in your next endeavor, let me know. I'll start preparing the way by holding some private conversations."

Zachary bowed. "Thank you, sir." There was more he wanted to say, but nothing seemed quite appropriate. "Thank you."

Agnar waved him away. "Go. And good luck. I hope this next part is as easy as you think it will be."

Zachary bowed again and left, a slight spring in his step.

∼

He returned home and spoke briefly with Edda, relating the progress he'd made with Agnar. She congratulated him. Like Agnar, she seemed amused by the order with which he'd tackled the steps of his plan.

As the day grew late, Zachary made his way to the barracks and the transport point. The Aysgarthian on duty didn't seem particularly pleased to see him but transported Zachary to Aysgarth all the same. When they arrived, she let go of his hand and transported straight back to Mioska. Zachary spoke to the guards, who pointed him in the right direction.

Zachary climbed the steps as he ascended one of the tallest towers in the city. When he was halfway to the top, he stopped and enjoyed the view. This high in the mountains, winter had already arrived, and the valley below was blanketed in a layer of puffy snow. Most of Aysgarth was huddled inside the walls, warmed by the fires of their hearths. Outside it was quiet, the snow muffling the few sounds there were. It was peaceful, and Zachary closed his eyes and basked in it.

Eventually, his arms grew cold. He continued the climb, and by the time he reached the flat roof of the tower, he could see his breath in the air. A pair of guards stopped him, and he waited patiently as Hel spoke with her generals, pointing out landmarks in the valley as she issued her orders.

Zachary enjoyed watching her. She spoke with authority, and the generals nodded whenever she looked to them for confirmation. Hel looked every bit the head of the council, and Zachary imagined her portrait hanging in a gallery somewhere. She wouldn't look as pensive as Agnar, he decided. She would be staring off into the future, pointing the way.

The meeting was short. Hel dismissed the generals, who nearly tripped over themselves in their hurry to get off the roof and into the warmth of their chambers. Hel looked out over the valley for a moment, then turned to follow. She saw Zachary for the first time, and her smile was wide. "What brings you here, stranger?"

The guards let Zachary onto the roof, and he opened his arms to embrace her. "I've been missing you."

She leaned into him, and with all the layers she was wearing, it was hard for him to wrap his arms around her. Her nose brushed against his cheek, and it was colder than ice.

"How long have you been out here?" he asked.

"Most of the evening," she confessed. "I find that having my meetings out here means they don't take long. People make their points a lot faster."

"That's brilliant, but you're freezing."

"I'll be fine." She stepped back. "As you can see, I dressed for the weather."

"Still, you mind heading in? Or do you want my meeting with you to also be over soon?"

Hel took his arm. "Of course not."

They made their way to the stairs, and the two guards followed at a respectful distance. Zachary glanced back at them. "They still with you all the time?"

"Much to my dismay," Hel said. "But even Valdis believes they're necessary. I'm starting to think she likes me."

Zachary chuckled. "So, it is the end of the world, then."

They reached a landing with a door that led them inside. As soon as they had walls between them and the winter, Zachary felt the warmth return to his limbs. "Damion should have built a second fortress someplace warmer."

"Believe it or not, the idea was actually considered," Hel said. "There was concern about having enough food year-round. But Damion was against it. Now that I know him a little better, I think part of it was his connection to the place, but part of it was his insistence that we keep our forces concentrated."

They wandered through the halls of Aysgarth, Hel leading them toward her chambers. As they walked, they caught up with each other on the events in their separate lives. Hel, it seemed, was having the easier time of it. The extra tehoin resulting from the change to their agreement had helped Valdis complete all the tasks she'd hoped to finish before winter set in. The food flowed steadily from Mioska, and no dragons had appeared in the sky.

Hel compared it to turning a massive cart around on a narrow road. It took them an enormous amount of time and effort, but they were working together, and every success built up to the next one.

Zachary told her of the growth of the cult and how his decision to show Hallr the dangers they faced had worked out poorly. She was a good listener, squeezing his arm tighter whenever he brought up something particularly difficult. He liked talking to her and liked it when they were able to share their burdens. He had no trouble imagining spending the rest of his life like this. And he couldn't be sure, but he believed she felt the same.

He finished about the time they reached her chambers. The guards took up station outside the door. Once it was closed behind them, Hel let go of his arm and looked up at him. "Why are you here?"

When the idea had first occurred to him, he'd thought this part would come easy. But he found himself stumbling over his words. He rubbed the back of his head and gazed down. "Well..."

She sat down on the side of her bed. She looked concerned, but not any more than usual when he was making a fool of himself.

Zachary gulped. This was a bad idea. He wasn't prepared. He hadn't even stopped to ask himself if there were any customs in Aysgarth to honor.

Then he looked at her, and all his doubts faded. Her presence gave him strength. They would figure it out together.

"Hel, you are one of the most impressive people I've ever met, and I'm more grateful than you can imagine that you stepped into my life that day in Vispeda. I'm not sure of much these days, but there is one thing I'm sure of. I love you, and I want to spend the rest of my life with you."

He got down on one knee before her. "Hel, will you marry me?"

13

Hakon and the band paralleled the road, following it toward the mysterious city in the distance. He split his attention between the city, the dragons overhead, and his friends beside him. He couldn't decide which of the three subjects he was most concerned about. The city was clearly a dragon nest. Or, more likely, given the numbers of the beasts flying over the tall spires, the home of several dragon nests. It also had to be the place they sought. The place Isira had heard of and the destination Cliona had pointed to. Hakon didn't know what they would find, but it felt like ice was running in his veins and settling in his stomach.

Approaching the city would have been worrying enough on its own, but it was the sight of so many dragons that made him consider turning around. They were already close enough that any of the dragons could see them. They walked in the tall grass, hoping it would provide some small amount of cover, but none of them deceived themselves. Dragons were capable of spotting smaller prey from farther away. As his feet grew sore from the long day, Hakon considered suggesting they return to the road. But he didn't.

Walking in the grass made them feel like they were doing something more than trusting their futures to chance.

The closer they came to the city, the more confused Hakon became. Even if they hadn't been tehoin, hated by dragons for as long as people had recorded stories, they were still food. Given the lack of game in the area and the number of dragons in the sky, Hakon would have assumed a couple of the dragons would have at least picked them up as a snack. He and the band were the equivalent of a flock of sheep finding their way into a kitchen and conveniently roasting themselves over a fire for the cook.

He wasn't the only one confused. Ari and Solveig muttered in hushed tones, and Irric stared at the dragons as though he was imagining them. He joined Hakon at the front of the line. "I'm not sure I'd be any more surprised if one of them came down, landed gently in front of us, and invited us to play cards."

Hakon turned to his friend. "I think I'd still find that a bit more surprising."

Irric's grin reminded Hakon of happier days. "Perhaps I went a bit too far, but that many dragons have picked this area clean of prey, and I'd guess that anything large enough to qualify as an appetizer for those beasts has long since learned to stay away from the area. Do you think they can't see us?

Meshell chimed in from directly behind them. "I'd guess they're able to smell us from here. It's been far too long since we've taken a bath."

"Speak for yourself," Irric said. "I'm certain I smell like a spring meadow after a rainstorm."

They quieted as they neared the outskirts of the city. Most cities Hakon was familiar with were surrounded by walls to protect the inhabitants more easily from the wild.

But even the smallest unwalled towns followed a similar pattern. Buildings near the edge of the settlement were smaller homes owned by a single family. It was only when one drew closer to the center of the city or town did one find taller buildings.

The stamfar who'd built this city didn't possess the same ideas about cities. The very first buildings that rose to greet them were ten to fifteen stories high. Only the crashed ship in the mountains could compare to them in size, and they were small beside the buildings farther in.

The dragons' flights didn't bring them too close to the band. It looked as though they circled something farther to the north. They paid no attention to the tehoin inching steadily toward their nests, but when the shadows of the buildings fell over Hakon and hid him from their sight, he breathed easier. Night was falling fast, and they decided it was best to find a place to take shelter for the evening.

They chose the first building they came to. It stood impossibly tall, made of stamfar glass and the same material that had built so many of their homes. A pair of doors served as the main entrance, and they opened silently as Hakon and the others approached. He glanced over at Solveig, who just shrugged. He went in. It was hardly the first time they'd encountered the stamfar mysteries.

The doors closed behind them as stamfar lights turned on above their heads. Hakon squinted against their brightness, but once his eyes adjusted, he looked around the room. It was as large as many of the homes he'd been in, but it stood without support from any columns or pillars. Chairs and small tables were in the corners. Hakon saw no signs of violence.

A hallway connected the large room to other rooms, still enormous by Hakon's standards but not as expansive as the first. The chairs and tables sat in various patterns, but Hakon could discern no larger order. Beside him, Meshell ran a finger along the tops of one of the tables.

She held it up for his inspection. "No dust."

"No bodies, either."

"Did they all just decide to get up and walk away?"

"Looks that way, even though it makes no sense."

"I'm starting to get used to that," Meshell said.

They met back with the others in the front room. Solveig's eyes were practically shining. "Ari and I want to examine a few of the nearby buildings. But we won't wander too far."

Irric slumped into a chair. "I'll rest for a bit, then put together some food. I'm assuming we're staying here tonight?"

"Seems as good a place as any," Solveig said.

Hakon pointed up. "Meshell and I can walk through the rest of the building and make sure there aren't any surprises."

The group split and Hakon and Meshell found a stairwell. It coiled around the walls, climbing all the way to the top of the building. Meshell sighed. "You're not going to make us look in every room, are you?"

"I figured we could check a few on the second floor, then climb to the top. I was hoping to get a better view of the city."

They climbed the stairs to the second floor and entered a smaller hallway than the one below. Hakon counted six doors on the floor, and he and Meshell went first to the one closest to the stairs. These doors didn't open on their own but were controlled by a pad like the ones they had seen in the crashed ship. Hakon pressed the stamfar symbol for "open," but the pad blinked red, and nothing happened. He tried again, with a similar result. They walked the length of the hallway, pressing each pad as they passed. All flashed red at them.

"Want to break one down?" Meshell asked.

"I do. I want to at least know what's inside them." He walked over to the stairs and called down to Irric, letting the cook know he didn't need to be alarmed. Then he returned to the first door and filled his body with teho. He lashed out with his foot, and the door cracked open. He and Meshell pushed their way through and into the remains of somebody's home.

Hakon's immediate sense of the place was that a family had once lived here. A variety of furniture sat along the walls and in the corner, and one table with four chairs sat in the middle of another room. Empty frames hung on the walls. There were no bodies and no dust. They went from room to room. Everything was in perfect order; there just weren't any remains.

"Are you starting to feel really uneasy about this?" Meshell asked.

"Been feeling uneasy about this for a while."

"Everyone left, but not in a hurry. Why?"

Hakon didn't have an answer. The place had two bedrooms and another room Hakon didn't understand. Tubes and fixtures were poking out of a cabinet of some sort. Hakon played with one of the fixtures, and water came out of it like a pump on a well. Meshell came at the sound. For a moment, they both stood there, staring at it like it had more mysteries to reveal. But it just kept pouring water. Eventually, Hakon turned it off.

They left through the broken door and climbed the stairs. The lights overhead flickered on whenever they passed underneath, turning off again after they passed.

They reached the top of the stairs and broke into another apartment. Though the furniture was different, and the details unique, the story remained the same.

Hakon pulled a chair to the large window in the main room and sat down. Outside, the sky had turned a lovely shade of dark purple as dusk illuminated the last of the clouds from the passing storm. The dragons still circled someplace deeper within the city, though Hakon thought there were fewer in the air than he'd seen earlier in the day. Either they had flown off to hunt, or they'd returned to their nest for the night. Regardless, the sight failed to instill a sense of confidence in the giant warrior.

Meshell pulled up a chair and sat down beside him. She'd examined the whole apartment for threats before allowing herself to relax. "They left."

"I suspect we'll see the same everywhere in this city."

"There's one question that keeps running through my mind. What would cause them to leave? In the mountain villages, they'd been killed. But here, they escaped. What were they fleeing from?"

"That's not it," Hakon said. He patted the chair he sat on. "They didn't just leave. They left *this*. They have running water. Lights. They could construct buildings we can't even come close to today. And whatever they faced was strong enough that leaving it behind seemed the best choice."

"And then they never returned." Meshell reached out and took Hakon's hand.

They watched the scene outside for some time in silence. Hakon studied both the dragons and the layout of the city. The dragons held on tightly to their secrets, but he was pleased to see that the city was mostly laid out in straight lines. Navigation in the morning should be a simple matter.

Meshell's chuckle surprised him. He glanced over at her.

"I was thinking about poor Ari. Solveig is probably pulling him all over the place right now."

Hakon's imagination had no problem painting the scene. Solveig, running from room to room like a child realizing they'd just found a whole city with sweets hidden in every corner. Ari, physically dragged along, grumbling under his breath the whole time. The thought brought a grin to his lips.

Meshell stood and stretched like a cat waking up from a nap. "It's getting dark. Not much point in staring out in the distance."

Hakon glanced up at her. "You're taking all of this better than I expected."

"Thought I'd be more like Irric?"

"You know?"

"He's going through a tough time. I can see it on his face, even though he tries to hide it."

"If we survive this, he wants me to kill him."

Meshell nodded. "There was a time when I almost asked Ari the same. When you were gone, and I wasn't sure if there was anything I wanted to live for."

She hadn't told him that before. "What changed?"

"You showed up. We ended up fighting dragons and stamfar again. Life got interesting."

"Not interesting enough for Irric, apparently."

"He's never found anyone to replace Brynja."

"I know. I just wish there was something more I could do for him."

"Be there for him. Otherwise, let him figure out his own path. Same as always."

Hakon ran his hands through his hair and immediately regretted it. Meshell had been right about them needing a bath. "You're right, of course. Still wish there was something more I could do."

"There is." Meshell gestured for him to follow her. "If there's running water, it means the baths here work, and I'm sure Irric would appreciate it if you were clean for supper. And besides, given how comfortable these chairs are, I want to test their beds. It would be a shame to get them dirty after all these years."

Hakon grinned and decided that she made a very good point indeed.

14

Zachary returned to Mioska with a spring in his step and a smile on his face. Not even the cold air of winter settling in for the season or the signs of the cult on almost every corner could diminish his cheer. He walked home, imagining Edda's reaction when he shared his good fortune with her.

As he neared the front gate, he saw Edda sitting up on her balcony. A thick blanket was draped over her shoulders as she composed a letter. When the guard at the gate opened it for him, she looked up from her work and waved. Zachary returned the gesture. Edda watched him for a moment, then shot bolt upright and ran into her room.

Zachary looked back at the gate guard to see if he'd also observed Edda's strange behavior. The guard was also staring up at the balcony, and when he noticed Zachary looking, he shrugged.

Their confusion was answered moments later when Edda flung the main doors open and ran down the steps. She grinned wide, the corners of her lips stretching almost ear to ear. She threw her arms out and leaped. Zachary had just enough time to brace himself. Slight as she was, her momentum almost knocked him back.

She wrapped her arms tight around his neck. "She said yes!"

Zachary figured his smile matched his sister's. "So much for that being a surprise."

He put Edda down, and she shivered. The sun hadn't yet had a chance to warm the air for the day, and the blanket she'd been wearing on the balcony had lost its grip on her shoulders somewhere along the path of her mad dash to the front door.

He took his traveling cloak off and draped it over her. "Let's get inside before you catch a chill."

Once inside, Zachary led Edda straight to the kitchen. It was between mealtimes, but he hadn't yet broken his fast. The food was better here, and he always felt a pang of guilt when eating Aysgarth's food. Rationally, one meal eaten by one person wouldn't make any difference to the fortress' fortunes, especially with the aid Mioska provided. But the memories of the gruel the tehoin there had once been forced to eat were too fresh in his mind. Besides, he and Hel had found better uses for their limited time together.

"How'd you guess?" he asked Edda in between bites of fresh bread.

"I've been waiting on the balcony all morning for you to return," Edda admitted. "And guessing was easy. You're practically glowing."

Zachary looked down at his hands, pretending to be blinded.

Edda rolled her eyes. "I want to know the details."

"We don't know many. There are a lot of questions to answer. We both feel our presence is vital to maintaining a sense of stability in our respective cities. Hel can't leave

Aysgarth any more than I could abandon Mioska. A lot will depend on what happens in the next few months, too."

"The next few months? I was expecting a wedding sooner."

"So was I, at first. Hel reminded me that preparations will take time, and even more for us, given how little time we have to spare. We also need Agnar to officially support us. For now, the announcement and the preparations will have to be enough to show others that life will go on. With luck, people will see us planning for the future and feel some hope again."

Edda pretended to pout. "I would plan it all, if you let me."

"You're almost busier than I am. Most days I'm convinced the only reason the other councilors listen to my ideas is because you've already convinced their spouses."

"So long as you realize it." She made to leave. "When are you going to tell Father?" She glanced quickly at the kitchen staff, who pretended to ignore the siblings.

"I hoped to do it today. No point in delaying."

A look passed between them that said more than they ever would have dared out loud. Though Father lingered on the brink of death, fighting his inevitable journey to the gate with every strength left to him, any whisper within hearing of any of the servants would still eventually reach his ears. Zachary knew she wished him well, knew that she understood the fight he was picking.

When Zachary discovered he was tehoin, Father had come close to throwing him out of the house. To this day, Zachary wasn't quite sure why Father hadn't. He suspected the gentler influence of his late mother, but she had rarely swayed Father in other matters, so he wasn't sure. Regardless, since Zachary had revealed he was tehoin, he'd often felt as though Father had just been waiting for Zachary to give him an excuse to exile him from the house. In his most cynical and bitter moments, he wondered if Edda's suitor had been chosen purposely to goad Zachary to action. That seemed a stretch, even by Zachary's expectations of Father's behavior, but he couldn't bring himself to rule it out completely.

So when Zachary told Father he was engaged to be married to another tehoin, he expected a fight. With the barest hint of a nod, Edda lent him her support.

Zachary sighed. He supposed there was little for it but to tell Father right away. If he delayed too long, word would reach him from the servants, and then there would be another fight about Zachary hiding important information. He finished his food and looked toward the main stairs. "I'll go look in on him and see if he's awake."

"If you want to talk after, I'll be up in my chambers," Edda said.

"I might take you up on that." Then, because he couldn't resist, he said, "If you hear him pull one of his swords from the wall and attack me, have no fear. I would consider that an acceptable reaction."

With that, Zachary let one of the servants take his food away and took the stairs up toward Father's bedroom. The door was closed, and Zachary rapped lightly. He heard no sound on the other side but decided it was best to peer in on Father. There'd been times in the past few days when he'd barely heard the call to enter. He twisted the knob and opened the door wide enough for him to peek through.

Despite the fact that it was midday, the room was almost as dark as night. No candles or lanterns burned in the room, and thick curtains had been pulled tight around the windows. Only a sliver of bright light burned along the seams, casting dim shadows around the room. He couldn't see if his father was awake.

A gruff voice from the bed settled the question. "What do you want, boy? Can't you see I'm resting?"

Zachary opened the door wider so that he could stand silhouetted in the light from the hallway. "Sorry, sir. I didn't know you were resting. I'd come with news, but it can wait."

A long series of grunts came from the bed that put Zachary in mind of a bear being disturbed from its winter slumber. "Well, I'm awake now, and if it was important enough for you to come yourself, I suppose I best hear it from your lips. Open the windows and give us some light."

Zachary walked over to the windows and drew the curtains aside. He blinked at the sudden light as he tied them open. "Shall I let in some fresh air?"

"Trying to kill me? Of course not. You'll leave those windows closed if you know what's good for you."

Zachary stared out the windows until he was calm enough to face Father. His voice was stronger than most days, and he sounded angry enough to kill a kitten. Telling Father the news now was as likely to end well as an attack against Ava led by a group of children armed with wooden swords. Retreat was the wisest option, but Father wouldn't be fooled. When Zachary was as ready as he was ever going to be, he turned to face his father.

His voice might have been strong, but one glance at him told another story. His once-strong limbs were thin. Skin that had once been stretched over strong muscles sagged. Father had always had a sharp face, but it had grown even narrower in recent weeks. Heavy bags hung under his eyes, and though the gaze missed little, it lacked the glittering intensity Zachary had once known. Disease accomplished what no councilor ever had: it had brought Father down.

As was often the case, Zachary couldn't believe his father lived. He believed that most people, ravaged in a similar fashion, would have long ago surrendered to the pull of the gate. But his father never lost a fight, and he seemed determined to drag this battle on so long that even the gate would surrender its inevitable victory. His father would be the first person to achieve true immortality through stubbornness alone.

The prospect terrified him.

The servants had placed a chair near Father's bed so that he could converse with advisors and guests. It wasn't frequently used, though Zachary was almost certain Edda stopped by at least once a day. Perhaps it was because she was the youngest, but she'd never angered Father the way the boys did. Zachary didn't believe she spent time by his bedside every day because of form, either. There was nothing for her to gain by doing so. She was simply a daughter, caring for her father at the end of his life.

Once, Zachary had wished his own relationship with Father could be so simple. The days of that desire were long past, though. There was no turning back the hands of time, no forgiving the decisions that stood between them as thick as any city wall. Zachary pulled up the chair and sat down. Neither of them had any patience for small talk.

"I've gotten engaged," he said.

"To who?"

Not "Congratulations" or "Well done!" Not that Zachary had expected either, but a childish part of him had dared to hope. His Father's first thought would be toward the advantages he could take from the new situation.

"To Hel."

"The tehoin bitch?"

Zachary breathed out slowly and forced his hands to

stay relaxed on his knees. "If you mean the head of the Aysgarth council and the woman who was instrumental in saving Mioska then yes, we're talking about the same person."

Father was silent, a range of emotions playing over his face. Zachary thought he saw anger, disgust, and disappointment, but it was difficult to discern Father's emotions as they twisted the already gaunt visage. Zachary steeled himself for an outburst. He wouldn't defend himself. There was no point. He was no longer a young man, deluded that Father didn't understand him.

No, Father understood him well. Just as he understood Father. It was why they would never see one another as equals.

Instead of an outburst, Father's face went slack, and Zachary feared he'd brought the news that had killed the old man.

He should have proposed sooner.

Father broke the silence with a sound that might have been a dog's bark. He barked again, then once more.

He was laughing. At first sharp and staccato, followed by rolling laughter that turned into a coughing fit. After the coughing subsided, his father continued to chuckle, even though he didn't smile. Only his father could make laughing seem bitter and unpleasant.

When even the chuckling had stopped, Father looked up at him. "You're a damned fool. Why her?"

"Because I love her."

"Even you're not that dumb, boy. Why her?"

"It is because I love her. I'll take the news public, let people know that life will go on. That we're going to keep fighting. It's to give people hope when there is none."

"By marrying a tehoin, you're guaranteeing you'll never

sit in Agnar's chair. The council will never vote you governor."

"You can't know that."

"But I can. Sure, you're the hero of Mioska now, and for a while, I thought you might even make that mean something. I thought maybe the wild had beaten the stupid out of you. Or at least that foolish idealism. I see I was wrong."

Zachary stood. There was no reason for him to sit through this. Father reached out and grabbed his wrist. His hand was hot and his grip surprisingly strong. Zachary could have broken the grip without problem, but something in Father's gaze kept him rooted in place.

"It's a good choice, though," Father said.

Zachary staggered before regaining his balance. He shook his head, certain he'd heard wrong. "You just called me a fool."

"And you are. I tried to raise you smarter than that, but apparently some lessons can't get through that thick skull. Maybe that's for the best."

Zachary blinked rapidly; still sure his senses failed him. In one breath, his father hurled insults with practiced ease, reinforcing the same beliefs Zachary had developed over years of bullying. Then in the next, it was as if Father was a different man. Zachary sat down, and though his vision was steady, it seemed as though the world spun around him. Father released his grip.

"You're a fool because there's no chance your marriage will inspire the city the way you think it will. Not to her. Not to a tehoin."

"Our marriage will tie Aysgarth and Mioska closer together. We need the tehoin if we're going to survive!"

"Boy, if there's one lesson I can teach you, one lesson that you'll actually listen to, it's this: open your eyes. You're so blinded by how you want the world to be you forget how it is."

Zachary was about to protest, but Father stopped him. "The truth is simple. You can't protect Mioska. Even if you brought every tehoin from Aysgarth to fight constantly for the city, it wouldn't matter. There's nothing you can do."

Zachary wanted to argue. They only lost when they gave up hope. Though they hadn't found a way to win yet didn't mean one didn't exist. But he'd been staring at the same fact daily. They had no ideas. He'd spoken with generals, tehoin, and councilors of every stripe. At best, they had the strength to save a single city, and even that was doubtful.

Father saw Zachary's acceptance and continued. "I know you think you need to keep fighting. That there's an honor in dying on your feet. And perhaps you're right. But even if your idealism had merit, your methods are those of a child. A public marriage can inspire and distract. I agree. But not to a tehoin."

Zachary didn't have the strength left to argue. "Why not?"

"Figure it out for yourself."

Zachary was too tired. "I don't know."

Father studied him for a moment, then sighed. "Maybe you can't. Let me ask you a question. Why do you think people hate tehoin?"

"They're jealous of what we can do and afraid of the power we have over them."

"Both true, but not complete. You don't understand. For those of us who are ahula, what you do is deeply unnatural. It's not like we can train hard and perform the same feats. It's that we can't do them at all. A child could spend his whole childhood trying to become a tehoin and would still be a failure. We can't trust tehoin, because to us, what tehoin can do is *wrong*."

"We can't help what we were born as!"

"Of course not. I'm not arguing that it's fair. Using teho might feel natural to you, but if you really want this dream of yours to come true, you need to think how the rest of us think. Making weapons appear out of thin air? Being able to defend yourself against a volley of arrows with just a thought? You think of them as abilities. The rest of us think they make you a monster."

"So they'll never approve of Hel and me?"

"No, and that's a good thing. Maybe it'll finally be the mistake that changes your life for the better."

Zachary slumped back in the chair. He'd come into this room expecting a fight, and right now he felt like he'd lived through one. His chest hurt, and there was a hole in his stomach where his breakfast should have been. "I don't understand."

"I'm dying, boy, in case you haven't noticed. It's made me realize another truth."

Thankfully, Father didn't wait for Zachary to goad him on. "Your efforts to save the city are noble. I'll give you that. I'm guessing you got that part of your personality from your mother. But it's pointless. You're going to lose. I've seen the reports. There's nothing to do, and the only reason this city is still standing is because of your antics last time. But even if this city was going to stand for another thousand years, it wouldn't matter one bit. I'd still tell you the same. Nothing you're doing matters."

"I'm trying to save humanity."

"Bah!" Father waved away the claim. "Save yourself instead. You're one of the few who might actually have the strength to live through this."

"You don't think I should try to save Mioska?"

"Look at me! I spent my whole life in the pursuit of my own goals, and here I am, dying with nothing to show for it. I never became governor. My oldest son can barely stand me. I sacrificed myself for years, and it came to nothing. You'll be in the same place soon if you're not careful."

"I think trying to save all of humanity is a better use of time than trying to become governor."

"Why? You can't save them any more than I could have outmaneuvered Agnar for his position. So you might as well get married and enjoy Hel's company while the world burns around you."

"You don't really believe that."

"I do. Look at me. Truly look at me. I know you see our lives as opposites, but that's you not thinking. We've both spent our days chasing after something we were never going to achieve. The only difference between us is that you have the chance to change. I'm begging you. Do something different than I did. We only have a short time on this brutal world. You might as well enjoy yourself. I never did."

Father slumped back in his bed, the last of his vitality spent. "I know you hate me, and for good enough reason, I suppose. But believe me now. I'm trying to help you. Not to mold you in my image, as I have in the past, but to tell you to avoid my mistakes."

He reached out, and Zachary took his offered hand. It was still burning. "Marry her if you want. But don't spare a thought for a city that will never love you."

Zachary swallowed a lump in his throat.

"Promise me you'll at least consider my words," Father asked. "Please."

"I will," Zachary said.

And he was surprised to realize he meant it.

15

The next day in the city dawned cold, cloudy, and windy. Overnight another storm had developed and blown in. Hakon didn't know if the tall buildings of the abandoned city somehow altered the ways of a storm or if this storm was simply worse than the last, but the wind whipped snow around the buildings like it was trying to topple them over. The wind whistled and howled, and Hakon swore their building swayed in response.

Irric prepared a meal for them to break their fast, and while they ate, they debated their next action. Solveig and Hakon both wanted to trek deeper into the city despite the storm, but Irric and Ari wanted to stay put until the storm passed.

"We don't know how long that will be," Hakon said. "None of us are familiar with the weather patterns here. And besides, it's just a little wind and snow."

"And we can't heat our bodies with teho the way you can," Ari muttered.

Irric argued Hakon's point. "We might not know this area, but we're familiar enough with winter storms on the plains. They always blow out after a day or two. There's no point risking ourselves when we have excellent shelter."

"I'm not sure that's true," Solveig said. "I've been doing my best to keep some sort of log of where we are, and I think we're a fair bit farther north than any place in the Six States. The storms might be different here. And even a delay of a few days might be costly. We don't know how bad the situation has become back home, but it makes sense to hurry."

"You just want to explore more of the city," Meshell accused.

"Of course. But that's beside the point. Given the nature of the city, I can't imagine it will be too difficult for us to find more shelter. A closer location might even allow us to observe the dragons more closely."

"A wiser person would be trying to find their way away from the dragons. Not closer to them," Irric said. But there was no heat to his argument. They'd come to find answers. The storm wasn't sufficient reason to wait.

After breakfast, they gathered their gear and prepared to leave. Ari inscribed a transport point near the lobby of the building, though none of them imagined using it. This close to that many dragons, a transport would attract them like moths to a lone flame in a dark room. But someday, perhaps they'd be able to return under better circumstances.

If they returned from this at all.

By the time Hakon led them to the front door, a drift of snow almost two feet high had built against it. When Hakon approached, though, the doors swung open, shoving aside the snow as though it wasn't there. The cold wind slammed into Hakon with physical force, and he briefly wondered if Irric and Ari hadn't had the right of it. They were committed now, though, so he lowered his head and stomped through the wind like a bull pulling a heavy plow. The others followed behind him, using him as a moving windbreak.

Thanks to the buildings, the wind and snow swirled and attacked from all angles. One moment Hakon would think he was in the lee of a building, only to catch a blast of stinging snow as the tall structures funneled a gust of wind straight at him. The snow gathered in tall drifts that slowed their advance. At times, they walked on the hard surface of the stamfar streets. Moments later, Hakon would trudge through drifts that came all the way to his waist.

He could have asked the others to take turns breaking the trail, but it seemed a more appropriate task for him. Teho kept him warm, and he could push his body harder than any of the others. They were here, following him. The least he could do was make it a little easier for them.

They took frequent breaks thanks to Solveig's curiosity. Any building she couldn't immediately discern the purpose of, she insisted they check. No one complained, as every investigation meant a respite from the relentless storm. Many of the buildings were clearly designed as living quarters, as the first one they'd encountered was. Others had purposes beyond Hakon's understanding, but the most interesting were those with enormous constructions within. Hakon didn't understand why they'd been built. Solveig claimed they might have been used to build other things, but Hakon didn't much care. He simply stood in awe of what their ancestors had achieved.

Someday, he hoped others would achieve the same.

Their stops were always short, frustrating Solveig to no end. There were mysteries enough here to last a lifetime, even one as long as hers.

In every building they surveyed, they found the same story. The people here had packed up and left. But why they had left and where they were going remained unanswerable.

Between the vicious storm and their frequent stops in unknown buildings, they didn't make nearly the distance Hakon had expected. Although it was hard to be sure in the tight confines of the narrow streets, he was reasonably sure they hadn't traveled more than two or three miles. They were much closer to the center of the city. At times, Hakon could sense the dragons in the air nearby. But they never stayed long, and they left the band alone.

Eventually, they called a halt to their advance. The storm hadn't abated, and their progress was more difficult than before. They chose one of the buildings they guessed were living quarters and were pleased when they found they were right. The building was much the same as the one they had spent the previous night in. This one was taller, and the apartments were smaller than before, but the principles of design were the same. They checked a few apartments, but they already knew what they would find. Once their findings were confirmed, they gathered again on the first floor.

They ate together, and then the band broke into smaller groups. Hakon and Meshell climbed the stairs all the way to the top floor, at Hakon's insistence. Part of his desire was that he wanted to see what he could from a higher vantage point. But another part was nothing more than sheer childlike curiosity. Here was a high point. He wanted to climb it because it was there.

The top floor wasn't like the others. It had the same hallway, but there were only four doors, whereas most floors had eight. Hakon kicked one open and whistled.

The space within was larger than the house he'd raised Cliona in. The dining room alone was probably half the size of his house. The lights flickered on when Hakon and Meshell made their way in, and they took a few moments to adjust to the size of the space.

"Makes climbing up all those steps worth it," Meshell said.

They walked deeper into the apartment. An enormous table stood in the middle of the dining room, reminding Hakon of the long table in Aysgarth at which he'd related the story of the band. Further examination of the apartment revealed a bed that was twice as big as any Hakon had ever slept in. He didn't even know how it had fit through the door.

He walked to the window, which went from floor to ceiling and wall to wall. The wind still whipped outside, and now that he stood still, he swore he could feel the building swaying slightly with the gusts. Strange as the sensation was, he didn't worry. These buildings had stood for hundreds of years. They weren't going to fall tonight. Unfortunately, he couldn't see any deeper into the city.

Meshell pressed herself against his left arm, and he raised it so she could nestle next to him. She'd already stripped off most of her layers.

"I take it we're staying here tonight?" he asked.

"Nicest room we've been in yet. Seems a shame to waste it."

They stared out the window together for a bit, but the storm had yet to calm, and there was little to see except streaks of white as light escaping from the window illuminated the nearest blowing snow. Meshell pulled him toward the bed, and he didn't complain at all.

$\sim$

He wasn't sure what woke him. When he opened his eyes, he was alert and ready for battle, but he sensed no enemy. The subtle rocking of the building had ceased, and when Hakon looked outside, it seemed the snow had stopped. But his internal sense of time told him it was still the middle of the night. He waited and listened, but nothing alarmed him.

He felt her then, like he had in the field. Teho, almost as familiar to him as his own. He rolled from the bed, grateful it was so large. Meshell didn't wake as he came to his feet. He pulled on his pants and slipped from the room.

Cliona sat on one of the chairs from the dining room table. The chair now sat by the window, looking out on the city. Before, Hakon was certain it had been at the table. He stared, not trusting himself to believe this was real. She turned from the window, and when she saw him, her smile was wide.

Tears came unbidden to his eyes, and he took one shambling step forward, his vision fuzzy. He reached out, then drew his hand back. "Are you...are you real?"

"I think so."

The voice was hers, exactly as he'd remembered it. The doubt holding him back snapped, and he rushed to her. She stood, and he wrapped his arms around her, picking her up and holding her close. She was solid in his arms, as heavy and as real as she'd been a year ago. He wept, unable to stop. She returned his embrace, her arms barely reaching across his broad back.

In time, she started to squirm. Hakon knew he'd held on too long, but if he let go, he might never hold his girl again. He couldn't let go.

"Dad," she said.

He meant to let her go, but he couldn't. He didn't dare.

"Dad," she said again. "I'm not leaving."

When he still couldn't let go, she formed teho and pulled his arms apart. Hakon blinked as he was gently lifted up and pushed back. It reminded him of being manipulated by Isira's teho, of encountering a well of power that had no bottom. She put him down, and his paralysis was broken. He wiped the tears from his eyes. A dozen questions battled for the right to be asked first, but all he wanted was to run to her and hold her again.

Cliona used thin bands of teho to pick up another one of the chairs and place it behind Hakon. The effort appeared to cost her nothing, and the sight focused Hakon's racing thoughts. The Cliona he'd lost couldn't do anything like that. She'd possessed the raw power, but she'd lacked the control. Like her father, her gifts largely involved the internal manipulation of teho. The woman standing before him was his little girl, but she also wasn't. She gestured for him to sit, and he did. The chair groaned under his weight but held.

"How?" he asked. "I buried you."

The memory of her funeral brought on a fresh round of tears, but he wiped them away. The questions were important but not as important as repairing what was broken between them.

Before she could answer, he was back on his knees in front of her. "I'm sorry, Cliona. I'm sorry I lied, and I'm sorry I couldn't protect you the way I should have." His breath caught in his throat. There was so much more to apologize for, but he couldn't find the words. "I'm sorry for everything."

She wrapped her arms around him, standing next to him and holding him tight. Then she put her arms under his armpits and lifted him up, just the way he had when she'd been a little girl. She put him down on his feet, the lift appearing as easy for her as if she'd been picking up a teacup.

She grinned at his disbelief. "I forgave you a long time ago, Dad. You need to let it go." She paused. "You'll need to let me go."

"I don't want to." Hakon's voice sounded petulant, even to him. But he'd lost control of his emotions the moment he saw Cliona sitting in that chair.

She gestured for him to sit again. "I'm not sure how much longer I'll be able to maintain this form, and there's much I need to say."

Hakon lowered himself back into the chair. Again, the damned tears came, and he swiped them away. "When will I see you again?"

"I don't know. Too much is hidden, even to my sight."

"What—what happened? How are you here?"

She held up her hand and examined it as though she'd never seen it before. Under the dim light coming from the window, Hakon caught the darker scar that ran along the back of it. It was a scar she'd earned six years past, running through the woods. She'd fallen and cut the back of her hand against an exposed root. She was so much his daughter, but not quite.

"I'm not sure," she said. "When my body died in Husavik, some part of me lived on inside the elder."

Hakon had thought as much but hearing it from her lips finally confirmed it was true. "How?"

"My teho and the dragon's were mixed when I died."

"What was it like?"

Her eyes lit up. "Words don't do the experience justice. Their senses are both wider and deeper than ours, and their thoughts are...richer. More varied, more alive. It reminded me of when I was a child, and you would pick me up and let me ride on your shoulders, and we'd run through the forest. It was the same forest I already knew but being so high changed my perspective. I felt like I was seeing the world for the first time."

Her words tried to pull him along, tried to share the wonder of her journey. But he couldn't get another memory out of his thoughts. The day he had killed the elder dragon, with her a part of it. He sniffed. "And then I killed you."

"And then you killed me," she repeated. "We were grateful. Ava had already fatally wounded us, and, weakened as we were, I don't know if we would have resisted her for much longer. You saved us."

"I wanted there to be another way."

"There was none. We'd searched for one ourselves, but sometimes life only leaves us one choice. You shouldn't grieve so, Dad. I know how hard it must have been, but that choice freed me so that I could become this."

"What are you?"

"I'm not sure myself. I went to the gate and stepped through. After that, memory fails me. But the gate is not what we believe it is. Yes, it's a passage for souls to whatever comes next, but it's more, too. I think that because I was tied so closely to the dragon, it gave me the strength to come back again."

She pointed to her head. "I still feel like I'm here, but here isn't something physical anymore. I made this form, and most of my attention is here, but I'm other places, too."

"I don't understand." Hakon's head was spinning as though he'd had too much to drink.

"I don't understand everything, either," Cliona admitted. "But I'm always learning. What's important is that I'm here. Not like I was before, but I'm still here, and I don't think I'm going anywhere. I'm trying to help as much as I can."

"You've been protecting us from the dragons." It was half a question but mostly his guess.

"Yes. Even though I'm not connected with the elder anymore, I can still understand them. And speak with them, in a way. So long as you don't attack any of them with teho, I think we've reached an understanding. I've told them you're here to help. It's a...very tentative truce."

Hakon ran his hand through his beard. "You don't sound all that certain."

"It's not like I can converse with dragons the way I can with you. It's more like we're exchanging ideas. They aren't happy about having you here, but I think they'll leave you in peace. At least, I've done the best I can to ensure that."

"Thanks for that."

She pointed out the window. Hakon followed her finger. Now that the blowing snow had cleared, he saw much farther than before. Thick clouds hung low overhead, and Hakon wondered if another storm was on the horizon. When he saw what she pointed at, all thoughts of storms fled. In the distance, perhaps a mile away, a pale blue glow emanated from near the center of the city. The light illuminated the bottom of the clouds, and Hakon realized the light he'd thought was from the moon was actually that glow.

"What's that?" Hakon asked.

"The heart of everything. The ancients called it a nexus. Every answer you've been searching for is there. If there's a way to save the Six States, it'll be there."

"But you're not sure?"

"I've learned more than I ever dreamed possible in the last year, but there's so much more I don't know. I can tell you that Isira was right. This is where you need to be. And I can warn you that there are other powers gathering here, each doing what it can to save the nexus. You won't have an easy time of it, but there's no one else."

"What do we need to do?"

"I wish I knew. The planet is dying. I'm not sure if it's Ava killing it or something else. But the planet is fighting back. It's why the wild is advancing upon the Six States. Save the planet, and you save the Six States."

She stood. "I wish there was more I could tell you, but I've done all I can for the moment. It's getting hard to hold this form, though, so I think it's time for me to go."

Hakon rushed to stand and embrace her. "I'm not sure I can handle losing you again."

Cliona shook her head. "Dad. You never lost me. The closest you came was when your lies were revealed. But that's forgiven. Though I can't promise I'll see you again in this world."

She bit her lower lip, and for the first time this night, she looked uncertain. "I'm sending you into more danger than you've ever faced. But I don't know what else to do."

Her eyes began to water. "I promise, though, that if you die, I'll be there to walk you to the gate. No matter what, you'll see me at least once more. And if I can do more to help here, I will."

Hakon held her close. "I love you, girl. More than anything else in the world."

"Love you, too, Dad."

One moment she was there, in his arms and as real as he'd ever known her. The next, he was standing in a dining room, embracing nothing, all alone.

16

———————

Zachary stared at the unopened pile of mail and letters on his desk and rolled his shoulders. He'd been at work most of the afternoon, and he was almost certain he had more letters to deal with now than he'd had when he started. There were letters from councilors suggesting motions they wanted to bring toward the council. Some practically begged for his support. Others came close to threats.

Besides those letters were notes and requests from the areas of Mioska he represented. Some were as mundane as store owners seeking to buy new property to expand their shops. Others dealt with claims of theft and assault by militia soldiers.

He'd read so many notes and letters and deciphered so many pages of poor penmanship that his eyes refused to focus. He sorted through the piles, looking for the most recent reports from the frontier. Those, at least, should be important enough to focus his attention. He found them and started leafing through the newest batch.

The news was no more than he'd come to expect. One village, one settlement at a time, the wild pushed them back. In a way, the wild's progress was slow. It wasn't as though some bastion of humanity fell every day. But bit by bit, they lost the land they'd fought so hard to tame.

The loss of life was troubling enough. But the burden on the survivors grew every week. People fled back toward the interior, burdening areas that were already near their capacity. Settlers moved west because, as difficult as carving out a new life was, it was usually a better future than they had in overcrowded cities.

No longer.

Those that survived the wild's assaults fled back east, content to take their chances in the places they'd just left. Many who hadn't yet been attacked packed up and returned. Zachary could hardly blame them. The militias couldn't protect the whole frontier. Better a familiar life of struggle than an almost certain death. But it meant losing vital farming acreage, and cities were stretched nearly to the breaking point.

It would take the wild years to eliminate humanity. But humans might tear each other apart long before that came to pass.

Before long, the words swam in his vision. He was staring at a paper, but the words no longer made any sense. He pushed the paper away and stood from his desk. His back was sore, reminding him he hadn't trained for several days. He rubbed his eyes and looked outside. Evening fast approached, and most days he'd be eager for his bed and sleep.

He didn't think sleep would come easily tonight, though. If he tried anytime soon, he'd just stare at the ceiling, the same damn thoughts coursing through his head. He needed air.

Zachary threw on a heavy cloak and a sword, then ran up one flight of stairs to let Edda know his plans. She wasn't pleased by his choice but was somewhat reassured by the sword resting at his hip. She urged caution but wished him well. They'd spoken at length after Zachary had finished with Father, so she understood the source of his agitation.

He slipped out of the servant's gate. He thought Edda's caution was a bit much, but there was no reason not to take basic precautions. He blended in with the flow of the late afternoon crowds, letting them take him where they pleased.

Mioska was as busy as ever, and no one looked to the skies the way Zachary frequently did. Most of the damage from the dragon attacks had been swept from the streets, and most of the damaged buildings were quickly being repaired. Even though Mioska was about as far from the frontier as one could possibly be, it too experienced the flood of new arrivals. Property was more valuable than he could remember it being. No damaged building would be allowed to stay empty for long.

If not for the persistent threat of destruction, it could have been any other night in Mioska, no different than the hundreds he'd lived through as a young man growing up here.

Except for the damned cult, of course.

As the crowds carried him to the outskirts of the markets, he saw more of the recent converts loudly proclaiming their bizarre beliefs. Almost every single one had an audience. One, in particular, caught his attention. She was a tall woman with blonde hair. She stood on a crate and wore a simple gray dress. Most of the cultists preferred bland clothing. Edda told him it was because they believed fashion and design to be frivolous wastes of time when the end approached.

This cultist held a piece of paper in her hand, waving it as though it was a sword.

"We already know why the dragons came here!" she proclaimed. "It's because of the tehoin. People like the councilor are the reason why so many of us lost husbands, wives, brothers, and sisters."

Zachary winced. As the only tehoin on the council, the subject of her hate was clear enough.

She jabbed her finger at the paper. "And now, this fool who risks all our lives wants to marry another tehoin! He wants to bring more of them here! What do we say to that?"

A chorus of curses rose from the crowd, some of them inventive enough that Zachary was impressed. He was grateful for the winter weather and the excuse to wear a heavy cloak. Had he wandered onto this corner without it, there might have been trouble. There still might be if he stuck around too long. He willed himself to be as small as a mouse as he snuck away from the gathering.

A bitter bile rose in his throat. Less than an hour ago, he'd been reading petitions written to him by people who might very well be in crowds like the one he'd just left. He hadn't become a councilor for thanks but was wanting not to be demonized too much to ask?

The scene had given him a destination, though, so he made his way toward Ingolf's inn. He passed several more of the cultists, most of whom had papers in their hands. He'd made a proclamation about the marriage just the day before, hoping it would turn people's gazes toward the future.

He reached Ingolf's and let himself in the main door. As

before, the common room was crowded, and Ingolf's servers danced nimbly from table to table. The room was warm, but Zachary fought the impulse to pull his hood down. He made his way toward the bar, where Ingolf was in three places at once. Zachary caught Ingolf's eye and gestured toward the back room.

Ingolf scowled but spoke with one of his servers, who smoothly took the innkeeper's place at the bar. Ingolf led him to the back room. "What do you want? Can't you see I'm busy?"

"Do people hate the tehoin?"

Ingolf screwed up his face. "Of course they do. What kind of question is that?"

"How bad is the hate against me, personally?"

"You don't need me to tell you. Ever since you announced your marriage to Hel, the streets have been talking about little else. Most seem pretty sure you're going to kill us all."

"I'm doomed, aren't I?"

Ingolf thought for a moment, then nodded.

"Was I always?"

Ingolf considered that. "For what you wanted to achieve, probably. There was a bit there, after the attacks, where you might have been able to launch a bid to become governor. People still remember what you did. But in time, they'll always remember that you're tehoin, and they've been afraid of tehoin for longer than you or I have been around. It would have taken you down eventually, no matter what."

Zachary wanted to ask Ingolf for a drink so they could sit down and reminisce. But he saw the way his friend was looking at the door to his bar. They had too much history for Ingolf to kick him out, but he wasn't welcome either. "Thanks. Sorry I bothered you."

Ingolf took away the last of his doubt. "You're welcome. But just so you know, I don't think you should stop around here so much. Nothing personal, you understand, but if people knew you were here, I'd have a fight on my hands the likes I don't want to have to pay to repair."

"I hear you."

Ingolf returned to his bar and Zachary took a moment to ensure the hood was well over his head. Then he returned to the common room, walked to the front door without hitting any drunk patrons, and escaped onto the street.

As the door closed behind him, he couldn't help but think Ingolf's dismissal felt very personal indeed.

Zachary had taken this walk to clear his head, but now his thoughts were more muddled than ever. Though his hood kept his face hidden, he glared at every passing stranger. Several people stepped away from him, though he made no visible threat. Laughter down an alley felt like broken glass raked across his skin. The shouts of the cultists were daggers in the night.

He walked quickly toward home, wanting to put thick walls and guards between him and the rest of the city.

Leaving had been a mistake.

Making his proposal public had been a mistake. Just as Father had said.

The thought brought him up short, and someone who'd been walking too close behind him swore at him. Zachary ignored them.

Father had been right about the wedding. Was he right about what Zachary should do? He imagined returning to Aysgarth and convincing Hel to leave with him. She received even less thanks for her role than he did here. They could find a quiet place, just like Hakon had after he'd been released from his imprisonment. And together, they would hold back the wild as long as they could, enjoying their days.

The temptation made him turn in place and look in the direction of the militia's barracks. Peace was only one transport away.

But turning revealed something more immediately concerning.

He wasn't alone.

The street was crowded with people, but most of them could be safely ignored. They were like a river of humanity, flowing from one place to the next. They broke around him like he was a boulder thrown into the middle of a stream.

But there were others like him. Those who only pretended to have reasons to stop. One young man was at a shop, but the shopkeeper was yelling at him and he didn't care. Another young man was leaning nonchalantly against a wall, but his eyes kept darting over to where Zachary stood.

Zachary didn't let his gaze linger on either of them. He pretended not to notice them at all. He made out four people, and those were only the ones easy to spot. There might be more, better skilled and able to blend in with the crowd.

He completed his turn and continued on. He turned a corner and used the opportunity to glance back. The same four young men were following him still. He didn't see any more.

Did he try to escape them, or did he catch them and interrogate them? Did they mean him harm, or were they just following him? And where did he go? He felt safe enough on the busier streets but going home would mean passing through several quieter neighborhoods. In other circumstances, he would have used Ingolf's inn as a place to hide, but he suspected he'd find no safe shelter there.

There was no other place to be than his house. And he would feel better if he was there protecting Edda.

Running it was, then. If he put enough distance between him and his followers by the time he reached the quiet neighborhoods, he could throw up a shield and not have to worry.

Unless some of them were tehoin. In which case, he might have to worry very much.

He never saw the archer. Before he took his first step, an arrow caught him in the left shoulder, only a few inches above his heart. Pain exploded in his chest, and the force of the hit drove him to his knees.

A woman next to him saw the arrow sticking out of his chest and screamed. Panic spread across the street like wildfire, and soon people were running in every direction. One young man ran in front of Zachary, his shoulder striking the fletching of the arrow in Zachary's shoulder. The impact twisted Zachary around and sent another wave of agony down his spine.

Fortunately, the panic prevented any of Zachary's followers from closing in. He looked up, searching for the archer. He'd underestimated them. He'd never expected someone to shoot at him in the middle of a crowd.

The archer stood on a rooftop a few buildings down. She'd already nocked another arrow and had the string pulled back to her cheek. Only the fact that Zachary had fallen to his knees in the middle of a panicked crowd protected him. As soon as she had a clear shot, he expected she would release her arrow.

But she stood still, as though she thought she was safe.

They had to know he was tehoin, but they didn't act like they knew. He supposed fighting a tehoin was different than any other opponent, but still. He formed a dark teho dart and aimed it at the archer. For a moment he held it, wondering if this was best.

But when he inquired of his conscience, nothing answered him. He didn't care, so he launched the dart, flinging it with all the speed he could summon. The archer's chest exploded as the dart struck, and the archer released the arrow as she fell backward. The arrow streaked across the sky, but Zachary didn't care where it went. He struggled to his feet, preparing for the battle yet to come.

The four attackers charged at him as the crowd cleared, daggers drawn.

Had the archer still been alive, perhaps the ambush would have worked better. Zachary wasn't sure he would have been able to divide his attention between attacks coming from two different directions. With the archer already down, though, the attackers were dead men. Zachary flung another teho dart as soon as the space between him and the nearest attacker cleared. It struck the young man in the chest, knocking him off his feet. He twitched once on the ground, then lay still.

Zachary's vision swam as he turned to the next attacker. He focused his teho into another dart. It sped toward the ambusher, who tried to block with his dagger. He was too slow, though, and the dart punched a hole in his chest. He ran forward another two steps before his body collapsed.

The effort of throwing the dart brought Zachary to his knees.

His body felt as though he'd been carrying a heavy pack for a full day without rest. He tried to rise to his feet, but his body refused to obey. His thoughts fragmented like clear glass shattered with a hammer. He shouldn't be this tired.

He looked down at the arrow. It was one of his worse injuries, but he'd been hurt worse with less effect.

Poison.

The word trickled through his thoughts and down his spine. He shivered and reached for the shaft. The last two attackers were moments away. He grabbed the shaft, shuddering at the pain. He closed his eyes and pulled with all his remaining strength.

Agony, brighter than the sun, turned his world white. He screamed as the arrowhead emerged, the tip glistening with a substance darker than blood. Zachary fell to the side as a dagger searched for his heart. The would-be assassin ran past him, looking at the point of his blade like it had betrayed him. He slid to a stop.

Zachary needed to get up. He needed to fight.

His body refused.

Zachary formed a teho dart, weak even by his standards. He launched it, catching the assassin in the stomach. The man dropped his dagger, which landed point down next to Zachary's right arm. He clutched at his stomach as he fell. It would be a slow and painful death.

One more.

Zachary flopped his head left, then right, but the last man who'd been following him was nowhere to be found.

A shadow crossed above him, the flash of a dagger in the dim light of the moon. Acting more by instinct than reason, Zachary formed a shield. It was pathetically small, but the tip of the dagger, aimed for Zachary's face, deflected off it. It hit the street and the man grunted.

Zachary grabbed the dagger the previous assassin had dropped and thrust it overhead. It punched into the man's stomach. He pulled it out and thrust again, and again, beyond reason. He didn't stop until the man fell over, collapsing near his head.

His breath came in labored gasps and his heart felt as though it was racing to get in as many beats as possible before it stopped for good. Sweat poured down his forehead, and the stars above danced in impossible patterns.

He needed to move. Home was the only place that was safe.

He rolled over onto his side, then pushed himself to sitting with his right arm. No one came to check on him, though they were surrounded by houses and shops. He and the corpses had the street all to themselves. He looked down at the bodies. The two he'd hit in the stomach were still alive, though they looked like they weren't pleased about it. The last assassin was pale and his fingers twitched as he grasped at the organs leaking from half a dozen stabs. Zachary saw the plain gray fabric underneath the man's other clothes.

Time for justice later. If there was a later. Zachary shifted to hands and knees, the effort just slightly less strenuous than picking up a mountain. He shouted, focusing his strength as he pushed himself to his feet.

For a moment he tottered, on the brink of falling over and never getting up again. But he kept his feet, and he stumbled toward home. One step at a time, he escaped the scene of the ambush. His vision narrowed until all he could see was his feet and the road right in front of him. A child with a stick and a grudge could have finished what the assassins started.

But he was alone, and his feet knew the way home, even if he could barely see. When he was in sight of the gate, the guards rushed to him.

"Poisoned," he croaked.

And then he surrendered himself to blissful oblivion.

17

Hakon told the others over breakfast about his conversation with Cliona. When he was done, Irric was the first to speak. "I've got to say this, Hakon. The decades when we were separated were some of the most boring in my life. I'm starting to think the difference is you."

Solveig rolled her eyes. "Do you think it was real?"

"I do. The chair was moved, and she was as solid as you or I are. I can't explain it, but I do believe she was there."

"Do you believe her?"

Hakon clenched his fists, then relaxed them. Solveig hadn't seen what he'd seen, and it stood to reason she would doubt him. Of them all, she was the one who most craved something solid she could grasp, something she could claim as proof. And Hakon was offering very little except a series of increasingly impossible stories. "Yes. She's my daughter."

The words came out harsher than he intended, and Solveig held her hands up in a placating gesture. "You know I have to ask."

He nodded. "I know. And if I hadn't seen it for myself, I'd probably share the same doubt. But she's also not telling us anything that we weren't already going to do. She's just confirming that the answers we're seeking are in the center of the city."

"She also warned us that we're not the only ones here," Ari said. "That's the part I'm most curious about. Because I haven't seen another soul in the last two days."

"Regardless, today we'll reach the center of the city, and perhaps we'll finally figure out what's happening."

Solveig sighed and stared at the ceiling. "I agree. But we should proceed cautiously. The storms have passed, and it doesn't seem like any more are on the way, so we've got that working in our favor, at least."

"Do you want me and Hakon to scout ahead of the group?" Meshell asked. "We're less likely to anger the dragons, and we'll be right underneath them today."

Solveig looked at Hakon before answering, as though judging his anger. "I don't think we should split up. If we can trust what Cliona told Hakon, the dragons aren't the threat we most need to worry about. Either way, though, I don't want us separated. If nothing else, I want us as close as possible so that Ari can transport us out if needed."

The others agreed, and after breakfast they spent a bit more time than usual preparing their weapons. Hakon did the same with his own sword. He had the feeling he'd be making use of it today.

Soon they were ready, and they headed out once again into the city. The snow was thicker and higher than the day before, but with the sun shining brightly overhead, Hakon barely minded trudging through the deep drifts. The sky was cloudless, and the wind was down, and in the sun, it was almost too warm for the layers they wore.

As much as possible, Hakon kept to the places where the drifts hadn't formed. At times, they were even able to walk on bare ground. He kept them heading toward the center of the city, always on the lookout for any of the mysterious other forces Cliona had referenced. The city seemed much the same as it had on the previous days, though. The only sounds were the wind between the buildings and their feet crunching through the snow. If there were any enemies nearby, they were well hidden.

Ari spotted the tracks first. He was walking along the left side of the street, and he noticed something in one of the cross streets they passed. He whistled loud enough for the others to hear, then gestured them down towards the side street. Hakon shivered as they stepped out of the light and into the shadow of the nearest building. Ari stopped next to the sight that had caught his attention. The others gathered around.

"Any idea what made that?" Ari asked.

The track was deep. Whatever had made it had punched all the way through the snow down to the street below. Given the depth of his own tracks, Hakon assumed that whatever had made the tracks was at least the weight of a human. Maybe a bit more. He didn't know what to make of the tracks. The closest comparison he could draw was that of a bird. The tracks had one rear talon, as well as three facing forward. But if this was a bird, it was the biggest and heaviest Hakon had ever seen. From the tip of the rear talon to the limit of the front talons was twice as long as Hakon's own foot.

"Dragon?" Irric said.

"Doesn't look like any dragon track I've ever seen," Meshell said. "Big as it is, the claws are too narrow."

"How else do you explain how the tracks start here?" Irric asked.

He gestured around. The tracks ran off to the west, but

Irric was right. They started here, as if the creature had appeared out of thin air.

Or landed.

But anything that large had to use teho to fly, and Hakon hadn't felt any teho recently.

Ari followed the tracks, and the rest of the band followed Ari. They came out on the next street, and Irric swore. Hakon could well understand why. The tracks of half a dozen similar creatures joined the first on the next street, and they all led toward the center of the city. The place had gone from abandoned to crowded in the space of one morning.

Hakon took the lead again, Meshell close behind. He kept an eye on the tracks, grateful he didn't see any more than before. Whatever the creatures were, there weren't too many of them. A few blocks later, the tracks separated, all going in different directions.

"Well, now that's just downright concerning," Irric griped.

Hakon agreed. As had become all too familiar lately, he had the feeling he was walking into a mystery where he didn't even know the right questions to ask. His hands itched to hold his sword. Still, there was nothing to do except advance. Their progress was slower now, but it hardly mattered. They were drawing close to the center of the city.

An enormous shadow passed over Hakon, and he very nearly pulled out his sword and prepared for battle. He looked up to see that the dragons now filled the sky. As before, none seemed particularly interested in him, but it did nothing to put him at ease. This close, he saw that most were younglings, though a few were elders. Fortunately, none of them were carrying boulders to drop on the band.

He hadn't felt this uncertain about an advance since he'd been a recruit in Brynja's unit. Several of the dragons overhead were big enough to eat him in one bite. He'd barely serve as an appetizer. But he kept placing one step in front of the other.

The center of the city grew ever closer. The road they were on led almost straight to it, curving just a few hundred yards ahead into what appeared to be some sort of giant city square.

The only warning Hakon had of danger was a flicker of movement in the corner of his vision. He filled his body with teho, just in time to get launched through the air like a child's doll. He flew over Ari and Irric's heads, giving him a brief moment of levity as he saw the expression on their faces. Then the pain of the blow registered, and he wasn't sure he'd ever laugh again. It felt like his chest had caved in and all his ribs broken. He landed in a snowdrift and came to a sudden halt. His world went white, then dark as the snow filled in behind him.

He tried to breathe, but that only gave the powdery snow a chance to fill his mouth. He coughed and rolled, spitting up bloody snow as he exited the drift. On hands and knees, he tried again to bring air into his lungs. Two coughing gasps later, cold, fresh air filled his chest. He coughed up more blood, but he could already feel his ribs stitching back together. He put his hand to his chest as it expanded.

His healing was too quick, but he wasn't about to question it. After another few deep breaths, he was able to stand, and he turned to look at what had hit him. His first glance gave him several answers. He wasn't sure if he was glad to have them or not.

The tracks they'd seen earlier hadn't been made by a giant bird, nor had they been made by a dragon. They'd been made by a teho demon, larger by far even than the ones that had guarded Ava's tomb in Husavik. Hakon guessed it stood at about thirty feet. Its legs were longer than Hakon was tall, but they weren't as wide as Hakon would have expected. In fact, given the size of the demon, they looked skinny. The legs were bent like a bird's, though, joints bending the opposite way a human's would.

The torso and four arms more than made up for whatever the legs lacked. The arms swiped at the band, who were almost all busy trying to avoid the same fate Hakon had just experienced. Only Meshell risked attacking, but even her teho-enhanced speed wasn't enough to get her safely inside the demon's reach.

Hakon frowned at the sight. Meshell could close with a dragon, so a teho demon shouldn't be a challenge, even one as big and quick as the one they faced. Something was wrong, but Hakon's mind was slow to catch up.

The rest of the band wasn't using teho.

Hakon looked up, where the indifferent dragons continued to circle overhead. They were afraid that if they used their teho to fight the demon, they'd bring the dragons down on them.

The only assurance they had that something different would happen was Hakon's dead daughter's word.

Hakon drew his sword. His arms moved without pain, and his chest felt fine. He couldn't explain why he wasn't laying in a snowdrift gasping for air, but he was ready to fight. He filled his limbs and sword with teho and sprinted into battle, passing the others once again.

Solveig shouted his name, but it sounded more like it was surprise than any sort of alarm or warning.

Her shout distracted Meshell for a moment, and the demon took full advantage. It struck Meshell with a backhanded blow that sent her into the side of a nearby building. If Meshell had braced herself with teho, she might still be alive. He didn't want to consider the alternative.

Haken swung his sword, hoping the demon was foolish enough to block it.

The demon danced back with impossible agility, then planted one of its hands in the snow and spun around it, lashing out with its feet.

Hakon had only enough time to flatten himself in the snow as the kick blasted over his head. Had he tried to block that with his sword, he'd be splattered all over the same building as Meshell. He pushed himself back to his feet, but the teho demon's technique wasn't finished. It landed smoothly on its feet and continued its rotation, swiping at him with two of its claws.

Hakon leaped back. He'd fought a handful of teho demons before, but they'd always been fairly mindless creatures. They were strong and plenty fearsome, but not usually hard to kill if one was careful.

This demon was as much like those opponents as Hakon was a toddler. Its movements were smart, its agility otherworldly. It was also sensitive enough to teho that it knew to stay away from the edge of Hakon's blade.

Lacking better ideas, Hakon attacked, his enormous sword carving intricate patterns between him and the demon. But the demon avoided the sword with ease, its eyes watching Hakon with a calm wariness.

When Hakon understood he wasn't making any progress, he stopped, sword ready for the next round.

The demon gave him no chance to recover. It sped forward, far faster on those thin legs than it should have been. It swiped at him with only one of its right arms. Hakon slid away, but one of its left arms had predicted his evasion and came at him with blinding speed. Momentum and biology would have prevented a human from doing anything similar, but of course, this creature ignored both.

Hakon couldn't dodge. He brought his sword up, and teho met teho with a familiar thunk. Hakon's sword bit into the demon's wrist but couldn't cut all the way through. The demon swiped at him with another arm and Hakon pulled his sword free as he leaped back.

The demon's wound healed before Hakon's eyes, and he swore at his luck. The center of the city was only a few hundred feet away. Why couldn't the creature have just let him get there?

He didn't dare turn his eyes from the demon, but he couldn't fight it alone. He raised his voice. "I could use some help over here."

None of the band answered his plea. Off to his side, rubble shifted as Meshell wobbled to her feet. It was good to see her alive, but she didn't look like she'd be fighting anytime soon.

"Trust Cliona!" he shouted.

The demon lurched forward, gathering speed as it prepared to strike. Hakon braced himself and sought an opening. Teho demons died if you landed a lethal blow but healed quickly from anything short of that. This demon protected its vitals well, always keeping one arm close to its body in case Hakon penetrated its guard. Alone, Hakon didn't see how to vanquish the creature.

As the demon raised an arm to strike, teho finally bloomed behind Hakon. Two darts flew over his shoulder and struck the demon in the chest. The darts penetrated the armor but faded before they reached the vitals. The demon roared and swiped at Hakon.

He dropped low and attacked the lower of the two arms.

He reinforced the edge of his blade with even more teho and was finally rewarded. His blade sliced cleanly through the demon's wrist.

The demon leaped back. It cradled its wounded arm as dark teho reformed the severed hand. Hakon wondered if it would flee, but it seemed only to be healing and gathering its strength for another attack.

Ari's dart had done more than sting the demon, though. It had broken the chains of fear holding the others back. High above the city, the dragons continued their flights. They certainly sensed the battle below, but Cliona had spoken true. They stayed in the sky, well above the deadly fight taking place in the streets. Irric and Solveig followed Ari's lead. Solveig's spear followed the demon as it leaped away, catching the upper right arm near where it connected with the demon's torso.

Irric charged past Hakon, a teho sword longer than Hakon was tall in each hand. "Stay back," Irric said as he passed.

Hakon was only too happy to take a moment to recover. He breathed deep, pushing teho through his body as he watched Irric's assault.

His friend was the best wielder of teho swords that Hakon had ever met. Most warriors, including tehoin, trained almost exclusively with wooden or steel practice swords. When they went into battle, even tehoin would form swords of equivalent dimensions, as it would be foolish to attack and defend with a weapon they weren't familiar with.

But teho blades were limited only by imagination and will. As weightless weapons, there was no reason a tehoin couldn't form a sword as long as a chimney. Those who tried were usually as much a danger to themselves and their allies as their enemies, though. Forming an impossibly long blade and using it well were two very different skills.

Irric was one of the few who had taken the time to master both. He leaped at the demon, his long blades hacking and carving at any exposed limb. Had Hakon been anywhere close, he would have only been in the way. Chunks of teho flew from the demon and unraveled into mist. Twice Irric struck for a vital target, but twice the demon sacrificed a limb to protect itself.

Solveig and Ari cooperated to throw a bundle of teho spears high into the air. Once they reached the apex, Solveig froze them in place and aimed them. Then she brought down her hand and the spears plummeted toward the demon faster than any volley of arrows would ever fall.

The demon raised its last functioning arm to protect its head. Three teho spears stabbed through the arm, while another half dozen embedded themselves deep in the demon's shoulder, back, and chest. It staggered, somehow still alive.

Irric solved that problem with his next strike. He darted forward and stabbed with his long sword. The tip of the blade slid easily through the demon's weakened armor, and Irric drove his sword all the way through the demon's chest and out its back.

The demon collapsed, and flecks of teho started to blow away as the creature dissolved. Ari and Irric both looked up to the sky, but Hakon knew what they would see. The dragons remained uninvolved.

He heard shuffling footsteps behind him. Meshell joined him. He glanced over her. One of her arms looked broken, but it was visibly healing. Hakon's eyes narrowed at the sight. She was healing as fast as he had.

"How are you?" he asked.

"I think I should be a lot worse off than I am."

"I was just thinking the same about me."

Meshell cast a glance to the sky. "Looks like trusting Cliona paid off."

"Let's hope it continues to."

They joined the others. Solveig examined Meshell and Hakon and pronounced them fit for battle. But she kept looking at them, even after her examination was finished.

"What?" Hakon asked.

"There's more teho flowing through your bodies than I've ever felt," she said. "You barely feel like kolma anymore."

Hakon looked down at his hands. "I don't feel any different," he said.

"Neither do I," Meshell reported.

"I don't feel different," Irric said, "but those swords I just formed were easily the strongest I've ever made, and they barely required any focus."

Solveig looked troubled, but Hakon simply put the phenomena in the ever-growing bucket of questions in his mind. Someday, he hoped he would find answers for them, but that time seemed hopelessly distant. For now, all that mattered was reaching the center of the city. They were so close. "Come on. We're almost there."

They fell into step behind him as he passed the remains of the teho demon, already nearly vanished. They reached the bend in the road and followed it as it curved toward the city center. Not long after, their final destination revealed itself.

Hakon and the others came to a complete stop at the sight. There was no telling what had once been here. It might have been a park, or it might have been the tallest building any of them had ever seen. Nothing of the center remained except a deep crater, glowing that same pale blue Hakon had seen the night before.

The edges of the crater were steep, but Hakon's attention was drawn to the tall buildings that surrounded the crater. Wherever they touched the edges of the crater, they'd been cut away. The cuts were sheer, and more strangely yet, there was no rubble. Entire parts of the buildings were simply gone.

An inhuman wail from below pulled Hakon's gaze down. He couldn't see to the bottom of the crater from where he stood, but he could see a fair way down, and the sight didn't fill him with confidence.

The crater was swarming with teho demons.

18

___

Zachary's world was a kaleidoscopic mix of colors, sounds, and impressions. He was staring up at a ceiling, and it was familiar, but it kept changing. One moment snakes crawled along the surface, hissing and snapping at him. The next, it was showing him memories he'd long forgotten. Pretending to be the band with his siblings, fighting in the great Rebellion. His mother reading him the histories of the great houses, her voice musical even when the subject was as mundane as the governor's lineage.

People were shouting, and Zachary knew they were shouting, but the sounds seemed to come from a long way away. It was like he was lost in the forest and his friends were shouting for him to return to camp.

Edda's face featured prominently in his illusions. Sometimes it filled almost his entire vision, her concern etched in every line and crease. He wanted to reach up to her and tell her she didn't have to worry. That she shouldn't have to worry. He was here for her and would be as long as she needed him. She deserved better than the mess that was this family.

Other times, she was crying, handkerchief covering her eyes. Oh, how he wanted to take her burdens from her! But he was an observer trapped in a body that felt less and less his own.

Pain brought brief moments of lucidity. He was in his chambers at home, and there were bandages around his shoulder. Fire burned in his skin where the arrow had struck him, but he couldn't move to ease the agony. After a few moments, he would plunge back into a world of dreams and shadows.

He didn't know how long he existed in the liminal state. His body fought the battle, and his mind wandered. In and out, he dipped between reality and illusion, rarely sure which was which. Always wondering in what realm he'd end up in. One day, though, he opened his eyes and his mind was sharp, and he knew something had changed.

He was standing on a lake of dark water, crystal clear and endlessly deep. Stars shone overhead, brighter than he'd ever seen them. They didn't twinkle but shone like lanterns in the darkness. He turned around, his feet leaving gentle ripples across the surface of the still water. Behind him, a glowing arch stood on the surface of the water. Its light was pale blue, as bright as a sun yet easy to look at. It pulled him toward it, and he obeyed.

As he drew closer, he knew what he was looking at.

The gate.

He would have expected the knowledge to pain him, but his heart was as still as the surface of the lake. There were those he would miss, but the pain and suffering of his past was finally behind him. He looked around, but the lake and the stars were endless, and he was all alone. He returned his gaze to the arch and continued toward it. The closer he came, the more demanding its pull.

"I didn't expect to see you here so soon," a familiar voice said.

Zachary would have jumped, but it was impossible to startle here, in this place. He looked to his left and saw Cliona walking beside him, as though she'd always been there. It was a sight he didn't understand, but nothing disturbed him. It was good to see her.

"I would have expected to see you on the other side," he said.

"I'm not sure I'll ever return there."

He didn't understand that, but it didn't matter. "If you're here, does that mean you're still alive?"

"Something like that."

"I went to your funeral."

She stepped in front of him and stopped him. "I'm afraid I can't let you continue."

Zachary scratched his head. "I'm pretty sure I don't have a choice. It wants me."

"You don't have a choice, but I do. And the gate can wait. It's nothing if not patient."

"What are you going to do?"

"Send you back, if you'll let me."

"I thought you said I don't have a choice."

"You don't. Not where the gate is involved. But I'm not sure I want to send you back if you don't give me permission."

He felt his first emotion since arriving here. It was a hurt, an ache like that of an old friend's betrayal. "Why would you take this from me?"

"The Six States needs you. Everyone else is only looking out for themselves. You're the only one able to look beyond that. If you walk through those gates, I don't see a way for the Six States to survive."

The hurt in his heart grew deeper. "I tried to save them. That's why I'm here."

Cliona looked down at her feet. "I know. And I'm sorry to ask you to delay your rest. I know the sacrifice I'm asking of you."

Zachary looked past her to the gates. Another dozen steps, maybe two, and there would be nothing to worry about ever again. Mother would be there, waiting for him. But Cliona wouldn't be there. Hel wouldn't be there. Edda would be all alone, with no one to share her burdens.

He bowed his head. "As you wish."

The words were some of the hardest he'd ever said.

"Thank you. I promise that if we meet in this place again, I won't stop you."

Something heavy lodged in Zachary's stomach. "Are you saying I won't see you again?"

"I'm not sure."

"I'm sorry for betraying you to Damion. If not for me, none of what had happened would have."

"You're forgiven," she said. She put a hand on his chest, and warmth and strength filled him.

The water that he'd been walking on since he arrived suddenly opened up, and he fell into the darkness.

When Zachary opened his eyes again, he was staring at the ceiling of his bedroom. No snakes writhed across it, and his vision was steady. He lifted his hand in front of his face, studying both the palm and the back. Holding it up tired him, so he let it drop by his side.

"You had me worried." The voice came from the corner

of the room. He flopped his head to the side so that he could see Edda.

She sat at the small table he often used for tea in the mornings. She had pulled the table away from the corner and wedged one of the two chairs there. The table in front of her was piled with papers, but her position allowed her to work and watch him at the same time. He smiled at the sight.

This was Edda, summed up in one sight. "Sorry," he said. His head hurt, so he turned back to face the ceiling. "That party got out of hand."

The chair scraped as Edda pushed it away from the table. She came to stand by the side of the bed. "What happened?"

He frowned, both at the question and the confusion it revealed. "You don't know?"

"All we know is that you left. When you came back, you were gravely wounded in your shoulder. If you hadn't told the guards about the poison, I don't think the healers would have even checked."

"What about the others?"

Edda mirrored his frown. "What others?"

"I was ambushed on the streets of Mioska by cultists. I killed five of them. There were dozens of witnesses, at least."

"There's been no news." Without asking permission, she rested her wrist against his forehead. "Are you sure?"

Had it been anyone else, he would have slapped her hand away. But one memory that lingered from his delirium was the sight of his sister, worried she was about to lose him. "I'm sure. But we can solve that later. How are you?"

Edda nodded and tried to make a brave face, but her watering eyes betrayed her.

"I'm sorry I worried you so. I promise I didn't go looking

for trouble, not this time." He raised his hand to her cheek, and she nuzzled against it. "You deserve better than to sit here and care for your infirm family."

The dam broke, and her tears dropped freely onto his bed sheets. "The healers said you were going to die. They had done all they could, but they said your body was too far gone!"

He pulled her head down to his chest and held her tightly. He wanted to tell her what he'd experienced. But she was nothing if not pragmatic. At best, she'd consider it a vision that had given him the strength to return. She wouldn't believe.

"Listen to my heart, sister. It still beats strong within me. I can't promise you I'll always return, but I can swear that I will always do everything I can to get back to you. Nothing short of the gate will stop me. If it's within my power, I'll never leave you alone."

He let her sob into his chest. While she did, he stared up at the ceiling and let his thoughts wander to the future. The path he'd chosen wasn't working. It would never succeed.

Something deep inside him had shifted. The hope he'd held for the future wasn't dead, but his fight and the journey to the gate had changed its shape. He felt like a sculptor working on a clay model that wasn't quite formed. He knew something strong and lasting could be formed from the materials at hand. What its final appearance would be, though, was still beyond him.

Edda finished and disentangled herself from his arms. "Sorry about that. It's been a tough few days."

"There's nothing to apologize for. How long has it been since the incident?"

"Three days."

"And there's been no word of an attack?"

"Not even a whisper. Trust me, I've been searching. We didn't know what had happened."

"Did anything else come up while I was out?"

She shook her head. "Outside of the household staff, no one knows you were hurt. And I suppose the witnesses you claim saw the event. But nothing in the city has changed."

When she saw the look on his face, she scolded him. "Let the city worry about itself for a few more days. You look like more of a corpse than Father. For now, focus on eating something and recovering. I've got an eye on the city."

He was glad to agree. He wasn't sure what good he'd do if he attempted anything, anyway. Edda gathered her papers and promised to send some food to his room. Then she left him to sleep.

The next few days were slow, but Zachary couldn't complain. He slept long hours and ate so much food he started to feel guilty he wasn't sharing it with others. His strength returned, and piece by piece, he started to rebuild his daily routine. He resumed training as soon as he was able, though he couldn't push himself long before draining his meager reserves of strength. He went on long walks around the grounds. The cold air invigorated him, and he always felt better after being outside for a few hours.

Most of the time, he tried to think about anything except the problems facing Mioska. He spoke at length with the groundskeepers on his walks, learning more about the plants on their estate. He learned his mother had been behind more of the design than he'd realized and learning about the gardens felt like learning about a past he didn't even know he possessed.

Edda began taking her meals with him, and they made a rule not to talk about anything important. They spoke most often about the books they had read, or the more pleasant experiences of their childhood.

The biggest surprise of his recovery was when he resumed training with teho. He formed a simple dart and was surprised by how strong it felt. He tried a shield next and found the same. The technique, which he normally struggled with, came naturally. Though it was hard for him to evaluate his own strength, he felt for sure like he'd become a nelja. Or maybe even kolma.

What had Cliona done to him?

Tehoin grew stronger through training their abilities, but they didn't jump from one class to another. Zachary had been born a vilda and was supposed to die a vilda.

Of course, he had died. Or at least, come as close to death as one could get and still be on this side of the gate. Like everything else that had happened to him, he held the knowledge of his new abilities close, not even telling Edda.

As he grew stronger, he let his thoughts churn in the back of his mind. It was something he discovered when he'd been wandering through the western frontier, seeking answers after Husavik. Thinking directly about the hard problems rarely worked. Better instead to fill his hours with other tasks. Eventually, he hoped the way forward would emerge.

On one of his long walks around the grounds, it finally did. He saw his mistakes as clear as day. And though he didn't know exactly how to move forward, he knew someone who would. The irony of the situation wasn't lost on him.

He finished his walk and went into the house. He climbed up the stairs and knocked on the door to Father's bedchambers. When he heard Father invite him in, he opened the door and stepped in.

Today, his father's voice was weak. It barely carried to

Zachary's ears. "For a while, I thought you might beat me to the gate."

"Only because you refuse to die."

At first, Zachary thought his father was suffering from a coughing fit. Then he realized his father was laughing.

He went to his father's bed and pulled up the chair. Father grunted. "You've changed."

He didn't bother denying it. Father was wrong about many things, but some things he'd always been right about. It only took Zachary nearly dying to see it.

"I want your help," he said.

Father gave him a sickly grin. "And I do believe that for the very first time, you might be ready for it."

19

────

Hakon inched toward the edge of the crater, trying to see to the bottom without getting killed by the legions of teho demons crawling along the walls. Right at the lip, he peered over. His first realization was that this wasn't a crater at all. It was a hole. The walls went straight down, through dirt, clay, and stone—all the way to the bottom, where it looked perfectly flat.

Except for the teho demons piled two high.

There had to be hundreds of the creatures. They took all shapes and sizes, a menagerie of nightmarish forms that almost guaranteed Hakon would never get a peaceful night of dreams for the rest of his life. He tried to remember if he'd ever seen more than two or three at once, and he couldn't. Here, there were so many that it looked as though the walls of the hole were alive.

The only hope Hakon saw in the situation was that none of them seemed interested in leaving the hole. Even though several ran along the walls just a few feet below him, they paid him no mind. He suspected that if he tried to lower himself in, though, they wouldn't ignore him for long.

"Well," Irric said. He left whatever else he was going to say to himself.

Meshell snorted. "Never boring."

Each of the band took a turn looking over the lip, voicing their disbelief, and stepping away. But they always returned to take another look. Hakon simply stared, looking for some way to the bottom. There were no stairs, and they had no rope. The hole had to be three hundred feet down, if not a bit deeper.

He pointed to the bottom of the hole. "I think that's where we need to go."

It sat in the center of the teho demons, but Hakon noticed that none of them dared touch it. From this height it looked like a pebble, but judging from the size of the demons, Hakon suspected the stone was bigger than him. It glowed brightly, but the sight didn't hurt his eyes.

Irric laughed, drawing all eyes toward him. "Of course we do. As if getting this far wasn't hard enough."

Hakon raised an eyebrow.

Irric waved away his concern. "Oh, don't worry about me. I'm just wishing we had one of Torsten's old court scribes here to write all this down."

Ari growled. "I wanted to kill at least half those scribes."

Irric chuckled. "Admittedly, your reactions to them were where I found the most enjoyment."

Hakon pointed down the hole. "Can we focus on how we're going to get down that?"

Solveig shook her head. "You know there's no way down that."

"Maybe I could make some really strong swords and jump down first to clear a path," Irric suggested.

Solveig didn't dignify the foolishness with a response.

Hakon looked at Ari. "Can you transport me down there? Right on top of it?"

The dour assassin looked as though he'd swallowed a lemon whole. "Sure, but what good will that do? They'll attack you the moment you're down there."

"Consider it a scouting expedition. You can jump us out before they reach us. We're not going to accomplish anything standing up here talking about it."

Ari glanced at Solveig, who shrugged. "Fine. You ready?"

Hakon bounced from foot to foot. "As I'll ever be."

Ari stood close to him and grabbed his hand.

Hakon blinked, and he was standing on top of the stone. As he'd guessed, it was far bigger than he was. The bottom of the hole was warm from the stone. He felt it through his boots.

A deafening chorus of screams filled the hole, echoing back and forth across the sheer walls. The teho demons had noticed them.

Hakon ignored the cacophony and looked down at the stone. He felt it pull him closer. He could resist, but this was why they were here. Why they had come all this way. He let go of Ari and reached down.

Ari shouted and twisted, but then Hakon's palm pressed against the stone and the world faded away.

The pale blue glow surrounded him, filling his body with more teho than he'd ever possessed. It filled his chest, arms, and legs, expanding his muscles until he felt like he would explode. His skin held him together, but it cracked as more teho poured into his body. Blue light shone through the cracks, and he felt his body unraveling like a teho demon's after it was dead.

"Stop fighting it. Let it flow through you," a familiar voice said.

He didn't question. Didn't doubt. Surrendering the fight sounded like death to him, but if she told him, he would listen. He stopped fighting, and the teho within his body calmed.

"You made it," Cliona said.

"We made it. I couldn't have done it without the others."

She reached down and picked him up. "Come with me. I have much to show you."

Hakon thought of Ari. "I'm afraid I don't have much time."

The corner of her lips turned up in a smile, and the expression reminded Hakon so much of Sera he almost cried. She made a gesture and the white surrounding them faded. Hakon saw him and Ari from a different perspective.

From the eyes of one of the teho demons. Dozens of them had leaped from the walls and were falling toward the two tehoin. Another dozen leaped from the bottom of the hole. Ari reached for him as he pressed his hand against the stone. At first, Hakon thought the scene was frozen, but he noticed subtle differences from moment to moment. Not frozen but moving very slowly.

"Time moves differently here. We have time, but we shouldn't dally."

Hakon nodded and followed Cliona.

The scene shifted, and Hakon knew, without words, that he was seeing through the eyes of a dragon. He flew high above the world, mountains below him. A bright light flashed in the sky, followed by an explosion in the distance.

"What am I looking at?" he asked.

"The arrival of the first humans to this planet."

The dragon flew over the scene of the explosion, and Hakon recognized the ship they'd once made their camp in.

It was outside the dragon nest. In this vision, it was still glowing orange.

"They were fleeing something," Cliona said, "but I haven't found out what. So far, I can only see from select viewpoints."

One scene after another followed, never more than a few moments. People spread out from the ship and went into the mountains.

"They hid in the mountains," Cliona explained. "There are whole cities underneath some of our mountain peaks, and we never had any idea. Whatever they feared, though, never found them here. Dragons and other creatures were the only danger they faced."

Hakon watched people stream from the mountains. They all headed west. He watched cities rise before his eyes. One looked very much like the one he'd been exploring for the last few days. "What happened to them?"

"The stamfar arrived."

The flashing passage of scenes slowed, and Hakon was once again a dragon, flying above a city. He wasn't sure, but he thought it was this one. Suddenly, a brilliant light shone in the sky above the city center. It flashed down, almost as quick as lightning but so much more powerful. Hakon looked down and saw the wound in the world, opened up by a lone tehoin.

Even after fighting Ava and Isira, he struggled to accept what Cliona showed him. The strength had to be impossible.

"I'm still tracking the development of the tehoin in the visions I can reach, but the humans that arrived on the planet were ahula."

"What?" He didn't hide his surprise.

"I know. Solveig and the others are going to be furious

when they find out everything they believe is wrong. Anyway. The stamfar came later. They were the first to realize they had this new strength, and to call them responsible with it would be a grave error. They discovered they were strongest in places with these glowing stones, and they started to fight amongst themselves. They killed thousands. Tens of thousands, perhaps. And they weren't even trying. The other settlers were just in the way."

"What happened here?"

"When the nexus was discovered here, people fled. They packed up their lives and left because they knew what was coming. In time, they became the settlers that would form what we now call the Six States. But that would only happen after a war the likes the world has never seen. Even your Rebellion was nothing in comparison. When the stamfar warred, the whole world trembled."

Cliona went silent, lost in thoughts Hakon couldn't begin to guess. She seemed an old soul now, burdened by years of memories that weren't her own. Strange, as in life she'd died before experiencing so much. He grieved for what she had lost but remained amazed at what she had become.

"They had something beautiful. They could travel between the stars and tame entire planets. But when this planet gave them a power beyond their knowledge, they couldn't handle it. Their abilities became our legends, but they did far more harm than good. Hundreds of years of progress were wiped out in a lifetime, and we still haven't come close to recovering it."

Her thoughts were wandering. Hakon thought of Ari, desperately reaching for him in another world. "Is that why the wild has been attacking humanity? Because we're so destructive?"

"Not the way you think, no."

She swept her hand across the scenes of destruction, and they blew away like dust in the wind. Hakon found himself in a void, looking down on a ball of many colors. Oceans of deep blue, deserts stained brown, and mountains topped with blinding white snow.

"This is our world," she said. "Small by the standards of those who first traveled here, but we've never explored more than a corner of it." The world dimmed and turned translucent, revealing a pulsing blue orb near the center. "And this is the source of all teho, the heart of the world. When humans arrived, it looked like this." With another gesture, the brightness of the orb increased until it was almost too much to look at.

With another gesture, the orb dimmed until it was barely glowing. "This is what it looks like now," she said.

"The planet is dying?"

"It gives something of itself to every creature born here. A fraction of a sliver, but still something. When the creature dies, the power is returned. Balance is maintained. Only two creatures break the balance."

Hakon's mind leaped ahead. "Dragons and humans."

She looked like a teacher whose slow student had finally answered a question correctly. "Dragons are aware of the balance and have developed their own ways of keeping it. Humans never have. Ever since the wars of the stamfar, we've grown and expanded. Tehoin steal chunks of teho and then try to live forever. The power Isira and Ava alone control is incredible."

The enormity of Cliona's words settled on Hakon's shoulders like a boulder. "It's trying to kill us to stay alive."

"And I think Ava realized something similar back in her

day. Her peers viewed it as heresy, but I think she was right when everyone else was wrong."

"So the only way for the planet to survive is for humanity to die out?"

Cliona grimaced. "That was Ava's solution. I'm looking for another."

"But if we keep fighting, and the planet can't wipe us out, what happens?"

"If the heart dies, so does all life on the planet."

"So, one way or another, all of humanity is dead?"

"Unless we can find another way to heal the planet, yes."

Cliona looked up, though Hakon saw nothing. "What?" he asked.

"Our time grows very short. You can talk with the others. Maybe you can find a way where I've found none."

"Wait! One more question. How are you able to show me all of this?"

"The stone carries the memories of the teho that has left and returned. I'm able to browse through it, like the world's best library."

"Could I do the same?"

"You could. Anything you can imagine and will, you can do here." She grinned as a sword, an exact duplicate of Hakon's, appeared in her hand. "See?"

"Do we have a moment?"

"Barely."

Hakon tried what Cliona suggested. He imagined Sera and sought her memories. They came to him, and he chose one at random, one close to the end of her life. They were in the home they'd built together, and Sera was in the kitchen with a much younger Cliona.

Sera was teaching her daughter how to make bread, and

though Cliona made a mess of the dough, Sera's grin was wide. She'd always been a patient teacher.

Tears rolled down Hakon's cheeks as he watched the two generations of his family work together. He wanted nothing more than to be with them in that moment, but it was not to be. This memory wasn't his, and he hadn't been here. But the warmth in his chest burned brighter than the fire in the kitchen. Sera had been happy. Right up until the end.

The scene faded, and Hakon found himself back in the void. He met Cliona's gaze and saw an understanding there—not just of what he had seen but also of his feelings towards it. Without another word, she embraced him. "We need to go."

"I know."

Cliona made one more gesture, and Hakon flew up and away, his awareness moving as fast as the ships his ancestors had ridden between the stars. He crashed through into the physical plane like a fish leaping out of the water, and he gasped as he saw teho demons falling toward him like enormous, deadly raindrops.

Ari grabbed him by the neck, and they were out of the hole.

Hakon's stomach twisted. He was used to transport, but getting thrown out of that strange realm and then transported a moment later was more change than his mind had been prepared to handle. He stayed on hands and knees and willed his stomach to relax.

The mutterings of the rest of the band reached him and he pushed himself to his feet. He stumbled back toward the lip of the crater, where Irric caught him before he fell to his death. The last of the teho demons were landing on the glowing stone where Ari and Hakon had stood. When they touched the stone, they screamed and dissolved as though they'd been killed by a blade.

"That's interesting," Meshell said.

Once the last of the ill-fated demons disappeared, the rest returned to patrolling the walls. Dozens had died in their attempt to kill the tehoin, but the rest seemed unperturbed. Thankfully, the provocation didn't encourage the demons to chase the band away from the lip.

"Well, that was a waste of time," Ari said.

"On the contrary," Hakon said, slapping Ari on the back. "That was the best thing we could have done."

"Did you learn something?" Solveig asked.

"I did. Now I know what the problem is. All we need to do is figure out how to fix it."

20

———

Zachary wrapped his cloak tight around him as the freezing wind blew hard from the north. Winter had settled in hard this year, and even the streets of Mioska were quiet. He shivered as he glanced behind him, afraid he'd see some archer climbing on the rooftops, preparing their shot.

But today was cold enough that even the assassins were huddling next to their fireplaces. Edda hadn't liked the idea of him heading out alone, and Zachary hadn't had the heart to tell her he didn't even trust their guards. The rot from the cultists had spread wide, and his trust was a fragile thing after the assassination attempt.

He stood on the wall, next to Rurik, the guard commander. Zachary liked Rurik but had the feeling the sentiments weren't mutual. Rurik had been serving in the guard when Father was a much younger man, and people often debated which would fall first, Rurik or the wall.

Today, Rurik stood tall, as though daring the wind to do its worst. He stared at the scene below. "This is as bad as I've ever seen it, but if what I'm hearing is true, it's far from what is still to come."

Rurik spoke true, but Zachary wished he didn't. The suffering at the gate wasn't something he'd wish on his worst enemy.

The refugees were a miserable sight. A long line of hunched figures, wrapped in what little clothing they had, were battered and beaten by the elements. Parents huddled around children, trying to provide some small protection from the bitter wind that lashed at them as they waited for entry into the city. Like the caravans that had arrived before, the trip had not been without its danger. He saw the signs of wild predation. Limbs that hung limp at sides, crutches supporting broken legs, and bloody scars left by claw and talon.

Worst though, was the look they had on their faces.

In their minds, they were safe. They had suffered mightily, but none of them had lost hope that they could find a safe haven within these ancient walls. And now that hope was almost realized.

Zachary watched with a heavy heart as families were let in one at a time, before being hustled away by the guards assigned to orient them. He saw mothers clutch babies tightly to their chests, fathers presenting a strong facade for their weary children, and siblings clinging to each other for comfort and security.

Zachary and the other council members had set up what shelters they could, and construction and repair of homes was happening as fast as builders could find the materials and the labor. But it would barely be enough for this group, not to mention those groups yet to come.

It was one thing to read the reports, but it was wholly another to see the problems with his own eyes. Their western front was still relatively quiet, but their northern was collapsing as the wild pushed south. The latest reports had towns less than a hundred miles north of Mioska falling. Even more concerning, there were stories of a woman riding the dragons. At first, Zachary hadn't believed, but as more reports trickled in from different towns, it became impossible to deny.

Ava had returned, and she was destroying his state one town at a time.

What he wanted, more than anything, was to fight the wild. With his newfound strength, he might even make a difference.

Not enough of one, though. Even if he was a nelja, even if he was a kolma, he couldn't stand alone against the dragons and Ava. The best that he could do right now was stand on this wall and make sure the refugees were cared for. It wasn't enough, but it was all he could do.

Rurik eventually retreated down below, out of the wind. He ordered his soldiers about, but Zachary paid him little mind. He'd do his work well.

When the last of the refugees had passed through the gates, Zachary started down the stairs. His legs were strong, and except for the slight ache in his shoulder, he felt healthy. His healing had gone better than he had any right to expect.

He stopped halfway down the stairs. A small group of cultists stood just inside the main gate, greeting the refugees as they arrived. They handed out blankets and warm bread, a friendly face at the conclusion of a difficult journey. And to each adult they met, they handed a flyer. Zachary made sure his hood was pulled as far over his head as it would go and clenched his fists. He could well imagine what the flyers said. More lies about the tehoin being responsible for the destruction of their lives.

The blankets and offerings of help were a nice touch.

Even if he wanted to go down there and disperse the cultists, it would only reflect poorly on him. He had little choice but to watch.

One of the cultists, a young man who looked like he might have been an off-duty guard, saw Zachary. He grinned wide and pantomimed drawing an arrow to his cheek and launching it. He laughed, then turned back to distributing blankets and food.

Zachary watched until the last of the refugees had left and the cultists had dispersed. Every day that passed without him doing something let them dig in deeper. It wouldn't be long before they controlled the city in all but name.

Agnar did nothing to stem the growing strength of the cult, and he continued to argue that he needed to speak to Hel and the council before he could support the marriage in public. Zachary began to suspect Agnar wasn't as much an ally as he'd hoped. As always, Agnar waited to see what ways the winds of power blew. Only when he was sure to win would he commit to anything.

Zachary had stopped trying to convince Agnar. Father had convinced him convincing the governor to stick out his neck was pointless. Agnar wouldn't change. It was too late for that path to work.

"You're looking for an official answer, something the government can do to stop the spread of the cultists," his father had said. "But you're thinking wrong. The cultists are a problem, sure, but what they represent is even more of a challenge."

"What do you mean?"

"They represent a belief. A belief that humanity is doomed and the tehoin are to blame. That's what you're really fighting against. A belief. And governments are terrible tools for fighting against beliefs."

Zachary considered the words again as he walked home. How did he fight a belief?

His thoughts were interrupted by a commotion farther down the street. It was getting dark, and most everyone on the street was flowing in one direction. The rest seemed in a hurry to be anywhere else. Merchants had closed up shops, and people were hurrying back home, gazes firmly locked on their feet.

"What's going on?" he asked a passerby.

The man shrugged. "There was a fight between a tehoin and some cultists."

"A fight?"

"They say it got ugly."

Zachary looked around. "Where are the guards?"

The passerby grunted. "At home with their families, if they know what's good for them."

With that, the man ran off, leaving Zachary on the empty street by himself. He debated for a moment, then followed the crowd who had gone deeper into the city. A looming sense of dread filled him, the silence before him deafening. A fight should be loud, with people cheering on the combatants. This reminded him more of the gate, reaching to claim its souls after the end of the battle.

He turned a corner and saw the crowd gathered, larger than he'd expected. Maybe a hundred people stood at the intersection of two large streets. They were almost completely silent, staring at something in the center. He saw a few heads bobbing near the middle of the group but couldn't make out anything else from this distance.

Zachary checked the roofs and alleys, but the shadows hid nothing unexpected. He formed a teho dart and held it in his right hand, taking comfort in the feel of the weapon in his palm. Wisdom told him he should turn and retreat, but curiosity and a sick certainty pulled him forward.

When he reached the edge of the crowd, he still couldn't see to the center. He stood on his toes, but too many people stood between him and the fight. Though it didn't sound like a fight. It didn't sound like anything at all.

He tried weaving through the crowd, but the bodies were packed too tight. All he earned for his efforts were glares from the people he tried to move aside.

If someone needed his help, he'd never get to them this way. Of course, if someone needed his help, it looked like he'd need to fight through quite the crowd. He swore under his breath. There was still plenty of time to turn around and walk away. He wasn't completely healed, and he hadn't tested his new strength against a real opponent.

If there was a tehoin there, they were more valuable than any wealth. And no one deserved to fight this crowd alone. He flung back his hood and stood up straight. He put his hand on the shoulder of the beefy man in front of him.

When the man twirled, fire in his eyes, Zachary met his stare. "Move, please."

Recognition flashed across the man's face, followed a moment later by undisguised hate. He balled his hands as though he was about to fight, but Zachary shook his head. The man saw reason and backed off. But the people in front of him weren't even aware of Zachary's presence. This wasn't going to work.

"MOVE!" Zachary bellowed.

That got their attention. Every face turned toward him, and it looked like well over half of them recognized his face. Of course, it had decorated quite a few flyers circulating around town. They should recognize him.

He suddenly felt very much like a piece of meat tossed into a circle of shadow wolves that hadn't eaten for a week. Several of the citizens looked like they were close to licking their lips.

And they still weren't moving.

Zachary extended a thin line of teho from his hand, then pulled it down like a curtain. He'd never tried anything like this before, but he found it easy, as though he'd done it every morning for years. He expanded the curtain, forcing the crowd apart. They cursed and swore, but they couldn't push back against his teho. After a few moments, he had a clear path to the center of the crowd.

What he saw made him question the wisdom of all his decisions. Two bodies lay in the center of the crowd. Blood covered them, and Zachary was certain they were dead. Then one coughed, a wet gurgling sound that made Zachary think one of his lungs had been punctured.

Before he could think about what he was doing, he rushed forward. The crowd let him pass, though he noticed they closed ranks behind him. He reached the two victims and kneeled between them. They were wearing the uniforms of city guards, adding a further insult to the scene. Not just tehoin, but tehoin who had pledged their lives to the protection of the city.

The guard on the left was dead. His eyes stared blankly at the sky above. His chest was a mess of cuts. He'd been stabbed dozens of times, at least. His face was a mottled collection of bruises, and he was missing several teeth.

The only advantage the guard on the right had was that he was still breathing, but he wouldn't be for long. Like his friend, his chest had been opened more viciously than a bear tearing into a meal. His breaths were heavy and labored, and Zachary thought he heard a whistling sound with every inhale. The young man was crying, his lips moving quickly.

Zachary wished there was something he could do, but it was already too late. The guard was dead, the gate just hadn't come for him yet. He grasped the man's hand, already cold. There was nothing he could say, but he could prevent the man from dying alone.

The guard's agony ended before long. He took his last breath and fell still, finally at peace.

Zachary stood up and looked down at his hand, covered in the guard's blood. Then he looked at the inner circle of the crowd. They stared back at him, many of them with bloody knives in their hands. A cold certainty came over Zachary, and he grew calm.

The first man to rush him earned a teho dart in the chest for his ambition. Zachary stabbed the second through the heart with a teho blade. Instead of discouraging them, it only taught the rest to charge at once.

He could have formed long teho blades and carved his way through them. These weren't tehoin he needed to fear. But they were still his citizens, and he'd sworn to protect them when he joined the council. He pushed out unfocused teho, a blast of power that sent everyone in the intersection flying away from him.

He hadn't even given the technique all his strength. When he had a chance, he would need to visit Aysgarth. This power had to be that of a kolma.

That would come later, though. He didn't fear dying here, with teho firmly in his grasp. The only question that remained was how many citizens would die before they saw reason.

Fortunately, the break in the fighting broke the back of their anger. They'd already claimed their blood tonight.

Those assembled had to know that despite their advantage in numbers, there was no defeating Zachary. He memorized the faces of those still holding bloody knives. If he weren't alone, he might try to apprehend them, but it invited too much risk. Better by far to break this up before the problem spread.

"Leave!" he shouted.

Too late, he realized that giving the order might have the opposite of the desired effect. They would hate listening to a tehoin.

He sent another blast of teho out from his body, knocking down those who had been struggling to their feet. "Leave!" he repeated.

As soon as the first few fled, the others quickly followed. Zachary stood guard over the bodies, a light shield protecting him from last-ditch attacks.

A quiet thunk from behind him told him that he'd chosen well. He glanced back to see a throwing dagger clattering to the ground. He glared at the boy who'd thrown it, and he went sprinting off, looking like he was about to wet his pants in terror.

Before long, he was alone, with only the bodies of the guards for company. The crowd had left, only a brave few shooting him angry glares as they disappeared behind corners. The wind cut at him, funneled down the street by the buildings.

He looked down at his hand, still covered in blood.

It was time to put an end to this cult.

21

———

They chose to relocate to one of the buildings adjacent to the crater. The corner of the building was gone, destroyed in a burst of teho Hakon had seen in Cliona's visions but still struggled to believe was possible. They used the gaping wound as an entrance, finding intact stairs on the other side of the building. A short climb took them to an undamaged room where they could look out at the crater.

Like every other apartment they'd visited, the rooms were clean and empty. Unlike the other spaces, Hakon noticed some signs of damage. A frame had fallen off of one wall. The glass had clearly shattered, but Hakon couldn't find any on the floor. They found enough chairs for all of them and pulled them up to a window.

Hakon explained what he'd seen and what Cliona had told him. His tale was met with skeptical looks, but after the events of the past year, no one argued or presented alternative interpretations. Their journey had taken them to places where the unfamiliar had become expected.

"So, we need to figure out a way to stop the heart from dying," Hakon concluded.

No one leaped to suggest a way of making the impossible real. They sat in silence, watching the demons patrol the crater while pondering possibilities.

"I suppose it all makes a certain sense," Solveig said. "We've been searching for a reason why the tehoin have been in decline. The heart is protecting itself."

"But the tehoin are almost gone," Ari argued. "There can't be more than one or two thousand vilda left, maybe a few hundred nelja, and no more than a dozen who are stronger. If the heart can hold out for a few more decades, there might be no more tehoin left."

Hakon didn't have a satisfactory response. "There's no way of knowing if that's true or not, but it doesn't change our problem. The heart believes tehoin are killing it, so it'll eliminate humanity to protect itself."

"Maybe you could just take this heart out for a night of drinks and have a nice long conversation about how we can do better," Irric said. "I'm sure it's quite reasonable once you get to know it."

Meshell punched Irric for all of them. He rubbed his shoulder and pretended to be wounded.

Hakon thought back to the various attacks they'd endured on their long journey west. The heart had sent an enormous number of creatures after them, more than willing to sacrifice them all if their deaths presented even the slightest opportunity of getting at the band. Though he understood Irric jested, he didn't think the heart would see reason.

Ari, who was sitting closest to the window, suddenly leaned forward, peering down into the crater.

"What?" Irric asked the question they all wondered, but he sounded exhausted.

"Their behavior changed," Ari answered.

The rest of the band scooted their chairs closer.

The demons no longer circled around the pit as though on patrol. Now, they had separated into two different groups. One climbed out of the pit, and Hakon tensed for battle. But they didn't spread out or seek the band. The demons simply left the pit and walked a few dozen feet away from the lip, then stopped. They sat down on whatever passed for their haunches and went as still as the frozen statues that decorated the tops of several nearby buildings.

"It seems like they're waiting," Meshell said.

Once Hakon's fears about the first group subsided, his attention turned more fully to the second group. These demons remained in the bottom of the pit, but they no longer swarmed across the entire floor. Instead, they gathered largely around the bottom edge of the pit. They were active, but Hakon struggled to see what kept them so engaged.

Ari's eyes were better. "They're digging," he said.

Hakon squinted. It looked like Ari might be right. Though the shapes of the demons took many forms, their intent was clear. Claws and talons cut through the walls of the pit. Others seemed to burrow in and out of the walls. But they all seemed intent on expanding the base of the pit.

The minutes passed and the frantic activity continued. The demons up top waited while the ones below labored frantically. There were fewer demons in the pit than ever, and those still within had their backs to the glowing stone. Hakon wasn't sure of much, but he was sure that any answers would be down there, and they would never get a better time to return.

He turned to Ari. "Ready for another transport?"

The assassin narrowed his eyes, then they went wide. "You can't be serious. You want to return?"

"We'll get more time than we did before. Their attention isn't on the stone anymore."

"It will be once we show up!"

Hakon didn't flinch, and Ari backed down.

"Fine."

Ari stood up, but before he could step toward Hakon, the building trembled around them. A subtle vibration, but one they all felt. They pressed themselves against the window as the demons' intent became clear. The walls of the pit started to collapse, burying the demons who'd been digging underneath. Tons of dirt, stone, and building collapsed into the pit, throwing up a cloud of dust and debris. Two of the buildings, which had lost most of their structure to the initial teho blast that formed the pit, finally surrendered to the destruction. They toppled, their death groans echoing and booming through the air.

Dust filled the air and prevented Hakon from seeing into the pit, but it had to be filled at least a third of the way. Even if all of them used teho to dig deeper, it would be days before they reached the stone. And that didn't take into consideration the hundreds of demons who still remained on the surface.

Since Cliona's explanations in the bottom of the pit, Hakon had believed there was a chance. She'd planted a seed of hope that had just started to bloom. The demons tore that hope away. There was no way the five of them would reach the stone again. Ari couldn't transport them under tons of rubble.

He was on the edge of despair when the floor started to shake again.

"What now?" Irric complained.

The shaking wasn't the same as the collapse of the pit moments earlier. It lacked the destructive force of the collapse and felt less random. Hakon pressed his face against the window, but the dust wouldn't clear for a while yet, and he couldn't see a thing. The shaking grew more pronounced.

"I'll go look," Hakon said.

Before anyone could argue, he tore out of the room, filling his body with teho. He sprinted down the stairs, leaping a floor at a time. His enormous legs flexed with every impact, but he was on the ground floor fast. He emerged from the stairwell and received his answer immediately.

The teho demons that had come out of the pit earlier weren't just keeping watch. They were in motion, hacking at the walls and foundation of the building that were closest to the pit. Their teho tore through the structures that had stood for hundreds of years as though they were paper. Whole chunks of wall fell as he watched, and he couldn't imagine the building would stand much longer.

He turned and sprinted back up the stairs, running as fast as his feet would carry him. He burst into the room they'd been using just in time to see a taller building across the pit collapse into the pit.

"They're dropping buildings into the pit as if they were giant trees," Solveig deduced.

"And this building is one of them," Hakon said. "It's time for us to go."

"Lead the way," Solveig commanded.

The building rumbled underneath their feet, and the whole room began to tilt.

"I don't think we have that much time," Hakon said. "Ari?"

The assassin nodded, and they all grabbed hands. Ari looked to him. "Where?"

"The building where we camped the first night in the city."

Their building began to tip, and Hakon saw them slowly start to tilt toward the dust cloud. As furniture started to slide toward them, Ari transported them away.

They landed in a heap in a familiar lobby. Hakon groaned. Meshell had fallen on top of him, and her elbow was digging into his stomach. He pushed her off. She swore as she untangled her legs from Solveig's.

Irric, of course, was the first to speak. "Interesting city, I'd say. But I don't think I ever want to visit again."

22

———

You should kill him.

The admonition echoed in Zachary's thoughts as he slid from shadow to shadow. Escaping his estate unobserved had proven more complicated than he'd expected. If news of his ambush had been squashed like an inconvenient bug by the cultists, the twisted story of what he'd done in the streets against his own citizens spread like an infestation of termites, chewing away at the foundation of his authority.

The story most often told was that Zachary had come across a crowd of well-meaning citizens who were waiting for the militia to arrive and protect the wounded soldiers. But when Zachary had seen that the victims were tehoin, he'd flown into a rage, killing several nearby innocents.

Zachary had circulated an official story, too, but no one seemed to know another version of the tale existed. Though he'd been instrumental in saving the city less than a year ago, everyone was ready to believe the worst in him.

Simply because he was tehoin.

Tonight, he took more decisive action. For too long, he'd

reacted to the moves of his enemies, trying to put out roaring fires of discontent. The difficulty of the task only became apparent when he climbed to the top of the walls of his estate. Citizens had taken it upon themselves to form a perimeter around his home. Several were armed, though as to why, Zachary couldn't imagine. None of them had a hope of defeating him in a duel.

He was tempted to break his way through, but the perimeter provided him with an alibi for tonight's action. How could he be guilty if a whole crowd of concerned citizens could testify he'd never left?

He no longer believed truth would ever find its way before a judge. Whether or not he committed a crime, he suspected there were more than a fair number of people ready to testify to his guilt. But there was no reason to make it easy for them. He dropped off the walls and went to the entrance to the caverns that had sheltered the very same citizens on the day the dragons attacked. His key let him in, and he lit a torch before proceeding into the darkness.

Zachary didn't know if it was design or coincidence that led to the wealthy of Mioska building directly over the caverns. Tonight, he didn't care. There were no entrances to the network of caverns except upon the lands of Mioska's wealthiest, and that served Zachary well tonight.

He followed the maze of passages. Most were natural, but in places it was clear tunnels had been dug and caves had been widened. Edda had given him a comprehensive tour once. He relied on that information today, grinning at the thought of the concerned citizens wandering overhead.

Eventually, he came to a set of stairs carved into the stone. A symbol had been etched in rock near the first step, a family crest Zachary recognized. He cast around with his torch until he found a small stone, then climbed the stairs. It only took him a moment to reach the door. He examined the latch with his torch, then extinguished the light. He was fortunate.

When the caves had been discovered, the nobles had rushed to find and establish their own entrances. They were designed to be safe havens in case the worst should come to pass. Many stored food and wealth down below so that they would be prepared if the wild ever tore down Mioska's thick walls. But most were far more concerned about thieves getting in than they were about others escaping. You wanted to be able to escape a hiding hole fast, so most were only locked on the outside. Zachary opened the door a crack and listened.

From the moonlight coming in through the crack, he knew he was somewhere on Hallr's grounds. The night was quiet, though, and he heard no one nearby. He waited a while longer to ensure no one was close. When he was as sure as he could be, he pushed the door open farther and crept out.

The entrance to the caverns had been hidden within a grove of trees in Hallr's garden. Zachary propped the door open with the stone he'd picked up below, then made his way through the grounds.

Plenty of guards wandered the wall, and more yet stood at the gate. Zachary counted a dozen on duty, and those were just the ones he could see. He got the sense Hallr was expecting trouble. Unfortunately, he'd only thought of that trouble coming from the street. It hadn't occurred to him yet that another noble might attack him through the caverns.

Zachary ran toward the house, eyes searching for an entrance. He'd been within the estate many times as a child, forced to endure countless balls and events hosted by Hallr and his wife. Those endless hours of suffering paid off handsomely now. He found an iron drain he'd played on as a child. He tested it and found it would still hold his weight.

He clambered up the home, reaching the roof faster than most people would have from taking the stairs. While he caught his breath, he looked around the grounds, searching for any sign his presence had been discovered. The night remained quiet. The guards had their attention fully on the walls and the street. A pair guarded the front door of the house, but none suspected an intruder already walked among them.

Zachary went to the door that he remembered. Hallr and his wife kept a small garden on the roof, a place where they could relax and look down on the city their family had governed for generations. The door was locked, but Zachary slid a teho blade through the deadbolt and opened the door without a sound. He stepped inside the house and shut the door behind him.

Once again, he listened to the sounds of the old house. Like his own, Hallr's estate was nearly as old as Mioska. The home had been refurbished, repaired, and added onto countless times over the generations, changing as the family's needs shifted. The result was a home that creaked and whispered, warm and alive despite the bitter cold of the evening. Its sounds weren't the same as the ones Zachary's house made, but they shared a type.

Zachary placed his hand on the wall, struck by a thought he'd never had before. In the past, he'd always believed that all that mattered were the lives within Mioska. Let the dragons and the wild destroy the city itself. So long as the people survived, Zachary would be satisfied. Now, he thought it would be a shame to lose some of these buildings. They carried just as much history as those that lived here. If he had to choose, he'd still choose lives over buildings, but the city itself deserved to survive. It was a monument to humans' prolonged presence, their defiance of the wild.

Once he was certain no one waited on the floor below, he made his way down the stairs, keeping close to the edge of the wall. A few of the stairs bent and creaked under his weight, but there was nothing he could do about it. At this hour, everyone on this floor should be asleep.

He was wrong. A lantern was on in Hallr's study. The door was shut, but the light flickered beneath the door.

That solved one of Zachary's problems. He walked quickly toward the study and listened one last time. If there were any guards on duty, they were likely far below, guarding the entrances to the house.

Zachary reached out and tested the door handle. It turned easily. The door was unlocked. Inside, someone shuffled around, huffing to themselves.

Zachary steeled himself. It was less to find the courage for what came next and more to keep his thoughts calm. Father's advice once again echoed loudly in Zachary's thoughts. "Just kill him," he'd said.

Maybe.

Zachary wouldn't commit to anything until he judged Hallr for himself.

He formed a ball of teho in his left hand, then flung the door open.

Hallr's study was a mess. Papers and books were scattered around the room. Zachary saw his own likeness on hundreds of posters. Not that there had ever been any doubt, but Zachary had just acquired all the proof he'd ever need.

Hallr stood in the center of the room, staring at Zachary as though he couldn't quite figure out if he was seeing things or not. Zachary launched the ball at Hallr's stomach. The councilman didn't even know he was under attack when he fell to the ground, gasping for a breath that his body refused to take.

Zachary closed the door behind him and locked it, just to be safe. He'd hit Hallr a little harder than he'd intended, and the councilman was weaker than he'd expected. He was still getting used to this new strength. It would be a few moments before he caught his breath. Zachary used the time to look at the posters. They were a new set, inflaming the citizenry against him for his murders in the street.

Zachary's blood turned colder than the frozen rivers running through Mioska. Hate suddenly seemed an insufficient word. A teho blade flickered in his hand, an unconscious reaction to the thoughts running through his head. He grunted and focused.

A younger him would have been ecstatic to possess such power. Now he found that all the power in the world meant nothing without control. It made him respect the band that much more, that they lived such normal lives when they weren't fighting.

He willed the blade away and squatted next to Hallr. "If you make so much as a peep, I'll kill you."

The older councilman looked into Zachary's eyes, and whatever he saw there was enough to convince him. It should be. Zachary was doing all he could not to kill Hallr. One wrong word would end his life.

"Give me one good reason why I shouldn't kill you for what you've done," Zachary demanded.

Hallr finally caught his breath and pushed himself up to sitting. He leaned back against one of his chairs, his gray hair disheveled. He groaned softly.

Zachary's hand tightened on a blade that wasn't there. Hallr was a coward, but he wasn't afraid. There were bags under his eyes, and now that he'd caught his breath, Zachary thought he heard a ragged edge to his inhale. His eyes narrowed. "You're dying."

Hallr coughed. "Seems a good time for it." He kept his eyes on Zachary, but pushed himself up into his chair, taking a long drink of water from the glass on the small table next to it. Once his thirst was quenched, he stared at Zachary. "I got the news a few days after we returned from that damned expedition of yours. The disease is eating me away. Made me realize I should do something worthwhile before I'm done."

"Something worthwhile?" Zachary's rage was like a bull threatening to break free of its pen. "Like encouraging everyone in Mioska to kill the only people that can protect them?"

Hallr made a sound that was half a laugh and half a cough. "You really believe that, don't you?"

"Of course. If not for us, the dragons would have destroyed this city."

"But have you ever asked yourself why they attack? It's not because they hate humanity. It's because they hate the tehoin."

Zachary formed a teho blade and pointed it at Hallr's chest. The coward didn't even flinch. "They'd attack whether or not we were here!"

"How can you say with such certainty? It's well-known that dragons target tehoin specifically. It's not much of a jump to say the tehoin are the only reason they attack. If the tehoin are gone, the rest of us can finally live in peace."

Zachary snarled and shook his head. "I didn't come here to debate such foolishness. I came here to tell you to calm down your cultists."

Hallr remained infuriatingly calm. "They aren't mine."

Zachary swung his sword around the room, capturing all the posters in the gesture. "Safe enough to say your word carries weight. The tehoin aren't to be touched. They're the only defenders we have."

"You would doom us all with your ignorance," Hallr said.

"You have no more evidence than I. But my way doesn't kill those who have done nothing but serve this city."

"But I do have evidence. Old texts, written in the age of the stamfar. We're not the first who have realized the truth. But the council of the stamfar fought to hide the truth back then. Just as you do today."

"There's no such text."

"There is. Recently discovered in the journals of Marjaana."

Zachary's eyes went wide, revelations striking him with the force of blows.

Hallr grinned, recognizing that Zachary understood.

Zachary felt his intent for the evening slipping away from him. But he couldn't be deterred. He inched his sword closer.

"No more tehoin get hurt," he demanded, pressing the tip of his blade into Hallr's chest. "I don't care how you make it happen. Just make it happen. If you don't, you won't be the only one who pays for it."

He turned on his heel and left, Hallr's dry chuckle loud in his ears as he exited the same way he'd come.

You should have killed him.

Zachary feared his father had been right again.

23

———

The tension among the band made Hakon think of the days leading up to his murder of Torsten. They didn't fight, but their supper was nearly silent. Their task was impossible, and no help they could think of was coming.

Hakon felt their failure like a stab to the chest. Despite everything, he'd always kept a flicker of hope alive for the future. But now, after lifetimes of fighting, it amounted to nothing. They'd been given more time and power than almost anyone else alive, and they'd squandered it.

Their only discussion that night was whether or not Isira could help. Ari had given her one of the stones he used to call for help, and he rolled it around his palm as they debated.

"She's the only one strong enough to have a chance," Irric argued.

Hakon shook his head. "There are too many unknowns. How sick is she? Will she even come? And will the dragons honor the truce if she shows up?"

Hakon paused when he thought of the dragons, then

continued. "Besides, she's admitted herself that she's been looking for the secret to immortality. I don't think she can reach the stone before something here kills her, but if she can, what's to say she doesn't do the opposite of what is needed? What if she tries to pull teho from the stone to keep herself alive?"

Meshell added another complication. "She's also the only one protecting the Six States right now. If we pull her aside, Ava might sweep in and make everything we're doing meaningless anyway."

They argued a bit longer, but there was no decision made. Hakon wasn't sure there was one to make. Calling Isira was their last possible option, and their discussion had sparked a new idea in him.

Mad, of course, but they had traveled far beyond the realm of reason.

They retired to the same rooms they'd had from a few nights before, and Hakon held on tightly to Meshell. It was late before Meshell finally fell asleep.

Hakon lay in the bed, hands behind his head, staring at the ceiling.

It had been good.

He'd been far more fortunate than he deserved. Being born meant a life of suffering followed by its inevitable end. But it had been worth it.

When he was sure Meshell was sound asleep, he rolled out of the bed. It was soft enough that his movement didn't cause her to stir. If they'd had more tomorrows, he'd insist on carrying this bed to wherever they made a new home. He took one last look at her before grabbing his sword and slipping out the door.

The building was quiet, the sound of his footsteps

swallowed by the soft material that made up the floors on the upper levels. He made his way down the stairs. He briefly considered grabbing his pack but decided against it. It would do the others more good than him.

All he needed was his sword.

He left through the front door, but didn't make it more than a few steps.

"I didn't think you'd actually do it," a voice said from next to the door. "I thought that maybe after all these years and all you'd been through, you'd finally learned."

Hakon snorted and looked over at Solveig. She was bundled in an impressive number of blankets and cloaks. He had the sudden thought that he could simply walk away, and she'd never catch him, bundled like that. It made him smile. "You're going to catch a cold out here."

"Seemed worth it."

Hakon looked around. "Ari nearby?"

"No. I told him to go to sleep."

"You were going to wait out here all night?"

"If I had to."

Hakon sighed. "Well, no point in you freezing. We can talk about this inside." He gestured for her to go first, and she did. Even now, she trusted him.

"How did you figure it out?" he asked.

"Noticed you pause when you talked about the dragons. Wasn't too hard to follow your thoughts from there. We can't rely on Isira, and even with our new strength, we don't have the ability to get to the stone. You've made a bit of a habit of riding dragons these past few years, so it's what you'd think about. But only you and Meshell can ride them, and it's suicidal, so you planned on doing it yourself."

"You forgot the part where it was noble and heroic, and you all sang my praises until the end of time."

"It was selfish. Just like when you left to kill Torsten, and just like when Isira released you and you didn't seek us out."

Hakon made to protest, but Solveig cut him off. "If it had been Sera and Cliona waiting for you, instead of us, when you emerged from Isira's cell, would you have stayed away?"

A lump formed in Hakon's throat. "No."

He slumped into one of the chairs. He rubbed his eyes, suddenly more tired than ever before. His body felt every single one of his years. "If there's a chance for any of you to live through this, I want you to have it. I don't want to see you come to harm."

"Do you think it's somehow different for us?"

The verbal blow hit hard. It took him a long time to find the right words. No apology seemed like it came close. "I suppose I was a bit selfish."

Solveig kneeled in front of him and took his hands in her own. "I won't complain that you want to keep me from getting hurt. But the way to keep us safe is to keep us together. We promised long ago to fight together. Nothing has changed since then."

Hakon ran his fingers through his hair and closed his eyes for a long moment. "You know, sometimes I think I don't deserve any of you."

Solveig stood up. "Of course you don't." Her smile took the sting out of her words. "But we're here anyway."

She broke away. "You should get back upstairs. Meshell is going to be worried sick."

Hakon's stomach sank. Bad enough Solveig had figured it out. He didn't want to face Meshell. "Did everyone know?"

"Probably. We've been together a long time, and you're not exactly turning over a new leaf."

Hakon grimaced, and Solveig stretched. "I trust that if I go to bed, you aren't going to go running off?"

"No, I'm here."

"Good." In another sign of her trust, she was the first to climb the stairs.

Hakon sat in the chair for a while, letting self-pity wash over him. He hadn't wanted to hurt anyone, yet he seemed to have a knack for it. With a sigh, he stood up. No point delaying the inevitable. He climbed the stairs and returned to the room he and Meshell shared.

As Solveig had guessed, she was up, sitting in a chair and watching the street in front of the building. He knew, without having to ask, that she had been waiting to see if he'd leave. When the door opened, she turned and looked at him. In the moonlight reflected off her face, he saw the tears running down her cheeks.

That sight, on Meshell's face, was almost more than he could stand. It hit harder than even Solveig's chastisements.

He bowed his head in shame. "I'm sorry."

She stood and strode toward him, and for a moment, he was certain that she was going to slap him across the face. He braced himself for it. It was no less than he deserved. But the blow never came. She stood in front of him, and he looked up to meet her gaze. She looked balanced on the edge of violence and grief. Hakon gave her the space to choose.

When she stepped forward, she reached her arms out wide and embraced him. He returned the gesture, holding her tight. She buried her head in his chest. "You said that you would never leave again."

There was no argument he could make. All he could do was hope he hadn't broken something that couldn't be repaired. "I know. I'm sorry."

"Never again," she said. And he knew it was half a question and half an ultimatum.

"Never again," he answered.

The next morning, when Hakon went downstairs, he went searching for Solveig. The others told him she was back outside.

Hakon went out the front door and found Solveig standing in the same place she'd been the night before. "Wanted to say thanks for last night. You stopped me from doing something foolish."

"You're welcome."

He was about to turn in, but the look on her face made him stop. "What's on your mind?"

She gestured toward the city. "I was just thinking about all of this."

"What about it?" It was usually dangerous getting Solveig started on the subject of history, but she seemed to have something specific on her mind.

"That our ancestors were able to do all of this without teho. Of course, we don't know how long they took to develop all these skills, but we've been fighting amongst ourselves for a long time. We know for sure the age of the stamfars was at least five hundred years ago, and likely much longer. Why haven't we been able to recover any of this?"

Hakon thought about the problem. He suspected Solveig already had a guess, but the question made him curious. "Because we've been too busy fighting?"

"No. Warfare usually results in incredible advances. We're at our most inventive when we're trying to kill one another."

"Then I've got nothing."

"I think it's because of teho," she said. "Why invent when you have such power at your fingertips?"

Hakon didn't have an answer, but Solveig had gotten started. He feared there would be no stopping her anytime soon.

"Teho granted us incredible powers, and the myths of the stamfar told us there were even greater powers we didn't understand. So that's what we focused on, instead of recreating these buildings, or these beds."

Hakon wasn't sure he believed Solveig's explanation. But it raised another question. "Do you think it would be better if we'd never had teho?"

Solveig looked lost. "I don't know. But I'm starting to wonder."

Just then, there was a shout from inside the building. Hakon and Solveig rushed back in, and Hakon received the biggest surprise of the day.

Cliona sat among the band, sipping tea as they stared at her in surprise. She seemed to be enjoying herself.

"Cliona?" Hakon couldn't bring himself to believe what he was seeing. This was the first time he'd seen her in daylight, and it made her more real than her previous appearances.

"Hi, Dad."

"Scared the crap out of us," Irric said. "She wasn't there a moment ago, and now here she is, sipping tea like she's been waiting all morning. I guess there isn't any doubting you anymore."

Hakon stood frozen where he'd first seen her. "You're here."

She nodded. "Taking this form has become easier. I think in time, I'll be able to maintain it for as long as I wish. But I haven't had much time to learn it."

Her voice, telling him about this new form as naturally as though she was summarizing a book she'd just read, pulled him forward. "Why not?"

"Ava is causing problems."

"How so?"

"The heart is throwing everything it has against the frontier. People are fleeing toward the remaining cities as fast as they can run. Ava sees it as her opportunity to finish what she started. There's one nest of dragons outside of Husavik she still commands, and she's using them to great effect. I'm trying to hold her off as well as I'm able." She looked at her hands. "But it doesn't leave me much time for this."

Hearing her so calmly describe the slow destruction of the Six States tore at his pride. They'd fought to found those states! They should be back there, holding the line.

As soon as the thought crossed his mind, he knew it for a fool's dream. They couldn't hold back the wild, not by themselves, and not with the strength remaining to humanity. It was why they'd come out here. The only way to save the Six States was to stop the heart.

Hopefully without dooming all of humanity in the process.

"Where's Isira?" Solveig asked.

"In her home," Cliona said. "She's still stamfar, but weakening steadily. I'm not sure there's much more she can do."

It confirmed their worst fears.

"Then we need to move," Hakon said. "There's no time to waste."

"Not much," Cliona agreed. "Ava is only a few days away from launching a major attack against Mioska. And as it stands, I don't think Mioska will be able to fight."

"Zachary hasn't found a way?" Ari asked.

"He has no strength to work with. I did what I could to help, but unless I'm there, it won't be enough." Cliona turned her attention to Hakon. "Irric tells me you want to use the dragons."

"Do you think it can work?" Hakon asked.

"Maybe," Cliona said. "The master is strong enough to reach the stone, but you'll have to convince him."

"Is that the one who attacked us on the way here?" Irric asked.

"It is."

"No thanks," Irric said. "It's faster to fall on my own sword."

"Doesn't matter," Solveig said. "Only Hakon and Meshell can mix their teho with that of a dragon. The rest of us can't help."

Irric wiped the back of his hand across his brow in an exaggerated motion. "Best news I've heard all morning."

"Cliona, would you be able to get to the stone?" Solveig asked.

His daughter looked at her hands again. "No. I still haven't found what the limits of this form are. But right now, I can't."

"So, it's simple," Hakon said. "We find the nest—"

"Not so simple," Cliona interrupted. "The teho demons have finished covering the hole, and now they're looking for you. To get between here and there, you'll have to fight."

"Still simple," Hakon continued. "We fight our way to the nest. Then, while you all protect me, I'll talk to the master, and then we'll get the dragon to make us a hole to the stone."

"And then what?" Solveig asked. "We still don't have a plan about what to do when you reach the stone."

A grin spread across Hakon's face. "Actually, I had a thought about that." He looked at Solveig, enjoying the confusion in her expression. "You see, you inspired me."

24

———

When he'd been younger, Zachary had enjoyed the attentions of the best tutors in Mioska. Father had spared no expense educating him, though much of the money had gone to waste. Zachary learned his letters eagerly enough, and basic sums had always come easily to him. The tutors who taught him about the physical world found him a willing student. But the tutors who tried to instill in him a working knowledge of history and philosophy typically ended their service after only a few weeks, claiming they couldn't work with such an impossible young man.

Father had been furious, of course, but Zachary had already developed a stubborn streak. The lessons continued, but with low-quality tutors who were simply eager to have steady pay. Zachary hadn't cared about the stories of people long dead, or the subtle nuances of knowledge. To his mind, people and government were simple. If one was strong enough to exert their will over others, they were obeyed.

Only one lesson from those years remained with

Zachary, and it was the one he was thinking about now. His tutor had been among the worst of a string of poor history tutors, and he'd shown up reeking of wine one morning. Zachary had complained about it, and the tutor had laughed at him. "You wouldn't listen to me if I was sober. So why shouldn't I enjoy myself, too?"

"Father will end your contract."

"He was going to anyway. So again, I ask, why shouldn't I enjoy myself for my last day or two?"

Zachary couldn't say why, but something about the tutor's attitude wormed under his skin, infuriating him. What was even more frustrating was that he couldn't articulate why it bothered him so much. "You shouldn't do that!"

"Why not, young master?" His tutor was mocking him!

Zachary stuttered but didn't have an answer.

The tutor laughed at him. "Cause and effect, Zachary. You haven't paid any attention, so I wouldn't expect you to understand."

"Of course I do!"

"Then explain to me why my behavior is perfectly rational. Why, even, it should have been predicted with your prodigious intellect."

Zachary stammered again.

His tutor tapped him hard on the forehead. The stench of alcohol was overpowering. "Listen well to your last lesson. I know your father plans to end my contract. You've made no progress, despite my efforts. What results?"

"You work harder to maintain your contract." It was what Zachary would expect.

"With a student who has no interest in learning, either from me or the tutors that came before? Be real, Zachary!"

He had never seen his tutor like this. This was more

dramatic, and more interesting, than any of the dry lectures that had come before. He put himself in his tutor's position. He couldn't think of any way that would allow him to keep the contract. "I don't know what I would do."

"Good. We make progress! Your tutor has no good options. His student has ignored and insulted him for weeks, a burden he's endured patiently due to the much-needed salary. But now it is all coming to an end. One more piece of information. Your tutor has a friend who visited the week before last, bringing with him a bottle of wine that remained unopened. Now, what effect follows?"

That answer was easy enough. "You drink the wine."

"I do! And you see, we have multiple causes. A contract that is doomed, a student who will not listen, and an unopened bottle of wine. Given those, how can you not predict the outcome?"

"It seems obvious, when put that way."

"And that, young Zachary, is the whole study of history! Cause after cause, some hidden and some known, which produce effects! The effects become the new causes, and it continues forward, a chain of cause and effect that trickles endlessly through time."

Zachary didn't bother to hide his disdain. "But why should I care?"

"If you understand the causes and what results, it gives you a power over others your father could only dream of!"

Zachary's ears perked up at that.

"The reasons for my drunkenness today are obvious now, are they not? You understand all the causes?"

Zachary agreed.

"So, if you could go back in time, you could, if you wanted, prevent me from being drunk today, correct?"

"Of course. I could either talk to my father and ensure

your contract will continue, or I could listen to your lectures."

"Exactly! And here's the magic—history repeats itself over and over again! If you know something that happened in the past, you can predict what will happen in a similar situation in the present. And in so knowing, you can take advantage of the world like no one else!"

Zachary had very nearly been pacing alongside his tutor when one of the household servants came in to deliver refreshments. She noted the wild behavior and the smell of alcohol, and the tutor had been thrown out within minutes.

There were times when Zachary wondered how he would have turned out if he'd been allowed to continue under the drunk tutor. The next tutor had been old, dry, and dusty as the pages of the ancient books he brought to read out loud to Zachary. His brief interest in history died once again.

But that idea of tracing cause and effect throughout history had always stuck with him. As he went through his correspondence for the day, he wondered what effect his visit to Hallr's would have. Hallr was a coward, but he'd shown surprising steel when Zachary had threatened him.

What would triumph? The coward who knew there was little he could do to prevent Zachary from killing him? Or the believer who looked forward only to the life to come?

Zachary wasn't sure, and his father's admonition to just kill Hallr still echoed in his memories. Given the money and time Hallr appeared to be funneling into the cultists, his murder would have disrupted their organization for a bit. But the cultists had been around before Hallr had joined them, which meant there were other leaders in the movement Zachary didn't know about. He nursed his uncertainties about how he'd handled Hallr, but still believed it was better to have the enemy he knew than the one he didn't.

He'd sent out a few of the household staff on errands that didn't really need to be done. He wanted their eyes and their ears in the streets, and they were still safe from the wrath of the cultists. Those that had returned reported nothing unusual. They said the streets were quiet and that their errands had been completed with a minimum of fuss. No one had noticed any of the posters Zachary had seen the night before.

He dared to hope that these were good omens. All day long, he kept returning to his window and looking out over the city. Every time he saw the quiet scene, he noticed his surprise. But by the time the sun went down, he was almost ready to believe his gambit had worked.

Which was when disaster struck. Thankfully, one of Edda's friends came by with an early warning. A mob gathered in the distance. As soon as Zachary heard, he climbed to the roof of their estate and looked out over the city. He could see the crowd gathered, and the light from the dozens of torches burned bright.

When he saw the mob, Zachary breathed out slowly. His shoulders slumped. It was over. After everything he'd tried, it hurt to have his efforts end this way. But there were fights one couldn't win. If there was more time, maybe he'd be able to change hearts, but time was one resource he had even less of than tehoin.

He returned to where Edda and her friend were huddled together. "I'm leaving," he said. "There's no place for me here, so I'm going to Aysgarth to live with Hel. I'll take Father, too, if he'll have it. Edda, what would you like to do?"

His wonderful sister didn't hesitate. "I would come with you, if you'd have me. It seems to me Mioska isn't much safer for me than it is for you, and I don't want to lose you again."

"Pack light, then. Nothing more than you can carry. Meet me at the front door in a few minutes."

He left Edda to say her goodbyes, then went to Father's room. He found Father standing next to the window. More torches had joined the ones Zachary had seen. The glow from the gathered lights burned brighter now. Father, it seemed, wasn't too surprised by the sight. "Been a long time since I've seen a mob in the streets of Mioska," he said.

"You know they're coming here?"

"Figured."

"There's no point in me staying any longer. Edda and I are escaping to Aysgarth. I would take you with us if you'd like."

Father turned. "I thought I taught you better than that."

If there was ever a worse time for a pointless lesson, Zachary didn't know of it. "How so?"

"Your opportunity for revenge is at hand! And yet you'd take me with you."

Zachary almost told Father he was a fool. That they'd never been enemies. That he'd never wanted revenge. But that was a lie, and they both knew it. A lie that would cheapen whatever relationship they'd built over the last few months.

"Regardless, the offer stands."

Father looked at him for a long time, then glanced out the window. "You're a better man than me. I keep waiting for this world to break you, but even now, you fight on."

Zachary grimaced. They didn't have time for this.

"I'll stay," Father said. "I was born in this house, and I've never left it. I should have died weeks ago. Today, I think I can go to the gate with as light a heart as is possible."

Zachary chewed on his lower lip. Father fought on, always. It was why he'd lived this long. The old bastard would probably live for another five years and take over Aysgarth in the process. At least, that was what Zachary had expected. This, he wasn't prepared for.

He'd thought so often about the revenge he would have on his father. Then he'd surrendered that childish fantasy as he'd reached a truce with the old man. It wasn't a full reconciliation. That was too much to ask. But it had been something, and now he was being asked to give it up.

Every parting phrase he could think of was untrue, though. In the end, he bowed deeply to his father, holding the bow for several long moments. When he rose, he swore he saw a tear on his father's cheek.

"Will you let Edda know? I'd like to see her, briefly, before you leave."

"Of course."

Zachary swallowed the stone forming in his throat. There was too much unsaid, but not enough time to even scratch the surface. He nodded, then turned on his heel and left.

Edda was already near the front door. Her friend, wisely, had left.

"Father says that he wishes to stay. He wants to see you. I'm going to dismiss the guards. Meet me out front as quickly as you can."

Her eyes went wide, but she ran back upstairs to Father's room. She might convince him to leave, but Zachary doubted it. He'd made his decision.

He watched her go, then turned to his own duties. They needed a few more minutes for him to complete his role as master of the house. He went up to his room and threw a few supplies in his pack. He'd never really settled back into his childhood home, so the process didn't take more than a moment. He flung the pack over his shoulders, then went to the front gate. The guards were gathered there, nervous.

"I'm afraid today probably marks the end of your service to the house," Zachary said. "I'd offer references, but I suspect they won't do any of you any good."

Nervous chuckles from the warriors.

"The mob will be here soon. I'll open the gates and leave them open. I'm afraid I won't be able to pay the last amounts due to you. If you want to take the risk, you're more than welcome to help yourself to anything valuable within the house. It's all I can offer."

"Thank you, sir," the commander bowed.

"Now, get out of here," Zachary said. "There isn't much time."

The guards scattered, leaving Zachary alone at the gate. He opened them wide. Already, a few people were gathering in the street outside. Not part of the main mob, but scouts in place to keep an eye on Zachary. They shouted at him, but he cast a shield around him like a bubble and ignored them. It didn't take long for Edda to come out of the house. She carried a pack that matched Zachary's. Tears streamed down her face. Her charms hadn't swayed Father, then.

"Ready?" he asked.

She nodded.

"Stay close to me. I expect there will be some trouble, but nothing I can't handle."

When he was certain she was prepared, he led her through the front gate. A couple of bricks bounced off his shield, barely strong enough for him to notice. One woman charged at him with a knife, but she bounced off his shield as harmlessly as the bricks. Edda's steps were uncertain as the people in the street started to gather closer. Zachary took her hand and pulled her after him. The crowd gathered stones and slammed them into the shield, but they lacked the strength to pose any threat.

The small crowd grew bolder, yelling and striking the shield with whatever was at hand. They couldn't break through, but if he didn't leave soon, it would be hard for Zachary to get through without hurting anyone.

Not only that, but they looked as though they planned on following him wherever he went, and he couldn't have that. "Out of my way! Otherwise, someone is going to get hurt."

He wasn't sure if they didn't care or if they thought he was bluffing. Either way, they didn't move. He pulled Edda closer, then thrust the teho of his shield away. It picked up everyone close and threw them back. They landed hard, but Zachary didn't think he'd hurt anyone seriously.

He formed a new shield and was pleased to see that this time they left him alone. They turned the corner, and for the moment, they were alone.

"Can you run?" he asked.

Edda nodded, and together they took off, putting as much distance between them and the mob as possible. Right away, there was one young man who tried to follow, but Zachary hit him with a teho ball hard enough that he wouldn't get up for a while.

Then the streets were quiet. Zachary led them to the militia barracks, desperately hoping he wouldn't run into any problems there.

Fortunately, the guards let him in without a fuss, and he woke up the two transporters resting in their tents. They were groggy but came to fast.

"I don't think there's going to be much need for

transport soon," Zachary said. "Let's get out of here while we can."

Neither of the transporters argued. If anything, they looked eager to leave. They all hurried to the departure point. Edda pulled her hand away from Zachary's and pointed. "Look."

He followed her finger. Far off in the distance, flames licked the sky. Zachary didn't have to wonder what was burning, or who was in it.

The last hope he'd held out for Mioska snapped. It wasn't as painful as he'd expected.

He grabbed the transporter's outstretched hand, then took Edda's. Then they transported away from Mioska for what Zachary expected was the last time.

25

———

Hakon slapped aside the clawed hand aimed at his face with his sword. The blow opened the teho demon's guard, and Ari threw one of his daggers deep into the demon's chest. The demon wailed, and Hakon cut off its head with the next swing of his giant blade. Before the demon had time to fall, he was on to the next one, leading with the tip of his sword. One stab sent it to the ground, but Hakon stabbed it one more time, just to prevent any surprises.

When he looked up, the battlefield was empty except for the band. The last remains of the demons were drifting away on a warm southerly breeze. Hakon spun slowly around one more time, then sheathed his weapon.

They had suffered a few scratches in the battle but were otherwise unharmed. Given the number of demons they'd just fought, there should have been more healing for Solveig to perform.

Irric kicked at the disintegrating corpse of one of the demons. "Either we got stronger, or they got weaker. None of them were as tough as the one Hakon faced on the way in."

"Maybe there are different classes of demon," Solveig suggested. "We've always known they vary in strength, but maybe the differences go deeper."

It was possible, but Hakon couldn't make a guess one way or the other. "Not going to complain about demons that die this easy, though."

The others muttered their agreement.

"Take a short break, then move on?" Hakon asked.

"I'm good to go," Meshell said.

The rest of the band echoed her sentiment.

"No rest, then. Let's go."

As usual, Hakon took point. After forming their plan with Cliona, they'd decided to circle around the center of the city. Though the demons were spreading out to search for them, the vast majority remained near the filled-in crater. There was no need to pick a bigger fight than the one they already had on their hands, and circling didn't add that much distance to the journey. One way or another, they should be to the nest by nightfall.

Hakon trudged through the snow, breaking fresh trail with every step. The sun was out today, shining bright under a clear sky, and the snow sparkled like crystal ahead. He squinted against the glare and pushed forward.

They encountered another small group of teho demons about a quarter mile later, but the three creatures fell to the band in a brief fight.

Hakon looked back to the center of the city. "You wonder if maybe they're retreating?"

"I think they're less interested in finding us than protecting their stone," Solveig said.

"That's sure how it feels," Hakon said.

Solveig shrugged. "Without Cliona to tell us, I'm not

sure how we would find out. She seems connected to what's happening here in ways I don't understand."

Hakon nodded. "What do you think about her?"

"I haven't had enough time to think about it. I have no doubt in my mind that the last part of her died with the elder dragon, but I can't deny what I've seen with my own eyes."

"Do you think it's her?" Hakon almost didn't ask the question, but Solveig knew Cliona best. She'd supervised and protected his girl when she ran to Vispeda to become an academic.

Solveig thought for a while. "That's not as straightforward a question as I think you mean it as. But I know what you mean, and yes, I think it's her. Her behaviors and mannerisms are all the same."

"Any idea *what* she is?"

Solveig shook her head. "She's the god we once made of the stamfars."

"You think?"

"Don't take my thoughts too seriously. Her appearance still makes me quake in my boots when I think about it too long. It's easier for me not to think about it. She makes me think twice about all the superstitions I thought I'd abandoned over a hundred years ago."

"It's the first time I've thought that she'll outlive me. There's a great deal of comfort in that."

"I can imagine."

He sensed Solveig wanted some time to herself, so he picked up his pace and walked ahead of the others for a while.

The walk was less trying than they expected. They came across one last group of demons that afternoon, but the fight was won in minutes. Hakon wouldn't complain about the ease of their battles, but it made him worry there was something worse to come. There was too much power in the area for anything to be this simple.

It was early evening when they came upon the dragon nest. The dragons hadn't been in the sky all day, but their nest was right where Cliona had told them it would be.

Hakon had seen a few nests in his life, but never one like this. In his experience, dragons preferred mountains for their nests. Once he'd seen a nest inside an abandoned castle, but he'd never seen them take up residence in a whole neighborhood.

They spotted the first nest while still plenty distant. A side of a building was gone, and a dragon's tail hung from the hole like an oversized and stiff rope. It swung back and forth and Hakon had no problem imagining the dragon munching on a carcass inside.

The building across the street had a similar hole, though they couldn't see the dragon within from below. As they advanced, more buildings revealed matching damage. Hakon didn't know if it was proper to call the collection one nest or if there were multiple families here. One way or the other, he'd never seen homes for this many dragons in one place. As he kept counting, he quickly realized there were more dragons here than they'd seen in the sky several days ago.

A different type of building came into view. Although the design of the structures within this city varied widely, the trend was largely the same. They were tall buildings that had the same foundation measurements as the largest manors in the big cities. This structure stood in stark contrast to the others. It was several stories tall but shorter than anything surrounding it. A graceful dome stretched across the top. It was the longest and widest structure they'd seen by far. It also had an enormous hole in one side.

Hakon stopped the band and pointed out what he'd seen. "Anybody have any guesses what lives in there?"

"Something too big to live in any of the other buildings, would be my guess," Irric answered.

"I think that's where we need to go."

Solveig disagreed. "I think that's where you and Meshell need to go."

"We're not separating," Hakon said.

Ari tapped Hakon on the shoulder and pointed upward. "Pay attention, friend."

Hakon looked up. They weren't quite to the nests, but only a few buildings separated them from the outskirts. Their advance hadn't gone unremarked. Dragon heads poked out of every building. More dragons than Hakon had ever seen in one place. Their nostrils flared, and none seemed particularly pleased to have the tehoin there.

"It's either you or Meshell that needs to get there," Solveig said. "And I think they're more likely to let you through if it's just you two. Whatever Cliona says, I can't imagine they'll like tehoin like us getting too close to their master, and it's not like we're going to be able to fight it until it submits. You two are the best choice."

"What will you do?"

"I'm sure we'll find some way to pass the time," Irric said. "I'm still worried about a demon attack, too. We'll find a place a safe distance away and prepare to defend against an attack."

Hakon looked between the others. They seemed set on this course, and although he hated separating, he agreed with Solveig's argument. "Don't you dare die on me. Not here."

Irric snorted. "Speak for yourself. I'd much rather fight an army of teho demons than meet that master face to face."

"Come on," Meshell said, already turning toward the odd structure. "We're losing daylight."

Hakon swallowed hard and stared at his friends, afraid this was the last time he would see them. He committed their familiar faces and this place to his memory so he wouldn't forget. Then he nodded and followed Meshell into the lair of the master dragon.

26

———————

Zachary's unexpected arrival in Aysgarth caused a commotion. Being so much farther west than Mioska, the last rays of daylight still shone above the mountain peaks, and it took his eyes a few moments to adjust to the brighter light. He squeezed Edda's hand tightly before letting it go. Then he took a deep breath of the cold mountain air and released everything he'd been holding within. He let the weight of Mioska's future fall off his shoulders.

It felt good. There would be long conversations with Hel and the council, and countless questions to answer, but once they were done, he would be truly free. The cult that had taken over Mioska had achieved what not even his exile could.

The first sign that all was not well was the look on the guards' faces. The tehoin who'd transported him and Edda ran off to report, but the guards blocked Zachary and Edda from leaving the transport area. Zachary frowned at the behavior, but his head was so jumbled that he accepted the orders without complaint. He kept close to

Edda and waited for someone to tell him what was happening.

Hel was the first to arrive, entering the transport area at close to a run. "Zachary! Why are you here?"

"The cultists mobbed my estate. Burned it to the ground."

Her eyes narrowed, which wasn't the reaction he'd expected. "Are you seeking aid? Tehoin to restore calm?"

"No." He shook his head. The understanding that something more was happening here slowly worked its way through the confusion of the past hour. "Wait. What? No. I came here because I'm done. Because I wanted to be with you."

Her smile reassured him but, at the same time, made him feel a little like he was a child who had done something well-intentioned but misguided.

"What's going on?" he asked.

"The council believes Mioska has broken the treaty. The last shipment of food was supposed to arrive several days ago but was never delivered for transport. We sent inquiries to Governor Agnar but have heard no reply. Our next shipment was supposed to arrive today, but it also hasn't been delivered."

Zachary recalled his flight from Mioska. He'd seen no crates anywhere near the militia barracks. It wasn't conclusive evidence, but it was more than enough for Zachary. The council was right to be concerned. "I'm sorry. I had no idea."

It might have been an accident or miscommunication, but Zachary didn't believe either. Perhaps Agnar was hedging his bets again, but he also could have been swayed by Hallr's arguments. Especially if Hallr was claiming to have evidence from the age of the stamfars.

Which led Zachary to his next point. "Also, I think Valdis, or someone aligned with her, has been working with the cultists."

Hel's first question was almost, "Why?" but she caught herself before it escaped and asked a more meaningful one. "How do you know?"

"I had an encounter with Hallr a day ago. He claimed to have evidence of his beliefs. That there were stamfar who believed that it was tehoin that attracted the wrath of the wild. He claims the proof was found among Marjaana's journals."

"Which are all here," Hel completed the thought for him. She swore softly. "It's good you aren't trying to recruit the tehoin. I don't think they'll aid Mioska anytime soon. Fortunately, we saved more of the food shipments than we ate, but it will still be a hard winter. Most are more willing to attack Mioska than they are to defend it."

A growl escaped from the back of Zachary's throat. It was all so damned pointless. "I don't even think we needed the dragons to attack. If Ava would have been a bit more patient, we would have destroyed ourselves for her."

Hel took his arm. "For now, none of that matters. You and Edda need rest, and if you aren't calling for aid, there's nothing that needs to be decided tonight. Come, let's find someplace for Edda."

Zachary let Hel lead them through the corridors of Aysgarth, through the fortress he might now have to call his home.

~

The next day the Aysgarthian council summoned Zachary before it. He and Hel had expected no less, and they'd spent most of their morning discussing the nuances and outcomes of different possible approaches.

Hel arranged for a guard she trusted to escort Edda around Aysgarth and give her a full tour of the fortress. They hadn't yet talked about their plans for the future, but the tour occupied Edda and introduced her to the area.

Hel left for the council before Zachary, and while she was gone Zachary paced the room. The night before, he had dreamed of his home on fire, the flames reaching up to lick the sky. He'd woken up twice in a sweat, and if he stopped moving for too long the memories returned.

Eventually, he would have to deal with his grief, but not now. Not until their immediate future was secure. He kept pacing, focusing his mind on the meeting to come. When the guard arrived to let him know the council was ready, he followed eagerly behind.

The council room was cold but familiar. He knew the faces and their beliefs, both through his own experiences before the council and through Hel's stories. A glance confirmed everything he'd suspected. He'd find no gratitude here, no receptiveness. Nor would he expect any. He'd convinced them to risk their lives and in exchange, they'd been betrayed. He studied Valdis for a moment. Perhaps that betrayal had more than one facet, but the agreement had been broken by Mioska first. The very people he'd convinced the council they could trust.

He stood up straight, clasping his hands behind his back.

Valdis started the proceedings. "I trust Hel has informed you of the breach of contract?"

"She has. I knew nothing of this before my arrival, but given the situation in Mioska when I left, I'll confess I'm not surprised."

"So you also believe Mioska has willingly broken the terms of our treaty?"

Zachary wasn't sure what direction Valdis hoped to point this inquiry in, but he and Hel had decided the truth was best. Mioska doomed itself. "I have no conclusive evidence one way or another, but it seems likely, yes."

Several of the councilors shared looks with one another, and part of Zachary wished he'd been able to listen to the discussion that took place before he arrived. Some seemed surprised he hadn't argued the accusation.

Valdis watched him closely. "And if you were in our position, how would you react? Why should we maintain an alliance Mioska has no interest in?"

Even though they'd prepared for this, the question still landed like a hammer. "For the last few weeks, I've watched hundreds, if not thousands, of refugees flee to the walls of Mioska. I've seen towns destroyed and lives ruined. I've seen children without parents and farms without farmers. While you sit here, judging what is best for you, humanity is dying. I cannot defend those who rule in Mioska, and their decision to break faith pains me. Not only because it's a betrayal, but because it robs the people hiding behind the walls of their best chance to survive."

He paused to let his words sink in. He had their attention, though there was no telling what would come from it.

"I had hoped, when I first came before you, that there could be benefits for all. That Mioska would buy a shield to protect itself from the encroaching dangers, and that in so doing it would allow Aysgarth to easily survive the rest of the winter. I cannot honestly stand before you and make the same claim today. But I still believe this: we've been given a strength that makes us special. If we don't use it to protect those weaker than us, we are nothing more than monsters."

"You would have us die to protect those that hate us?" Valdis sneered.

He fixed her with a hard stare. Once, she had terrified him. But in the midst of the chaos, that terror had dissipated. He didn't understand why she had helped Hallr, but he was certain of her guilt when he looked at her. "I would ask you to protect those that can't protect themselves. It doesn't matter what they think of it."

Valdis didn't care. "He's admitted that it's likely Mioska has broken the treaty. Does anyone else have questions for him?"

There were none, so he was dismissed.

When the council door closed behind him, he thought he'd feel some sort of despair. He felt sorry for the people of Mioska and wished there was something more he could do. But before his sorrow could reach deep into his heart, he saw the lights of the mob and the flames devouring his house, his father no doubt inside. He shook his head.

It didn't matter. There wasn't anything left for him to do.

The guard offered to escort him back to Hel's quarters, but Zachary passed.

He knew the way.

He looked up when someone knocked on the door. The only person he expected was Hel, but there was no reason for her to knock on her own door. He put the book he'd been reading down and opened the door.

Valdis was about the last person he expected, but she stood in the hall all alone. Before he could invite her in, she pushed him back and stepped inside, closing the door behind her.

A quiet voice in the back of his head screamed that he should be worried, but the rest of him was too tired, too drained to care. "What do you want?" he asked.

She looked around the quarters as though making sure they were empty. "I wanted to be the one to tell you that the council has decided to break the treaty with Mioska. The letter has already been drafted and will be in front of Agnar before the end of the day."

The news came as no surprise. "And?"

His response startled her. "You're not furious?"

All he could manage was a shrug. "Furious. Depressed. Frustrated. All that and more."

"So what will you do?"

"Live what is left of my life in as much peace as I can."

A razor-sharp teho blade appeared in her hand. She pointed it at him. "You fought for this alliance for months. You expect me to believe you would surrender it so easily?"

"It wasn't surrendered easily. But you guaranteed this outcome when you cooperated with the cultists."

She was fast. Zachary vaguely remembered that once she'd given an unsuspecting Hakon a hard time. He'd expected the attack, though, and he had the skills necessary to fight a warrior like her. He brought his own teho blade up, cutting through hers with ease.

Before she could recover, he had his blade pointed at her throat. She retreated, but he followed until she slammed into the wall behind her.

She stammered, trying and failing to understand. For as long as she'd known him, he'd been nothing but a weak vilda. And she'd been looking for an excuse to kill him for as long as she'd known him.

Defeating her was the first glimmer of satisfaction he'd felt in a long time. He pressed the blade hard enough against her neck that it drew blood. Then he let the blade vanish and he stepped back. "Get out of here."

She snarled. "You make me sick! All that strength and you still moan about protecting the weak. When will you realize that tehoin have become something different? Something better?"

He didn't answer, and she left without another word. Hopefully, that would be the end of her attempts on his life. She would probably always hate him, but there was no need to fight.

27

———

Hakon looked up at the dragons in the buildings. They'd built nests in every structure, and most nests had more than one dragon. The creatures stirred as he and Meshell passed, often staring down with their golden eyes. They didn't attack, though Hakon kept thinking they were just waiting for him and Meshell to fall deeper into their trap.

It was a foolish thought. It wasn't as if the dragons needed to set a trap for humans, even if the humans were tehoin.

"What are you thinking about right now?" he asked.

Meshell shook her head. "You really don't want to know."

"You're filled with a deep love and admiration of my decisions?"

She snorted. "Something like that."

A dragon above them spun in a circle, chasing its tail almost like a dog before settling into its nest. Hakon stifled his next comment. Though he didn't think the dragons would attack him for being too loud, it wasn't worth antagonizing them.

They passed between the rest of the buildings without a dragon challenging them. Meshell stopped outside the hole in the enormous structure. This close, they could both feel the enormous teho of the dragon resting inside. It made Hakon's stomach drop. He stepped toward the hole, afraid that if he waited for too long he'd never advance. She held out a hand to stop him.

"It needs to be me," she said.

"What are you talking about?"

"If we're going to blast out that stone, it needs to be me."

"I'm the only one who's ridden a dragon like this before. And we're talking about the biggest one we've ever seen."

"I'm not saying I'm excited about it. I'm saying we don't have a choice. Even if you can cooperate with the dragon, it won't matter. You can't form teho. You can't do anything with the power it gives you."

Suddenly, Hakon was a youth again, on his first mission for the empire, and Brynja was telling him to stay back while the others fought. After a lifetime of battle, training, and discovery, he was still useless. Now, when it mattered more than ever.

The despair passed in a moment. True as it was, it meant nothing, because now he stood with Meshell. The only person he'd ever met who could use teho both internally and externally. He didn't believe in fate, but at that moment, it seemed like everything they'd ever done was to reach this point. To bring her here.

"Besides," Meshell said, trying to soften the blow. "You're the one who needs to touch that stone. Can't do that if you're riding the dragon and protecting the rest of the band."

Hakon shook off the last of his disappointment. He

grinned, and it wasn't forced. "You just want to be the one to ride the dragon."

"It does look like fun," she admitted.

"Then let's do it." He led the way into the building.

Once inside, Hakon paused, looked around, and identified the type of building they had entered. "This is some kind of arena," he said.

The dragon hadn't just torn a hole through the wall. It had cleared a path all the way to the center of the building, where an enormous flat length of ground stretched before them. Thousands of seats surrounded them, looking far more comfortable than the hard benches in the arenas he was familiar with.

"Irric's going to be jealous they made arenas this big," Meshell whispered. "Can you imagine what he'd sacrifice to show off his skills in front of a crowd this big?"

Incredible as the arena was, it paled in comparison to the dragon resting at its center. The dragon was every bit as big as Hakon remembered, a building of muscle, armored hide, and teho capable of destroying anything on this planet.

Often, when the weight of the world had threatened to crush Hakon, he looked up to the stars. Even before he knew that people had traveled between them, he'd known just how vast the universe was. He looked at the sky and tried to imagine the enormity of *everything*, and when he did, he realized that nothing in his own life mattered all that much.

Looking at the master dragon made him feel the same. The power of the stamfar was incredible and beyond anything Hakon ever dreamed of wielding. But it was still understandable. He could compare it to his own strength, and the comparison made sense.

There was no point comparing himself to this. To call his strength a drop in an ocean seemed insufficient. Even at rest, teho warped the air around the dragon.

Its eyes flicked toward Hakon, and Hakon almost bent a knee at the force of that gaze. It carried a physical weight.

Meshell muttered a curse under her breath. Then she whispered, "I'm starting to reconsider this plan."

"If it wanted to kill us, it would have already."

"I don't think it would even have to move."

They stood rooted in place. Hakon tried to take a step forward, but his feet refused to budge. "The longer we wait, the more time we leave for something bad to happen," he said.

She gritted her teeth. "I can't move."

"Its gaze," Hakon said. "Damn."

The dragon's chest expanded, and Hakon feared it was going to unleash a blast of teho that would tear the flesh off their bones. Instead, the dragon's lids closed over its eyes. The weight lifted from Hakon's shoulders, and he could once again step forward.

Meshell advanced, and it looked to him like she was stepping in front of a charging army of teho demons. He tried to follow, but it wasn't a lack of strength that failed him now. It was a failure of courage. His feet could move. He just couldn't convince himself to accompany Meshell.

One cautious step at a time, she approached the master dragon. And then she was standing next to it. She closed her eyes, reached out, and touched its neck.

Hakon braced himself for whatever might happen. He realized, for the first time, he was standing between the dragon and the exit, and finally his feet started to shuffle him out of the way.

Meshell's voice stopped him. It sounded like it came

from a long way away, muffled by thick walls. He couldn't hear what she said.

He looked over at her. She was standing in the same position, hand against the neck of the dragon. The dragon's tail was swishing across the ground as though it was agitated.

Meshell's face was pale. She repeated herself, and the words finally reached his mind. He felt the blood draining from his own face.

"I can't do it," she said. "I can't join with its teho."

28

For two wonderful days, Zachary pretended that all was well with his life. Hel's role on the council meant constant demands on her time, but whatever she could spare, she spent with him. They walked for hours, talking not about the threats that loomed over every waking moment but about the small details of their time apart. Whenever the subject came too close to Ava, the dragons, or the fates of Mioska and Aysgarth, they veered away like a scout avoiding an enemy army.

He and Edda both settled quickly into new routines. Aysgarth had tremendous needs, and Hel found them roles to suit their abilities. Despite her concerns, Hel followed Zachary's suggestion to put him to work with the laborers repairing the walls. He'd requested the work because he wanted something to do, something as physical as possible and as far away from politics as he could run. He no longer represented anyone except himself. The long days of working with heavy stone suited him perfectly.

Edda helped Hel as an administrator. She had a natural affinity for numbers and organization. Hel privately claimed

Edda had done more for Aysgarth in one day of work than the council had done in a month. Zachary stopped by to check on Edda during his mid-day break and found her working at a frightening pace. But she found the same peace in numbers he found in his labors, so he didn't disturb her.

Grief remained a constant presence, always lurking in the back of his mind. But so long as he kept busy, it never became a problem. Someday he would have to confront what had happened to his home and his father, but the wounds were too fresh and raw for him to look at.

Despite his efforts to distance himself from the news, there was no avoiding the knowledge of what was happening in the Six States. Aysgarth kept its web of spies active, and the transport areas were busy day and night with messages shuttling back and forth. Hel and the rest of the council did nothing to stop the flow of information, and he inevitably heard the latest.

The Six States continued to fall, faster than before. The wild forces, attacking from all corners of the frontier, joined as they moved farther east. Settlers fled for the cities as fast as their feet could carry them. The northwestern state of Bravol, sparsely populated, was almost gone. Zachary heard rumors of isolated villages that held out, but not often. The wild had pushed forward and entered Holar both through Bravol and the wastes to the north. Many of the hordes from Bravol had stalled against Holar's westernmost cities, but the surge from the wastes was accompanied by dragons, and that was the wedge driving toward Mioska.

The news wasn't always grim. Vispeda had organized a defense that had pushed the wild back. Zachary was impressed. The militia there had been in rough shape when he'd last visited.

Only one argument ruined his otherwise peaceful days

in Aysgarth. Edda wanted him to find Tollak and bring him to Aysgarth. Zachary argued that Tollak had hired a band of mercenaries to kill him the last time they'd met, but Edda remained firm. He was family, and at the very least, he deserved to know what happened to Father.

Zachary only relented when Hel got involved. She told him they wouldn't rest until they'd at least visited the village where Zachary had exiled his brother. Reluctantly, he agreed.

That evening, after Hel finished her work with the council, she and Zachary transported to the village. As he'd feared, they were far too late. The village had been attacked, and the wooden wall which had protected the village was broken in places. Zachary didn't see any signs of dragons, but from the blood that stained the streets, it hadn't mattered. The wild had taken any corpses and gorged on them, and though they searched the village thoroughly, they found no sign of Tollak dead or alive. If he'd stayed and fought, he was almost certainly dead and devoured. If he'd run, there was no telling where in the Six States he was. They returned to Aysgarth to report the news to Edda.

The news hit his sister harder than Zachary expected. She'd had no problems when he'd exiled Tollak to the far frontier for his crimes, but apparently, that was only because she knew he'd been alive. Despite the attempted murder of his sibling, she still believed he was worth saving.

Edda saw the best in everyone, a trait Zachary admired. It was even more impressive considering the environment in which they'd grown up. Father had taught them to judge and manipulate people with the same skill Edda juggled her numbers. Somehow, it hadn't colored her perspective the way it had Zachary's.

Hel assured Edda that she would create posters of Tollak

to distribute among her web of transporters. If he had escaped and he was alive, they would do all they could to find him. Edda wasn't satisfied, but she acknowledged it was all they could do.

With that done, Zachary settled once more into the routine of Aysgarth. He thrived in the long days and took satisfaction in the visible progress of their work.

He couldn't always stop his thoughts from wandering, though. Guilt gnawed at him. Despite all he'd suffered at the hands of Mioska's citizens, it still seemed wrong to hide here in Aysgarth as the world he'd known his whole life burned to the ground. Every day he received word of another town falling, and his heart grew calloused to the reports.

His life became a paradox.

Holar, the state where he'd always dreamed about being governor, was in the middle of its collapse. Its defense should have consumed his life and attention.

Instead, he had nothing to do with any of it. His greatest concerns were the shape and fit of the stones of a wall hundreds of miles from Holar's borders. And he was happier for it.

Thousands died by the day.

He enjoyed meals with his fiancée and sister.

He felt the paradox as a tension inside him, a twisting feeling in his stomach like he was falling. But he chiseled away at rocks and moved stone from one part of the wall to another. If he never looked closely, he could fall forever and always be fine.

The tension finally snapped one morning. It had started like any other. He'd broken his fast with the people closest to him. Hel went to receive the latest batches of reports, Edda went to work on the enormous ledgers Hel had her maintain, and Zachary went to the wall, eager to fit a particularly troublesome piece of rubble back into the wall.

Hel found him just as they'd finished putting mortar around the stone. Her face was pale, and the tension in Zachary twisted until he thought he might throw up. His first thought was for his family.

"Tollak?" he asked.

She shook her head. "Our scouts spotted the dragons. Ava is with them, riding upon an elder. They'll strike Mioska today."

29

Hakon wanted to shout at Meshell, but the presence of the master stilled his tongue. There couldn't be a "can't." Not when everything rode on her shoulders.

He also didn't want to walk toward Meshell and the dragon, but he was out of choices. He forced one foot forward, then the other. The dragon's eyes remained closed, and it didn't take him long to reach Meshell's side. There was barely enough light to see by as the world turned dark outside.

He leaned close and barely dared a whisper. "What do you mean *you can't*?"

She didn't seem to fear louder sounds, and she responded at a normal volume. "I can't. I try to mix my teho with its, just like you said. But the moment I do, it overwhelms me. All I can do is separate myself."

"Did you let it flow through you?"

Her glare was answer enough. They'd spoken of this before meeting the dragon.

Hakon considered the problem. Meshell had spoken true when she'd said it must be her riding the dragon.

Hakon might be able to utilize the dragon's strength, but he couldn't shape it in the way that was needed. It had to be Meshell. He only had one idea. "We can try it together."

She didn't look particularly enthused by the idea, but she held out her hand. He took it, and they each reached out to touch the dragon. The amount of teho flowing through the dragon almost burned his hand, though there was no heat. He forced his eyes closed so he could focus on the flow of teho.

He mixed his and Meshell's first, a technique that made his arm tingle. Immediately, he noticed a problem. Skilled as she was at manipulating the teho inside her body, there were channels where teho didn't flow smoothly. At her current strength, it meant little. But with the teho of a dragon coursing through her, those small imperfections would become turbulent and painful places. Without words, he brought her attention to those spots. Together, they smoothed out the flow of teho. It was slow work. He felt her grimace at the pain but bore it silently.

When the flow was as smooth as he could make it, he whispered again. "Ready?"

"I think so."

Before either of them had time to doubt, he let the barriers between them and the dragon fall. The experience was similar to him joining with the elder or touching the stone, but the sheer power of the joining made this feel wholly different. The dragon's teho filled him in less than the space of a heartbeat, and his own teho channels burned with the new strength. It was no wonder Meshell had needed to break away. The slight imperfections in her teho channels must have felt as though she was being torn limb from limb.

Together they bore the agony, sharing the excess

between them. Hakon couldn't say if they had been joined for a moment or a day, but once the initial agony passed, he found himself at peace. He stood in a vast emptiness, a construct of the master dragon's creation. He spun, the direction meaningless. Then Meshell appeared next to him, and they were both still.

Hakon wanted to talk to Meshell, but words seemed disrespectful in this place. It had the feel of the sacred, and he felt honored simply to be here. He reached out his hand and entwined his fingers with her, awaiting what came next. They waited for what felt like hours, but Hakon suspected the dragon's perspective of time was different from his own.

Without any warning, his body vanished. He became a rider on the back of a being far vaster than any mere human. His awareness expanded, encompassing not just the familiar sensations of sight, sound, and touch. He saw the world with new eyes, teho pulsing through the planet like blood through his veins. The heart beat, strong, rich, and generous with its gifts. Life flourished, in forms both familiar and not. He flew above it all, both intimately connected with everything below and something separate.

Streaks of fire burned across the sky, a familiar memory from a different angle. Years passed in moments, a perspective the historian in Solveig would have killed to experience. Ages of human history, all little more than the blink of an eye for this creature. Humans expanded, unified by a purpose that rose above their petty squabbles. Then shrank, as one purpose became many.

The cycles repeated, so often Hakon wanted to rage at what he saw. The expansions were times of prosperity, of new creations and new knowledge. But for every expansion, there was a matching contraction. A period of war and destruction.

Until one war broke all the others, erasing the years of progress and so much more. Lives and history were lost, the survivors fleeing east across the mountains, all under the watchful eyes of the master and its kin.

More cycles followed, the expansion reaching once again outward. Until the Rebellion and the division of the Six States. Hakon saw his own sword, cracking the foundation of the empire. Humans fought and bled as the web of teho weakened all around them. It pooled among those who could already access it. The stamfar grew stronger as their peers died. The master gained strength with the death of every dragon. Not enough was returned.

Looking down at it now, the whole Rebellion seemed so *pointless.* All that blood spilled, all that progress lost, for ideals that now seemed so very far away.

The scenes ended, and he was back in his own body, looking down at his hands as though he expected them to be covered with blood. Meshell stood beside him. As far as Hakon could sense, there was no one else with them in the space, but the question hung unspoken in the air.

This is what you have done. What can you do now to fix what has been broken?

Hakon stepped forward. Though this construct was a void, it wasn't empty. Here he felt at peace, only matched by the feeling he'd felt when he'd once neared the gate. Though the master had every reason to despise humanity, Hakon sensed none. It cared only about restoring a balance lost long ago. That equanimity toward his species gave Hakon hope.

He showed the dragon what he planned. As with the stone, his imagination and will painted the scene directly upon the dragon's awareness. Language couldn't cross the void between them, but intent could.

The void rumbled as Hakon finished showing the master his plan. The dragon seemed satisfied by Hakon's offering.

He turned back to Meshell. "Your turn."

She joined him. "How did you do that?"

"Imagine it, put your will into it as though you were forming a teho blade. It will respond."

She did, and Hakon was treated to the sight of her riding the master into battle and using the master's strength to uncover the stone.

The void rumbled again, and this time Hakon thought he sensed a hint of amusement in the dragon's acceptance.

Thick blood appeared, running in a narrow stream between their feet. Hakon didn't know what it represented, but Meshell understood. She formed a knife and cut across the palm of her left hand. She squeezed it into a fist and dripped the blood into the stream.

She looked up at Hakon, a wry smile on her face. "No backing out now."

Hakon imagined a blade, and one appeared in his hand. He grunted to himself. After all this time, he finally felt what it was like to be a normal tehoin. He mirrored Meshell's action.

As soon as his blood struck the stream, a fresh wave of strength filled his limbs. But there was a binding inherent in the strength. Meshell was right.

They were all committed now.

30

I n the back of his mind, Zachary had known the decision
was coming. The attack on Mioska was as inevitable as
the sun rising every morning. For days, he'd wondered if he
would truly be able to sit by and watch as the city he still
called home was destroyed for good. Most days, he believed
that he could.

When the moment came, he was surprised at how easy
the choice was. He pulled off the gloves that protected his
hands, then brushed his palms off on his pants. "Will you
take me?"

Hel nodded. "Someone has to bring you back."

"We need to tell Edda."

Hel reached out her hand, then transported them both
into her quarters. "Go," she said. "I'll come to her workroom
when I'm ready. There are a few details I need to take care of
before I leave."

She left the rest unspoken. Aysgarth needed to be
prepared in case she didn't return. Zachary would have
argued with her. This was his fight and his fight alone.
Pointless as his presence was, he couldn't live with himself if

he didn't try to help. But Hel wouldn't listen if he tried. She'd made her decision. While he'd try to protect Mioska, she'd protect him.

Zachary ran through the halls. At this time of day, Edda wouldn't be in her quarters. Hel had supplied her with a small study close to her own, and Edda would no doubt be pouring over her ledgers for the day. He entered the tiny room without knocking. She jumped, then put her hand to her chest when she saw who it was. "What happened?"

"Mioska is under attack."

He didn't have the chance to say the rest. She rose and embraced him. "Come back, if you can."

He held her tightly. "I will. Don't lose faith."

She broke away. "Is Hel going with you?"

"She is." Something about the scene bothered him, but it took him a moment to figure out what. "Wait. You're not surprised?"

Edda shrugged. "A little, maybe, but I'd hoped you would fight. I'm not sure I'd want to be around you if you didn't."

Hel appeared behind them before Zachary could answer. "I'm ready," she said.

"Must be Valdis' greatest day ever," Zachary muttered.

"Not when we return," Hel said. She held out her hand.

Zachary took it. He grinned at Edda, braced himself, then nodded to Hel.

The peace of Aysgarth vanished, replaced by the familiar sights of the militia barracks. Zachary summoned a teho sword to his hand, but all his action earned was the confused look of a single guard.

Zachary lifted his gaze. Mioska seemed exactly the way it had been when he'd left it. Embarrassment flushed his cheeks and he turned to look at Hel. It seemed her web of spies wasn't as good as she thought it was.

Before he could chastise her, his world shook, and he almost lost his balance. The loudest thunder he'd ever heard blasted his eardrums, and he clapped his ears to the side of his head. When the echoes finally faded, he looked behind him.

The walls of Mioska still stood, but flashes of light, brighter than the sun, sparked across the sky. Another wave of thunder crashed over him. He felt the sound in his bones.

A chunk of wall exploded off the top, flying well over Zachary's head and landing in the streets on the other side of the barracks. Human figures were flung from the flying wall, landing with sickening thuds. Both he and Hel crouched low as though it would make a difference.

He pointed to a section of intact wall. "Can you get us there?"

Hel nodded, grabbed his wrist, and they appeared on the wall between two sets of guards. They jumped at the new arrivals, but Zachary cast a shield around both him and Hel. He wasn't eager to trust any of the militia anytime soon. The shield also protected him, a bit, from the fight before him.

He spotted Ava and her dragons first. Five of them circled in the air, and at least one of them was clearly an elder. It took him a moment to understand why they hadn't leveled the city, though.

His answer came when he saw a diminutive figure standing in the fields outside the city walls. Isira's childlike form stood as the last line of defense against the dragons. Teho spears sped into the air faster than any arrow. The dragons spun and scattered, clearly not interested in being struck by the weapons.

When the spears missed, they twisted in the air, then came crashing down. Ava, riding the elder, formed her own spears to intercept Isira's. Zachary guessed what was to come and strengthened his shield. The spears struck one another, lighting up the sky once again like lightning on a clear day.

The blasts buffeted his shield, but Zachary held it easily. He tore his gaze away from that duel to study the rest of the battlefield. For now, the only enemies he saw were Ava and the dragons. The flood of wild animals he feared wasn't here yet. It wasn't much of a difference, but it gave him a glimmer of hope.

Ava leaped from the elder. She fell from the sky, as graceful as a falling stone. Then teho wings bloomed from her back, and she landed softly in front of Isira.

From a distance, the two opponents looked foolish next to one another. Ava was a tall woman, and Isira was a short child. But Zachary figured the result of their duel would change not just the fate of Mioska, but all the Six States. He was about to ask Hel to transport him to the duel when she tugged on his arm and pointed up.

He swore.

Isira's efforts hadn't slain any dragons, but they had kept them away from Mioska. Now she didn't dare make any move away from Ava, which left the dragons free to do as they pleased. The elder led them down toward the city. They folded their wings in, diving faster. They spread out as they fell.

Zachary formed a teho spear. From this distance, he wasn't sure there was anything he could do. But he hadn't come all this way not to try. He threw the spear with all his might, blowing snow away from his feet as he launched it. It flew almost as fast as Isira's had.

He'd thrown at one of the outer dragons. Strengthened as his brush with death might have left him, he had no chance of taking down an elder in flight.

The dragon didn't try to evade the spear, and Zachary subtly adjusted its flight as it neared the falling beast.

He hit it true, right near the center of its chest.

The dragon shrugged the blow off as though it had been playfully slapped.

A moment later, both it and its siblings struck Mioska. The force of teho blew down buildings as they passed, and they lowered their heads to break through anything sturdy enough not to bow before them.

They tore through the city without slowing, leaving wide gouges of destruction behind them. Besides Zachary's spear, not a single teho weapon sought to bring the dragons down. The tehoin were either dead or in hiding.

The dragons finished their pass and lifted up into the air. They circled around and dived again.

Zachary stood open-mouthed, he couldn't imagine how many had died in that first pass. The devastation was only just beginning. His new strength, and his appearance here, were both meaningless.

Mioska was doomed.

31

Hakon broke apart from Meshell and the master dragon. The sudden lack of teho made him feel empty inside. But he didn't dare reach for the dragon again. The bargain had been struck. He envied Meshell for her connection. He stepped away from the master, no longer afraid. Outside, the sun was rising on a new day. Their negotiations with the dragon had lasted the whole night.

Meshell opened her eyes and scrambled up the dragon's neck. Its armored scales were large enough that she had no problem finding hand and foot holds. When she reached the top of the neck, she looked down at him.

Her eyes seemed to see through him, and he felt a push against his teho. "You should go. The others will be nervous."

Hakon bowed to her, then turned and ran. He felt when the dragon opened its eyes and began to shift. Teho flooded the arena, and a wave of power swept him out the exit. He barely kept his feet. He came to a stop just outside the hole, then realized how poor a place that was for him to be. If the master came flying out, he'd be squashed flatter than a piece of parchment.

He ran off to the side to get out of the way, then ran toward the others. Solveig waved from the side of a building well away from the arena. They stood when he approached.

Before they could ask, the master sped from the hole in the arena wall like an enormous arrow shot from a bow. Hakon caught a brief glimpse of Meshell pressed tight against the master's neck, a wide grin on her face. In all their years together, he wasn't sure he'd ever seen such an expression of unbridled joy.

"I take it the master agreed?" Irric said.

In answer to the question, the dragons in their nests began to stir. Small pieces of debris fell from above, and the band pressed themselves against the buildings. One by one, the dragons emerged, stretching their wings and flexing teho to take to the air. They chased after the master, who was barely more than a speck in the sky. They circled like carrion eaters over a particularly tasty morsel.

Solveig was the first to tear her eyes away from the sight. "We need to get as close to the center of the city as we can. When Meshell reveals the stone, we want to reach it quickly."

Before they left, Hakon addressed them. "Thank you, again, for everything. You've followed me a lot longer than I've possibly deserved."

The others shared a look, and it was Ari that answered. "About time you figured it out."

Irric clapped Hakon on the shoulder hard enough that it stung. "I can't believe I'm saying this, but I'd do it all over again, even if I knew what was to come."

Ari grunted but kept his comments to himself.

They ran toward the center of the city. Meshell, the

master, and all the other dragons remained far above, waiting. The band was still a good half mile from the crater when they ran into their next problem.

Teho demons stood in ranks, blocking their advance.

More than before.

When the band caught sight of the first demons, they took cover behind the corner of a building. The demons didn't pursue.

They watched for a while, long enough to confirm that the remaining streets between them and the crater were also flooded with demons.

"Did they make a bunch of little teho demon babies while we weren't looking?" Irric asked.

"Nothing little about those demons," Hakon answered.

"Or the heart is capable of creating the demons," Solveig said. "We've always wondered where the first ones came from."

"It's doing everything it can to keep us away," Hakon said. He pulled at his beard. "Wish there was some way we could convince it we're trying to help."

"If you want to go talk to one of those demons, I'd be more than happy to watch," Irric said.

"Thanks," Hakon said.

Solveig looked up. "We can't reach the heart anyway. No point in committing suicide for a task we can't complete. I think this is as close as we get until the dragons decide what they're going to do."

They didn't wait long. Hakon felt teho gathering above. When he looked up, the dragons had spread out. The master flew alone, surrounded by unbelievable amounts of teho.

Hakon had no doubt that the master possessed the strength necessary to reach the heart. But a dragon couldn't shape teho. That ability was unique to humans. Which meant the most important unanswered question was whether or not Meshell could shape and focus the enormous strength that was about to be channeled through her. It was a level of power far beyond anything she'd ever attempted. Though she would be little more than a passage for the dragon's teho, even that role might be too much for her body to handle.

They would know soon enough.

Hakon held his breath as he saw the master turn toward the center of the city and begin its descent. The teho demons looked up, screaming in unison, a shrill, trilling sound that made Hakon wince. The demons started climbing the surrounding buildings as though they intended to leap onto the master when it came too close.

More teho gathered around the master. Hakon swore he caught another glimpse of Meshell, glowing with white light. They fell together, growing stronger with every foot they dropped. The power built and built, focused by Meshell's will. Though it seemed impossible she could continue, she accepted even more teho. It was already the most powerful attack Hakon had ever felt, and it only continued to grow. He kept thinking she had to release it, but the moment never came.

He feared that she would push herself too hard. That she would die before releasing the teho. He thought of his own emptiness when he'd broken away from the dragon. That kind of power wasn't just a temptation. It was a physical pull, a sudden need you didn't even know you'd possessed.

The light above the dragon flashed, and teho twisted in Hakon's gut so strongly he fell to his knees. "Take cover!" he shouted.

He took his own advice, pressing himself tight against the building and curling into as small a ball as he could. He filled his body with teho. Ari, Irric, and Solveig all cast overlapping shields over the group.

The world went white.

The air cracked so loud it felt as though all the bones in his body had broken into pieces. A hundred thunderstorms rumbled at once and the ground heaved Hakon into the air. He smacked the back of his head on Irric's inner shield.

Then that was it. The others dropped their shields, looking at the buildings around them as though surprised they were still standing.

Hakon peeked out around the corner, rubbing the back of his head. He expected dust and debris but saw nothing. The air was clean, and the sun still sparkled off the snow in the street. Had it worked?

His only hint came from the teho demons. As one, they had turned toward the city center and were pouring that way.

Hope blossomed in his heart. If they were hurrying to defend the stone, Meshell must have reached it. He looked up in time to see the master return to the sky, Meshell still upon its back. It roared, and dozens of answering roars came from the other dragons.

Younglings and elders alike banked in the air and dove into the streets of the city, devouring and scattering teho demons with reckless abandon. One cleared the street between Hakon and the heart, and he took off behind it, buffeted by the force of its passing. It snapped one teho demon up in its jaws, then raked its talons across two more. They all died, flaking away in the passing of the dragon.

Hakon made it half the distance to the center before he had to draw his sword. But before he could swing, a pair of teho spears blasted over his shoulder and into the demon's head. It fell silently, and Hakon turned his attention to the next demon between him and the heart. The demon ran toward the heart, ignoring Hakon. It paid with its life.

Another dragon swooped in, using a cross street in front of Hakon. It killed another handful of demons before it crashed into the ground.

Hakon was confused until he saw the demons crawling along the dragon's back. They plunged claw and talon into the dragon's armored scales, ripping and tearing out flesh as though a chest of gold had been hidden underneath.

Hakon ran past the dragon. Allies or not, all that mattered was reaching the heart.

He watched similar scenes happen across the center of the city. The dragons were far more powerful and mobile, but there were so many demons, and they were damned clever. They launched themselves from buildings anytime a dragon passed by, and if two or three could latch on, they were enough to bring a youngling down. Five or six could kill an elder.

Hakon and the band were still able to advance, though. The sacrifice of the dragons prepared the way. The demons who weren't interested in the dragons were focused on reaching the heart instead of fighting the band.

He looked up, hoping the master and Meshell might be able to tilt the battle permanently in their favor. But when he saw them, they were over another part of the city all together.

He realized why when he came into the city center and climbed over the first layer of rubble.

The heart hadn't just called on teho demons. It had called *everything*. Herds of deer. Packs of wolves and shadow wolves. Bears. Everything ran toward the center of the city.

From his perch on top of part of a destroyed building, he saw the hole Meshell had made. The blue glow emanated from it, confirming that she had reached the heart. But teho demons were jumping into the hole one after the other.

Hakon waved to the others to follow him. The dragons could handle the demons that remained.

Off in the distance, the master and Meshell unleashed another devastating assault of teho. But the band didn't have long. There were simply too many creatures on the way. Hakon had minutes at most to reach the heart and end this.

They scrambled over the rubble, reaching the hole together. Unlike the first crater, which had been dozens of feet wide, this one wasn't much wider than the heart. But it was filled with dozens of demons, an impassable maelstrom of death.

Through the whirling limbs, Hakon caught sight of another problem. One demon, bigger than all the rest, had wedged itself just above the stone. It had four arms, all ending in sharp talons, and it was looking up, just waiting for someone to dive into the hole.

If Meshell had been here, he would have asked her to clear it again. But she was elsewhere, protecting them against waves of the wild. And he wasn't sure they had time for her to reach them. The demons were carving into the walls of the tunnel, hoping to collapse it once again.

Irric formed a half dozen spears above the mouth of the tunnel. "We'll clear the way."

He didn't wait for an answer. He launched his first spears into the tunnel, killing two demons with his first assault. More spears appeared in the air. The swordsman didn't give himself a moment to rest.

Ari and Solveig joined in.

The three of them working together rained sharpened

teho into the tunnel, tearing through the first layers of demons.

Hakon risked a glance up. Far fewer dragons flew in the air above them, and those that did looked too wary to approach closer. Meshell and the master flew a ways away, but the first of the wild creatures was already reaching the edge of the rubble.

He filled his body with teho and looked back down into the hole. The relentless assault of teho shredded the demons, but they were rapidly running out of time, and the others were tiring. They'd fought whole battles in the past using less teho than they'd used in the last few heartbeats. But all three kept pouring their souls into the effort.

Ari stumbled, almost following one of his spears into the hole. Solveig grabbed him, but that was enough for Hakon. Most of the demons in the hole were dead.

"Protect yourselves!" he shouted as he jumped into the hole.

He felt a band of Irric's teho wrap around his waist and slow his fall. When he was about thirty feet above the heart, Irric let go, and Hakon dropped into the last of the demons, his enormous sword pointed down. He pierced the last demon even as it tore through his arms with its talons.

Hakon didn't feel the pain. He and the demon fell together into the heart, where the demon died in agony. Hakon lay on his side, the demon's final attack draining blood from dozens of cuts, some of them through his organs.

He ignored his wounds, closed his eyes, and drove his teho into the heart.

32

Zachary stood, frozen, upon the walls of the Mioska. The commander of the walls had finally recognized him, and as he was desperate for direction, he was shouting at Zachary for orders. But Zachary had none to give.

Once, there might have been a chance. They could have united tehoin and militia and developed strategies for fighting against the dragons. Terrifying as the creatures were, they still died, especially under coordinated assaults. Ava had only brought five. A frightening number, but he could imagine ways to beat them.

Now, though, they had nothing. Divided, what little chance they might have had vanished like smoke in the wind.

The dragons struck again, sowing destruction wherever they passed. Buildings crumbled as they passed. From the screams echoing down the streets, Zachary assumed no one had gotten to the caverns. If this council had even opened them for protection.

He stammered, desperately wanting there to be

something he could do. Stronger than ever, and at best he might distract one of the younglings for a time.

More eruptions slammed into his back, and when he turned, he saw that Isira had been joined by two other tehoin. Zachary didn't recognize them, but a moment of studying the battle told him they wouldn't be enough. Ava was still more powerful.

"Zachary." Hel's voice focused him back on Mioska.

He saw the cause of her concern. One of the younglings was standing on top of two houses, staring at them. It spread its wings, and Zachary felt the teho gathering. It launched itself at Zachary, and he flung a spear at its face. It shifted its face to the side and Zachary's spear glanced off its armor. He froze in place as enormous jaws opened wide to swallow him whole.

Hel grabbed him and transported them a moment before the dragon struck. The transport hadn't been far because Zachary still felt the teho of the dragon's passing. She'd only moved them a dozen feet to the side, still on the wall. Now they stood next to the pale-faced commander. The section of wall they'd been standing on was halfway gone.

The youngling rose into the air and banked around for another pass.

"Any ideas?" Zachary asked through clenched teeth.

"Outside of leaving, no."

Zachary formed another spear and flung it at the falling dragon, but it skipped harmlessly off the dragon's scales. If he could hit something vital, he thought he could wound the creature, but it wasn't giving him any opportunities.

He was just about to grab Hel's hand for a transport back to Aysgarth when a bright light shone from behind them. He suddenly cast a long shadow that stretched almost to where the battle between Ava and the others was taking place. The youngling spread its wings and took to the sky. Zachary glanced back, but the light was blinding. It was pure white and almost painful to look at.

Whatever it was, the dragons didn't like it. All five had taken to the sky and were circling high above. They roared but dared not come closer. Zachary couldn't tell why, though. The light was bright, but it released no teho.

The light drifted toward the wall where Zachary stood. It dimmed as it approached, revealing a human figure.

Cliona landed beside him as softly as though she'd been gently placed there by a giant hand. "Good to see you again, Zachary."

"You, too."

Cliona turned to Hel. "And you must be Hel." She gave a bow, deep enough to honor the head of the Aysgarthian council. "It's a pleasure to finally meet you."

Hel handled the appearance of the stranger with surprising calm. "Cliona, I assume?"

"Yes." But Cliona's attention was on the battle happening outside the walls, between the stamfar. The ground still rumbled with the exchange of blows.

"Are you here to save us?" Zachary asked.

Cliona shook her head. "I'm not strong enough. I can't fight Ava. But there is something I can do." She lifted her hand and pointed at the dragons. "I can wrest control of those dragons away from her."

"What will that do?" Hel asked.

"There's...a truce between humanity and the dragons at the moment. The pact was formed less than an hour ago. If I remove Ava's control, the dragons should abandon their assault of Mioska."

Somehow, Zachary knew the pact had been forged by

the band. It seemed like something they would do. But part of Cliona's answer bothered him. "Should?" Zachary asked.

Cliona shrugged. "Can't guarantee any more than that. Quiet, please. This isn't easy."

Hel and Zachary watched as Cliona stood there. It didn't look like she was doing anything, and Zachary couldn't feel any manipulation of teho. He looked around and saw the commander staring at him, wide-eyed and open-mouthed. When he looked back toward Mioska, he saw no small number of citizens and militia doing the same from the streets.

He supposed Cliona had made quite the entrance.

She spoke. "It's done."

Zachary looked up. The dragons circled for a moment more, then roared and turned west. Before long, they were out of sight.

"Thanks," Zachary said.

"It's not enough, but it's a start." Cliona looked at Zachary. "I don't know how you'll do this, but it's up to you and the others to kill Ava."

She was already fading. Zachary could see through her to the broken wall beyond.

"I'll do what I can," he said.

The last part of her that disappeared was her smile.

When she was gone, Zachary turned to Hel. The battle still raged in the fields beyond the wall. "You don't have to help me with this."

"Already here," she said. She held out her hand and he took it.

They transported into the battle.

For several moments, Zachary could do nothing but stand in amazement and watch. Teho darts, spears, and shields were everywhere. The power was beyond compare, but it was matched with lifetimes of skill and experience. When teho met teho, the world exploded, but the warriors stood their ground, protected by the shields they maintained.

Isira unleashed the greatest amount of teho, slamming dart after dart on top of Ava's shields. She attacked so relentlessly that it seemed impossible that Ava could do anything but defend. But Ava's shield held under the assault, and she returned everything she took and more. She even had time to launch attacks at the other tehoin who had gathered behind Isira.

Those tehoin were kolma, and Zachary had little trouble deciphering their strategy. They attacked as often as possible but never tried to block Ava's responses. He imagined that if they tried, they'd pay dearly. At least one of the tehoin was a transporter, and he saved the other several times.

Zachary didn't know what else to do except add his strength to the battle. He created a spear, as strong as his current strength allowed, and flung it at Ava.

As he expected, it bounced harmlessly off her shield. The only recognition he received for his efforts was a brief glance in his direction. A teho dart strong enough to destroy Mioska's wall dropped from the sky a moment later.

Zachary took his elders' tactics to heart and didn't try to defend. The moment he felt it, he dove away. The dart blew a crater in the ground, sending dirt and snow high into the air. Zachary rolled to his feet and prepared another spear, looking for some opening.

There was none, and Zachary didn't know how much longer they had to find one. Isira's attacks were noticeably weaker than when the battle had started, and Zachary didn't sense any weakening from Ava.

He threw his spear, but this time Ava didn't even flick her eyes toward him.

Isira screamed, a sound that made Zachary shiver coming from such a small girl. She unleashed another assault, greater than all she'd launched before. The mysterious tehoin joined in, and Zachary contributed two spears to the cause. Hel threw one of her own, too.

Hel's shield absorbed all the blows, and Zachary had to throw up a shield of his own to keep from being knocked backward by the force of the explosion.

When the smoke and dust cleared, Ava wasn't where she'd made her final stand, and Zachary dared to hope.

But then he saw her ten paces in front of Isira. Not only had Ava blocked the attack, but she'd also sent a spear of her own straight through Isira's weakened shield and into her chest. Blood poured from the girl and the rest of the shield dropped.

Ava vanished and appeared right before Isira, not even wasting the time to step forward. A teho blade was in her hand.

She brought it down, cutting through Isira from crown to crotch.

As the two halves of humanity's last stamfar defender fell to each side, Ava looked at the other tehoin gathered, death in her gaze.

33

———————

Hakon passed through the levels of the heart with little difficulty. His daughter had shown him the way. He relaxed and let the power flow through him, diving deeper through the layers it used to protect itself. He needed to reach the center of everything. His pain faded away, and an overwhelming sense of rightness washed over him.

His journey ended in a void, similar to the one he'd been in with the master dragon. Cliona's words came to him.

"Will and imagination," he whispered to himself.

The scene was easy enough to remember. He thought of it often. The void vanished, replaced by the kitchen in the house he'd built for Sera. Laughter echoed from down the hall, but Hakon didn't dare follow it. If he found his wife and daughter healthy and happy, he might not have the strength to do what needed to be done. He would rather stay here forever and let the world burn.

The sounds of trees cracking outside caught his attention. He ran from the kitchen and out the front door, jumping off the porch and staring in the direction of the sound.

Something was coming. Something big.

He wished he had his sword.

It was in his hand. He looked at it and shook his head. "Right. Will and imagination."

A teho demon, larger than any they'd seen in the city, broke through the last of the line of trees. Its arms were twice as long as Hakon's sword, and there was no way he'd reach it before it tore him into shreds.

Time to test Cliona's claim. His sword became four times as long while maintaining its familiar weight. He swung the weapon and cleaved the teho demon in half. He let the sword disappear, then let the forest vanish, too.

The void returned. It was better he be here. Too many emotions were tied to his home.

If he lived, he wanted to return. Those had been the happiest days of his life, as brief as the years had been. He didn't think he would, but it didn't hurt to have a dream, even at the end.

He needed to speak to the heart, so he summoned it, unsure if there was anything to even summon.

Ava appeared before him, and Hakon brought the sword to his hands once more.

The image blurred, and he realized he wasn't actually looking at Ava, but something imagined.

He held his sword at the ready, not quite ready to trust the projection of the heart. Ava stared at him but said nothing. Then she gestured, and three more teho demons appeared, all as big as the one he'd seen outside his house.

Hakon lengthened his sword once again, cutting through all three with a single swing.

Ava looked angry, but she made no other motion.

Something about the scene struck Hakon as unusual, but it took him a few moments to understand. When he did, he let the sword drop from his grip. "No wonder you hate us so," he said and walked up to her.

He thought of Meshell, riding the dragon. Necessary as the passage for the dragon's teho. All that power and wisdom, but the dragon couldn't shape it. Only humans could.

It was the same story with the heart. More power than a stamfar's most audacious dream. The ability to influence the wild and create teho demons. But it couldn't shape its strength. In a way, even the vildas were capable of more.

He touched Ava's shoulder and felt the heart thrumming with power beneath his hand. The temptation was almost painful in its intensity. As he expected, there was nothing she could do against him directly.

If he wished, he could grab hold of this power and become a god that would make even the stamfar tremble. Between his will and the strength of the heart, there was nothing they couldn't accomplish. The future of the Six States would be assured.

The heart, Ava, sensed his intent and tried to pull away, but there was no place for it to run. Cliona had given him the key to the greatest possible power, and his will and imagination made him invincible.

He let go of Ava's shoulder.

"I know we're killing you."

Her eyes widened.

"I've come to end it."

He gestured, and the void disappeared. He showed her what he intended and asked if it would be possible.

Ava thought for a moment and pointed a finger at herself. She shook her head. Then she pointed the finger at him and nodded.

He understood.

She didn't possess a will. Not the way he did. It would take a human to end the silent war she'd been fighting for countless generations.

"I want protection," Hakon said. "Not for myself, but for humanity. That's my price."

She thought for a moment more, then nodded. She held out her palm, and Hakon saw that it was bloody. A cut had appeared across it, and she offered him her hand. Hakon nodded. He imagined his own palm cut open, and a similar cut appeared. He took her hand in his own and they shook.

Hakon had expected to feel something more, but he felt nothing more unusual than the situation he found himself in. The deal was done.

"Show me how," Hakon said.

His imagining of what was to happen vanished, replaced by something that looked almost like a map of the continent. It was similar to what Cliona had shown him, but in such a way that one glowing blue light stood at the very left edge of his vision. Thousands upon thousands of whisker-thin strings emanated from the blue light and traveled west.

For a moment, Hakon was mesmerized by the beauty before him. This was a web, vaster and more intricate than anything he could imagine.

Ava nodded at him.

Once more, temptation struck.

This, this was the moment of her greatest weakness. His greatest opportunity. It didn't even matter if she pulled the construct away. Now that he had seen it, he could duplicate it.

Unlimited power, not just for himself but for all of humanity. He thought of the band and all the accomplishments they had achieved working together.

Imagine, their strength in the hands of everyone he granted it to.

Ava must have sensed the direction of his thoughts because she trembled as he neared.

But if he had learned one thing since returning to the world it was that he had no idea how best to guide it. A thousand well-intentioned ideas ended in nothing but disaster, not to mention the ever-present temptation of using his abilities to advance a cause only he believed in.

He had betrayed the band once. He would never do so again.

With his left hand, he gathered up the countless strings of teho connecting all of humanity to the heart. He felt the pull on his own teho when he grasped his string and held it in his fist.

When he had them all he closed his fist and pulled, stretching the lines tight. He had no idea what would happen next, but he knew this was right. He formed his sword in his hand and sharpened its edge until nothing in the world could stand against it. He debated for one more moment and then brought his sword down with all his strength, cutting through everything with one blow.

34

Unlike with the dragons, Zachary didn't hesitate. Even though the rational part of his mind understood that Ava was even more dangerous than a dragon, there was something about facing a human that was reassuring. There was a glow of satisfaction in her eyes, a brief moment of opportunity when he thought he might land one fatal blow. He formed a teho spear and whipped it with all the strength remaining to him. The spear leaped through the air, and his aim was true.

Ava batted it away without a second thought. She looked at him and gestured as though dismissing a rude servant from her quarters. Hundreds of teho darts erupted from her fingertips, speeding towards them all like a wall of death. There was no dodging such an assault, and all Zachary could think of doing was throwing up a shield. Hel stood behind him, adding her shield on top of his.

As Zachary braced himself for the impact, he felt a strange twisting in his stomach. He didn't have time to question what it was before the darts struck.

Hel's shield was the outer of the two, and the impact sent

her straight to her knees as it overwhelmed her. But she had stopped enough of the darts that when the rest hit Zachary's shield, he was able to handle them without much difficulty. He was grateful that Ava had created so many, distributing her power so that he could handle the blow.

His defense did little but mildly annoy her. With a snap of her fingers, a spear of incredible power appeared over her head.

Zachary couldn't be sure, but it felt to him as though her power had grown in the past few minutes. That spear was beyond anything she had used against Isira. And there was absolutely nothing he could do about it. Hel could have transported them away, but his impulse to be a part of the battle had meant she committed to defending him. She wasn't dead, but she wouldn't be transporting anyone soon.

He was determined to meet his fate with eyes wide open. He planted his feet and threw a shield, not over him, but over Hel.

The other tehoin transported away, leaving him and Hel alone against Ava. Not that it made any difference.

And then it felt as though someone had punched a hole through Zachary's stomach. He looked down, expecting to see through his torso. His legs gave out and he fell onto his hands and knees. He tried to rise and summon teho, but he couldn't.

The realization hit him like a hammer to the side of the head. It wasn't that he was too weak. It was that he *couldn't*. There was nothing to grab at. Nothing to focus.

He reached again, but it was like grasping for a cloud in the dark.

His connection to teho was gone.

When he looked up, Ava's teho spear was also gone, and she was on her knees, vomiting. When she'd emptied her stomach, she screamed at the sky like a woman mourning the loss of her lover. For the briefest of moments, Zachary almost felt sorry for her. Losing teho had made him feel sick, but her loss was greater than his.

The moment soon passed. This was the woman who'd dropped dragons on Mioska. The one who had tried to kill Cliona. He didn't know how long he had before their connection to teho returned, but right now, she was no stamfar. She was just a woman who'd tried to destroy the Six States.

He pushed himself to his feet, feeling like he'd just run a dozen miles to get here. He drew the dagger from his belt and stumbled toward her like a drunk man. She screamed at the sky again, then bent over as she clutched at her stomach.

Ava looked up as Zachary stood over her. He was twice her size, and she'd never seemed smaller. She tried to scramble away, but he caught her hair and pulled her to her feet. She clawed at him, but he drove the dagger into her stomach.

All the fight went out of her. It might have been a fatal wound, so long as she never embraced teho again. But Zachary wanted to be sure. As she dropped to her knees, he got behind her and put his dagger to her throat. He pulled hard, digging deep and slicing through both sides of her neck.

Blood fountained, and Ava fell forward, burying herself in the snow. Zachary watched for a moment to make sure she didn't move. He searched for teho but still couldn't find it. The action that had once felt so natural now seemed as though he was trying to speak an ancient language for the first time.

But it guaranteed the only thing that mattered. The last of the stamfar was dead.

And if Cliona spoke true, the threat to Mioska was gone, too.

He looked out to the walls, where he saw soldiers staring at him. He lifted the bloody dagger and roared.

The wall erupted in cheers, and Zachary stabbed the dagger high into the air again.

"You seem to have won some new admirers," a soft voice said behind him.

He brought the dagger down as he turned around. The pair of tehoin who'd been fighting Ava with Isira emerged from behind the ruins of a building.

Zachary put himself between them and Hel, who was slowly getting back to her feet.

"Who are you?" he asked.

The younger man bowed. "My name is Eliav, and she's Dagrun."

The names were vaguely familiar. "You're kolma?"

The two of them shared a look, and Zachary had the distinct feeling he was looking at a couple that had been together for far more years than he'd been alive. Ari and Solveig looked at each other the same way. So did Hakon and Meshell. The woman answered. "I believe it's more accurate to say that we *were* kolma."

"You can't reach teho, either?"

"No. And I get the sense we never will again."

Zachary put that aside for the moment. "Why are you here?"

"Isira asked for our help. A long time ago, she was our commander."

He was finally able to place the names. They knew the band. Hakon had met with them over a year ago when he'd been searching for Cliona. He raised his dagger. "You fought Hakon."

Instead of taking offense, the comment brought a smile to Dagrun's lips. "Long ago, yes. But you have nothing to fear. For one, you're a strong young lad, and I'm a much older woman. More importantly, though, it was Hakon who convinced Isira to risk her life fighting Ava. We're all on the same side now."

Zachary thought about it and then put his dagger away. "I suppose so."

They all looked around, no one quite sure what happened next. Dagrun scratched her head. Then she glanced at Eliav. "If we can't use teho, we've got a very long walk ahead of us."

"I was just thinking the same," Eliav said.

"Where do you live?" Hel asked. She was pale but looked otherwise unharmed.

"In the great forest east of Vispeda," Dagrun answered.

Hel looked at Zachary, then back to the walls. Her question went unspoken.

Zachary turned to the walls. At his gaze, the soldiers broke out into another round of cheers. He could imagine how it looked to them. He knew the woman who turned the dragons around, and he'd killed a warrior of unimaginable power.

Word would spread like wildfire.

If he wanted Agnar's seat, today was the day.

Everything he'd always wanted since he was young.

He reached out and took Hel's hand. "There are a few details I want to straighten out in Mioska, but Hel and I will be heading the same way soon. We live in Aysgarth. I think I'll be able to equip us for the journey if you wouldn't mind having us as companions."

EPILOGUE

Hakon rotated the spit, studying the meat closely. It was just about done, but he figured a bit more time wouldn't hurt anything. Laughter echoed from behind the corner of the house, and Solveig's was loudest of all. She'd been drinking since the sun rose that morning, and Ari hadn't done anything to slow her down.

Of course, the assassin had spent most of the afternoon holding his head in his hands and cursing last night's excess, so perhaps he wasn't the one best suited for containing Solveig's exuberance.

Irric came around the corner of the house, a wide grin on his face. "If Solveig has much more to drink, she'll probably tell us anything we ever wanted to know about Ari."

"A tempting idea, but some secrets are best left buried, don't you think?"

Irric raised his wine glass. "You're getting wise in your old age."

"One of us has to."

Irric came and offered to take a turn at the spit. Hakon

surrendered his spot and used the opportunity to take a long sip of ale.

"It's good to see you," Irric said. He took a sip of wine before continuing. "It's been too long."

Hakon chuckled. "It's not even been half a year."

Irric's smile faded. "But it feels different, doesn't it? When you left us after our imprisonment, I was angry, but I think I also knew that if enough time passed, I'd see you again. Nothing was likely to kill us, and time didn't matter all that much. Now though, I feel like time is an assassin, always trailing behind me. All these years, and now I'm afraid I don't have enough left."

"You regret your choice?"

"Not for a moment. Traveling to that city, I was done. Had the demons killed me, I would have died with a smile. But when you took teho away, everything changed." Irric snorted. "Now, I don't want to die."

Irric swallowed hard. "Thank you for being willing to fulfill my wishes. And thank you for understanding when they changed."

"After all you've done for me, I think it's the least I can do."

Further discussion was ended by a crowd of others coming around the corner. Solveig leaned heavily on Ari, who looked like he was about to collapse. She spoke loudly. "So, there we were, surrounded by teho demons, an army of shadow wolves and bears charging hard, when all of a sudden, none of us can use teho anymore."

Hel nodded politely. She kept glancing toward the woods, where Zachary had disappeared quite a while ago.

Solveig was in no condition to notice her audience's distraction. "Irric looks like he's ready to dive into the oncoming wolves with only a dagger, and Ari is swearing like I've never heard before—"

"And you kept trying to throw teho spears that wouldn't appear," Ari interjected.

Solveig ignored him. "We didn't know what we were going to do, but then the teho demons form this wedge against the wild animals, and they run past us without even getting close. But the best part—" Solveig leaned close to Hel, who wrinkled her nose at the alcohol on Solveig's breath. "—is Hakon. He's down in the bottom of this pit without a way to get up. He's wounded and can't climb that far, and we don't have any rope to get him."

Solveig paused for dramatic effect but only succeeded in nearly losing Hel's attention completely.

"Then a teho demon goes down into the hole, picks Hakon up, and carries him all the way out of the hole. It held him like a baby!"

Hakon remembered almost pissing his pants but decided Solveig's story didn't need any further embellishment.

A shout from the woods captured all their attention. Even Solveig stopped her story. A few moments later, Zachary appeared, cheeks flushed red. Cliona followed behind him, doubled over in laughter.

At Hakon's questioning look, Zachary shook his head. "She rose out of her grave while I was there paying my respects."

Hakon snorted, trying to contain his laughter. Over the years, Cliona had developed a wide variety of new skills, one of which was reappearing in various half-formed states. He'd also almost pissed his pants a month ago when he'd stepped into his bedroom and found her head on the wall grinning at him.

The others started to laugh at Zachary, but Hakon turned his eyes to Cliona. He still didn't understand what she'd become, but there was no doubt in his mind that she was still his daughter. The pranks she pulled now were reminiscent of the girl she'd been before Sera had died.

"I'm sorry," Cliona said, "but the opportunity was too good to pass on."

"It was your own grave!" Zachary argued.

Cliona shrugged.

Hakon got everyone's attention. "Food's ready, everyone. Let's sit down."

It took longer than it should have, but eventually they were all gathered around the table, passing bowls of food around and loading up their plates. Hakon and Meshell had decided gardening wasn't for them, but they traded their game for more produce than they knew what to do with. Neither were great cooks, but Irric had arrived a few days earlier to help with the preparation.

Hakon took a giant bite of meat, enjoying the talk around the table. Zachary had recovered from his fright and was telling Ari about the most recent developments in Aysgarth.

"Edda is expecting her first child this winter, so we're very excited about that," he said, playfully slapping Hel's hand away as she reached for some of the food on his plate. "But mostly, we've been busy trying to survive. It took two years for our fields to recover, and a lot of our tehoin had to relearn how to hunt and handle a bow. But the walls are rebuilt, and it looks like Hel will be on the council for the foreseeable future. The place has really grown on me."

"Do you ever miss Mioska?" Cliona asked. She didn't eat anymore, so she didn't have a plate in front of her. "I heard they were just about ready to make you governor after killing Ava."

"They talked about it," Zachary admitted. "But after everything, I was done with the city."

"It's changed since you left," Cliona argued. "The cult withered and mostly died when the dragons stopped attacking. Even the wild isn't as aggressive as it once was. Hallr lost his council seat once the governor regained full control of the city. I'm surprised you weren't tempted."

Zachary shrugged. "I have more unpleasant memories in that city than good ones. And I decided there were better ways to spend my time than that mess of council politics. Besides, everyone in Mioska was mostly impressed with you." He stared pointedly at Cliona. "You know there are people calling you a god, now. I've passed a few of your shrines. The idea has spread far beyond Mioska. Give it a generation or two, and you'll be as legendary as the stamfar."

Cliona looked like she'd swallowed something bitter. "That was never the point. But you didn't answer my question."

"There are days," Zachary admitted. "But we've got our daughter, and I've come to appreciate the quiet of Aysgarth. I think I'm a better father than a governor."

"Debatable," Hel said between bites.

"How is little Cliona?" Hakon asked.

"Ready to climb the walls and explore the whole world if we let her," Zachary answered. He thrust a bite of potato in his mouth before Hel could grab it off his plate. "Oh, and we found Tollak still alive!"

"Really?" Solveig asked.

"He escaped with most of the village before the attack came. Turns out, he became a decent archer and helped them out. I sent a letter inviting him to Aysgarth to meet all his new family members, but I don't know if he'll take me up on it. He's still not my most ardent supporter."

Zachary turned the conversation away from him. "How's Vispeda, Solveig?"

"Recovering, the same as Aysgarth. We have more resources at our disposal, but it's been busy."

"How much longer do you think you'll stay there?" Meshell asked.

"Not long," Solveig said. "I've been preparing to take an expedition back west. There's a lifetime of study there, and I want to get started soon."

"Is that safe?" Zachary asked. "We still don't wander too far west of Aysgarth."

"No more dangerous than anywhere else," Solveig replied. "We'll be prepared." She turned to Hakon. "You and Meshell are more than welcome to join us. If you do, we might even convince Irric to leave with us. One more adventure for the band."

Hakon gave a noncommittal smile. "We'll see. I suppose it mostly depends on how bored Meshell gets here. I'll confess I'm not too interested. I've hung up my sword for good."

Ari shook his head. "I still can't believe you carried that damn thing all the way back here. You can't even swing it anymore."

"Sentimental value," Hakon said.

"Where is it now?" Ari asked.

"I buried it under the house, just like when Cliona was born. It's where it belongs."

"You carried it all that way so you could bury it?" Ari looked horrified. "That's a legendary blade!"

Hakon ignored the question.

They caught up on the events in their lives, and Hakon was struck by how mundane much of their news was. It wasn't until Zachary asked Cliona about her last few months that they were reminded of the deep currents running under the surface.

"The heart is recovering," Cliona said. "I've been watching it closely, and Dad's gamble looks like it worked. I'll keep watching it. Besides that, it's a lot like I'm back in the academy. I spend almost all my time learning more about what happened to me, and what's happening with this world. I did find another person like me, who died and came back again."

That was news to Hakon. "Really?"

"She's not from this world. Her name is Alena, and although it's difficult for us to communicate, she's been invaluable. I think I'll learn a lot from her."

Hakon stared in wonder. His girl was on a journey he couldn't even begin to imagine. When he'd left this house in pursuit of her so many years ago, he'd never imagined this would be the result. His heart still ached when he looked at her. Though she sat at their table, her place was empty. She was here, but she'd also died.

He grew used to the strange mix of emotions that resulted from the paradoxes. He and Sera had known, back before Cliona had ever been born, that Hakon would have to say goodbye to his daughter. But he'd never imagined it would be because he would pass through the gate for good first.

Still, there was something right about it. In one sense, he'd outlived her, but she would go on long after he was gone. And that was as it should be. A father should never outlive his daughter.

He looked around the table at the band, as close to him

as any family he'd ever had. Zachary and Hel were part of their table, too, and soon they'd bring little Cliona with them. The family around this table would grow, and it would divide and go its separate ways.

Just as families had since the day the first stamfar crashed onto the planet.

He smiled wide.

This life hadn't been what he'd planned.

But it was good.

ALSO BY RYAN KIRK

Saga of the Broken Gods

Band of Broken Gods

Last Sword in the West

Last Sword in the West

Eyes of the Hidden World

A Sword Named Vengeance

Wraith's Revenge

Frontier's End

Oblivion's Gate

The Gate Beyond Oblivion

The Gates of Memory

The Gate to Redemption

Relentless

Relentless Souls

Heart of Defiance

Their Spirit Unbroken

The Nightblade Series

Nightblade

World's Edge

The Wind and the Void

Blades of the Fallen

Nightblade's Vengeance

Nightblade's Honor

Nightblade's End

Standalone Novels

Blades of Shadow

The Primal Series

Primal Dawn

Primal Darkness

Primal Destiny

ABOUT THE AUTHOR

Ryan Kirk is the bestselling author of the *Nightblade* series of books. When he isn't writing, you can probably find him playing disc golf or hiking through the woods.

www.waterstonemedia.net
contact@waterstonemedia.net

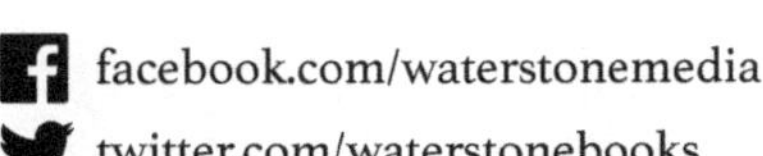
facebook.com/waterstonemedia
twitter.com/waterstonebooks
instagram.com/waterstonebooks

www.ingramcontent.com/pod-product-compliance
Lightning Source LLC
Chambersburg PA
CBHW061523210726
48287CB00006B/1800